The Past She Carries

Agnes Pomeroy

Contents

Chapter 1

The wind howled. It was a more vicious wind than Belle had heard in a long time. It was more than a storm. It had to be a hurricane blowing into Saint-Martin.

Rain simultaneously pelted the earth with unyielding aggression, soaking the dirt beneath her feet. Belle was nearly sinking into the mud, her bare feet frozen, and she could hardly see three steps in front of her as she trekked through the fields in the dead of the night. Her hair was plastered to her face, and her dress was completely soaked through.

But she wouldn't stop. Belle ought to have been afraid of dying in such a storm. Any normal person would have been afraid to be out in such weather. But she was not afraid. She could never fear death. She knew that there were far worse fates than death.

Faster. Be faster. Belle willed herself to be faster with every step she took. Every step was one step further away. Her rapid heartbeat rivalled the sounds of the thunder above as she pushed herself to keep going.

This was it. It was now or never. Belle had waited years for an opportunity like this. She had waited, suffered, endured her life for years without ever having a moment to run. It had taken a hurricane coming for Belle to have a chance.

And she did see trekking through a hurricane as a chance. She would rather die here, die now trying to escape during this storm, then remain behind and wish every day that she were dead.

A loud clap of thunder startled Belle awake, and it took a moment for her to grasp her bearings. She was not in Saint-Martin and had not been for a long time. She was in England, in a little Hertfordshire village called Ashwood, the place that had been her home for the last three months. The thunder that she had heard was from a summer thunderstorm which had appeared out of nowhere and had done quite well at frightening off any of the usual shoppers who would be out and about in the village. That same thunder had triggered her memories of a time that she so longed to forget.

"If you've got nothing better to do than sleep on the job, girl, then I'd sooner lease that space to someone who was going to make me a penny."

Belle looked up to see Ashwood's grocer, Mr Andrews, standing by a display of baked goods. He was a man of about thirty or so, with light coloured hair and pale blue eyes. He wore an apron over his white shirt, his sleeves rolled up out of the way as he cleaned, as evidenced by the broom he held in his right hand.

"I'm sorry," Belle apologised. "It won't happen again." She knew why she was tired. She was up most nights sewing Susanna's wedding dress. She would never begrudge making

Susanna's gown. In fact, she was honoured to have been asked. Designing gowns, like the one that she was creating for Susanna, was exactly what Belle loved and wanted to do. She had always loved drawing, and her own imagination for these sorts of things had helped her create an escape for herself long before she had ever been free.

If her circumstances were different, Belle would have loved to do what she was doing for Susanna for other ladies. She would have loved to be able to create and make beautiful wedding gowns, ball gowns, and debutante gowns.

But they weren't, and Belle would never allow herself to feel ungrateful for even a moment. She might not have had her own shop, but she was working, and she was sewing. It did not matter that the sewing she was employed to do was fixing buttons and hems.

The dowager duchess, Cecily, had arranged it all. Really, she had bullied Mr Andrews into agreeing with her. She was a hard woman to refuse.

There had once been a tailor in the village of Ashwood, quite a long time ago, Belle understood, and he had been the father of the young duchess, Grace. The shop he had once leased had long been occupied by another vendor, and so Cecily had persuaded Mr Andrews to give Belle space at the grocer to establish herself as a seamstress.

Mr Andrews had been amenable to the idea, just not the seamstress. Belle was used to apprehension, mistrust ... and disgust. Her appearance was startling to many.

Her eyes, Belle found, often made people uncomfortable, wary, or uneasy. She was quite used to this, as there were many people where she had grown up who were raised to be fearful of witches. Belle was uncertain how possessing golden coloured eyes made her a witch, but such was the assumption of someone who had such a startling feature, made even more prominent by her cool, dark complexion. Belle had become accustomed to looking down whenever she engaged with a white person.

She was one of three black people in the village of Ash-wood, who were all still quite getting used to the fact that there were people beyond their village borders who looked differently to them. Lady Susanna Beresford's engagement announcement to Alex Whitfield two months earlier had caused quite the stir. A stir, really, was an understatement. Many thought Susanna mad, though they would never dare insult a lady of her rank by saying so to her face.

Belle heard the gossip in the shop. People didn't watch their words in front of her. Perhaps it was because she spoke with a heavy French accent and so they thought she would not understand, or perhaps it was because they thought her invisible or insignificant.

Belle could not be wounded by either. Words could never hurt her. She knew pain, and this was not it.

Belle quickly returned her attention to the spencer coat that she had been in the process of mending before she had nodded off. As much as she could dream of the sorts of gowns she would like to create, once again, Belle would never be ungrateful for paid work, even if she was only able to keep thirty-five percent of what she earned.

That had been Mr Andrews' condition upon allowing Belle to operate within his shop. He would take sixty-five percent of her earnings as compensation for any lost business he would suffer for having a black girl work from within his store.

Thirty-five percent was more than Belle had ever thought possible for her. Paid work was a blessing. Belle was grateful for her blessings.

As she sewed, the sound of the storm outside did cause her mind to wander, as it had done when she had fallen asleep. It had been more than a year since her flight from Saint-Martin.

Belle had been almost certain that she would have been caught trying to escape. People were caught, and shot, for such crimes all the time. Had she been caught; she would have wished for such a fate. After all, she did not fear death.

But just because she did not fear death, it did not mean that Belle was fearless. Quite the opposite. Belle feared greatly. She could be sick with it. She could induce night terrors from her own memories. But memories she could survive. It had been more than a year since Belle's fears had been her reality.

Belle was determined that what she had endured on Saint-Martin would never be her reality again. Never would she speak of it. Never would anyone know. That life, and the person it had belonged to, was dead, as far as Belle was concerned.

But sadly, ghosts always lingered.

Belle spent the rest of the day mending the garments that had been left for her, and she ensured that they were neatly folded ready for their owners to collect them the following day. What with the weather, Belle did not expect anyone to venture out.

Peering out the shop window, Belle observed that the rain had eased, but there was still a good, constant drizzle falling from the sky. She could hardly believe it considering it was July. She was certainly not in the Caribbean anymore, and thank God for that. Rain, Belle decided, was just another kind of good weather.

Despite the fact that the rain had let up, it was still a fair walk back to Ashwood House, so Belle knew that she should have thought to have brought an umbrella with her. Mr Andrews sold them, but after Belle had passed on what she owed to Mr Andrews, she really could not afford it today.

No sooner had the thought crossed her mind, did the shop door open, and the little bell above chime. Belle smiled as she saw Alex Whitfield cross the threshold, carrying exactly what she needed. An umbrella.

If it was possible, Alex looked as though he had grown even taller in the three months they had been in England. Perhaps it was that he had grown wider in his brawn as he regained much of the muscular strength that Belle remembered seeing on him when they had first met on the smugglers' ship.

No, she decided, he was definitely taller. He stood taller, prouder, as an honest working man.

The moment that Alex and Susanna's engagement had been announced, it was then quickly decided that it was highly inappropriate for the engaged couple to be living under the same roof. Susanna's brother, the duke, then decided on gifting Alex and Susanna their wedding present early.

Land.

Belle knew that she could understand best what land meant to Alex, what it meant to be his own master. And he now carried himself with that pride.

Belle was not entirely certain what had drawn her to Alex when she had first encountered him on the ship. Of course, she was concerned for his health, but something within her told her that this man was safe. Such a feeling was entirely foreign to Belle. She had never known a safe man. She had never felt safe with a man.

Even now, sharing a space with Mr Andrews, Belle did not feel at ease, even though she knew in her deepest soul that nothing bad was going to happen. It was something that was now intrinsically ingrained into her. It was how she had survived. Men were not safe.

But Alex was. Belle looked upon him as an older brother, a protector, which was someone that she had never had. Belle had been abandoned as an infant. She had never known family, and yet she had felt the connection of family for the first time with Alex. Their shared experiences bonded them in a way nobody else could understand.

Even now, Alex really did know very little about Belle. This was because she didn't share. This was because she wouldn't share. But Alex knew not to ask.

"Are you finished for the day?" Alex asked her. "I had thought I had better walk you back, what with this weather."

"Yes, I am," Belle confirmed, nodding. "Thank you."

"How do you do, Mr Andrews," Alex greeted the grocer politely.

Mr Andrews nodded his head. "Be on your way now," he urged stiffly.

Belle pocketed her money tin and left the shop, followed closely by Alex who put up the umbrella as soon as they were out in the street. They walked together in the middle of the road, which was abandoned, of course, due to the weather. There were still people about, however. Belle could see them at the windows, looking out, and down, on their new black neighbours with mixed expressions of curiosity and distrust.

People seemed to distrust and dislike those they did not understand. In a way, Belle was glad for them. If they did not understand, then it meant that they had never known the life that she had once lived. She would never wish that on her worst enemy.

Stares she could live with. Stares she could cope with. Because while they stared, Belle walked the street as a free woman. That feeling alone was worth more to her than they would ever know.

"Are you alright?" Alex asked Belle as they walked. "You seem very lost in your thoughts today."

Belle immediately nodded as she met Alex's dark eyes. She smiled to reassure him, though she could feel it in her own facial muscles that it was not a convincing smile. "Just a bad dream," she murmured dismissively.

Alex nodded knowingly. "I have those dreams sometimes," he replied.

Belle didn't reply. She couldn't. She did not want to have such a conversation, and Alex knew that about her. He didn't ask. He didn't expect her to say anything more.

"Do you think the news will have reached Ashwood today?" he asked, changing the subject. "Were there any letters before you left this morning?"

The Beresfords were anxiously awaiting the news of the birth of Jack and Claire's second child. The last letter had arrived not a week ago with the news that the birth was imminent.

The dowager duchess had been very put out when her son had specifically asked that the family stay away for the birth. Belle understood that the birth of their first child had been quite traumatic. The letter had stated that once Claire and the new child were both well enough, they would visit.

"I left before breakfast," replied Belle, "so I did not see if there had been any letters delivered."

"Before breakfast? Did you eat?" queried Alex.

"Yes, of course," retorted Belle. Her thin appearance was frequently commented on, and it bothered her greatly. It made her feel very self-conscious. Belle had been naturally slender and small all her life, and when she looked in the mirror, she resembled the size and weight that she had been before being starved on that smuggling ship. She knew that her cheekbones protruded, but they always had, and they, along with her strange eyes made her face very startling to look at. Belle had never had a womanly figure, even if she was only nineteen. Her waist and hip measurements were nearly identical. She disliked her bony arms and wrists, and how people liked to collect them and wrap their hands around them to demonstrate just how little she was.

She hated to be touched when she was not expecting it. It made her panic inside. It made her feel unsafe.

Belle understood that to be fuller was to be attractive, and that the way she looked was very unattractive. She didn't like to be reminded that she was unattractive. Despite not wanting to care, she did not like to think that no one would ever find her desirable, even if the very idea of a man thinking that way frightened her to death.

"Alright," Alex replied, leaving the subject there, clearly observing that Belle did not like to discuss it. "Come on," he urged. "Faster. Before either one of us catches our death."

And with just the mention of the word, Belle could vividly feel her bare feet trudging through mud once more, as she willed herself to move faster. How powerful were nightmares when they could haunt a person while they were awake?

Chapter 2

P eter Denham was a typically productive man of business, even if he was only twenty years old. He looked every one of his twenty years, sometimes a few less, which often vexed him when it came time to conducting important meetings as many assumed Peter was not old enough to be privy to such information, nor old enough to manage the business that he did.

Despite his young age, Peter was every bit capable of running a business. He had always been clever. School had never particularly challenged him. He had always known the answers, to the point where the vicar would often have to ask him to put his hand down to give others a chance when it came to answering questions. Peter had always been a vociferous reader, poring over whatever few books he could get his hands on, enjoying literature as much as he did textbooks. It had been Peter's dream to finish his schooling and go on to university to study business, so that he might establish himself properly in a city like London.

Except that Peter had known his dream was exactly that; a dream. Peter was the eldest son of a poor family. University could never be a reality. Peter left school early, shortly after his elder sister, Kate, married the blacksmith, Jim Ellis. Through this connection, Peter secured an apprenticeship, and his future was set.

Peter could never be ungrateful for Jim's patience and instruction. He did not dislike the work. In fact, he was rather good with his hands, and his talents had come in handy when some of the printing presses had jammed. But as the years went on, Peter could not deny that he wanted more for his life.

Were it not for the advantageous marriages of his other sisters, Grace and Claire, Peter never would have even considered leaving Jim and his apprenticeship. But with Grace and Claire married well, and the security of his mother assured, Peter came to the decision that he had to try. He had to wet his feet in London, to see if he could do it, to see if he could really be a man of business.

Peter was so grateful to his brother-in-law, Jim, for his graciousness as he left, and he was doubly grateful to his brother-in-law, Jack Beresford, for giving Peter the opportunity to be his partner at Beresford Press.

Peter had been in his role at Beresford Press now for a little over a year. Next month it would be the anniversary of the first book that Beresford Press had published. To date, they had now published four. Jack was responsible for finding the books. He had the eye, the taste. He knew what he liked to read.

It was Peter's responsibility to handle the money. In hindsight, Jack had taken an enormous gamble on Peter. He had been only nineteen at the time and was still only twenty. To be given the responsibility of handling capital of upwards of twenty thousand pounds was simply unheard of. But Jack had done it, and Peter hadn't let him down yet, and he certainly did not intend to.

"It will be anonymous, you are certain?" checked Hattie Granger.

Miss Granger sat opposite Peter's desk in his small office above the printing room. From where they were, they could hear the printers below chatting jovially as they went about their roles.

Miss Granger was in her late twenties, by Peter's estimation, and was oddly dressed as a widow, complete with a veil, despite herself being a Miss. But Peter could attribute that to her wanting to appear incognito.

Miss Granger had written the fifth book that Beresford Press had purchased in order to publish, a manuscript entitled, "Confessions of a Lady".

Peter did not need to wonder as to why Jack had been intrigued by such a book. Four of the five books that Beresford Press had published had been written by women. Ordinarily, books authored by women did not sell well at all, and that was where Peter worked hard. Taking out advertisements in women's magazines had been one of his many brainwaves to ensure that the books they published sold well.

Jack seemed to be fascinated by women authors. Peter believed it was because he was now the father of a future young woman. Jack enjoyed reading and promoting stories written by, about, and for women.

Miss Granger's novel was the first non-fiction book that Beresford Press would be publishing, so this was another gamble. But Jack was determined, and Peter knew that with a little hard work, he could get the results.

"Yes, of course, Miss Granger," Peter confirmed. "In fact, I have the title page here for you to see, if you would like." Peter fished the book's title page from the manuscript and handed it to Miss Granger, who accepted it in her black gloved hand.

Peter had read the book himself and had thoroughly enjoyed it. In his opinion, the messages did not only apply to women. Miss Granger had written somewhat of an autobiography of a woman raised in the upper classes. She wrote about forgoing the traditional route of a debutante, seeking further education, and establishing independence. Of course, Peter could not relate to a great deal of the book, what he did enjoy was the emphasis on education.

If he were ever fortunate enough to have a child one day, no expense would be spared on ensuring he or she was properly educated. He would not care if he had two broken legs and couldn't walk, no child of his would be forced to forgo anything to support him.

"It is our aim to print some three and a half thousand copies over the next two years," Peter explained. "Through these sales, we can project that you will earn some fourteen hundred pounds in royalties."

Though her face was veiled, Peter could see the bottom of Miss Granger's jaw, and it had opened in shock. Peter could not imagine what a single woman would do with such a sum. But he imagined that it would help her in her endeavour to stay independent. His projections, of course, were always on the side of cautious. Peter never liked to over-estimate. For all he knew, her book sales would be higher.

"I thank you, Mr Denham," Miss Granger said gratefully. "Is Lord Beresford about? I should like to thank him as well."

"No, he is not in today," replied Peter. "His wife is in her confinement. They expect a child any day." Jack had not been into the office for nearly a week, though Peter did not be-grudge him that. Their family were all aware of the traumatic circumstances of Claire's first birthing experience.

Peter had not been present, of course, but the very knowl-edge that his sister had given birth to a child who had nearly died was terrifying. He could only hope that the next child was born fat, pink, and happy.

"Oh, do pass on my congratulations to the happy couple, then," Miss Granger urged. "I ought to be going. You have my address should you need anything further from me. I thank you again."

"Congratulations, Miss Granger. This is a very exciting time." Peter rose from his chair and shuffled awkwardly around his desk to reach the door for Miss Granger. It was a cramped space, really, even if Peter did do his best to keep it organised.

Peter showed Miss Granger out before he returned to the printing floor. The printers had been, perhaps, the most chal-lenging people from which to garner respect. The youngest man they employed was perhaps thirty or thirty-five, and no man of that sort of age wanted to take orders from a man they deemed a child.

But Peter had proved himself. He wasn't just book smart. Perhaps he was young, but five years as a blacksmith's apprentice meant he was lean, strong, and knew his way around a machine. It hadn't happened overnight, but Peter had spent many months rolling up his sleeves and helping the printers meet deadlines, and somewhere along the way, they had stopped calling him "Boy".

As Peter and his head printer, John Jessop, planned for the run of "Confessions of a Lady", they were startled by the sudden violent opening of the door. The door swung open so quickly that it smashed into the woodwork, no doubt causing some damage by the handle.

Jack leaned against the threshold, huffing and puffing as though he had run the route from their house in Mayfair directly to the publishing house without bothering to hail a hackney.

Peter could only assume it meant one thing. Jack did not look sad, or the devastated that he would be if something had happened to either Claire or their child. He looked absolutely elated, even if he was sucking in air for dear life.

The printers all stopped, joining in on the curious cheers as they all realised what Jack's coming would mean.

"What is it?" asked one.

"Boy or girl?" asked another.

"Does it look like you, sir?" joked one more.

Jack let out a delighted laugh as he called out, "Girl!"

The printing room filled with claps, cheers, and shouts of congratulations, and Peter felt his own smile widened and he realised he had a new niece.

In addition to his one nephew, Peter had four nieces now. Perrie, Lily, Jackie ... and now the new baby girl. Peter felt rather giddy at this news. He had grown up with older sisters. Whenever Grace or Claire had their first son, the lucky boy would have older sisters to look after him.

Once Jack had caught his breath, he entered the printing room and made his way directly to Peter. Peter smiled at his brother-in-law and enveloped him in a tight hug. "Congratulations, Jack. Two girls. You are certainly blessed."

"I know it, do not you worry," replied Jack, the smile never fading. "But I have three girls, you know. My world now consists of my three girls."

Peter knew that Jack was not saying such sentiments for Peter's benefit because Jack was married to Peter's sister. Jack meant every word, and Peter admired how openly he loved his wife and adored his child, now children. It was enough to make a man envious at times.

"How is Claire?" Peter asked.

"Well, perfect," Jack beamed. "She did wonderfully. She is exhausted, but she asked me to fetch you. She wants you to come and meet Maria Frances."

"Maria Frances Beresford," repeated Peter, glad to hear that Claire was safe and well. "I know Frances is after Claire. How did you choose Maria?"

"How else? A book," Jack grinned. "An author, really. Maria Edgeworth. A fantastic writer and thinker. I encourage you to read her if you have not."

Peter had not heard of her, though he was not surprised that Jack seemed well-versed. It was, after all, his job now to read.

Peter followed Jack into the bedroom that he shared with Claire. Claire sat up in her bed, cradling a small, swaddled bundle while being attended to by her maid.

Claire had been dreadfully uncomfortable in the last week, but now she looked flushed and radiant. "Oh, Peter, you're back! Come and see! Come and see her! She is perfect!"

Jack walked around the other side of the bed to sit down next to Claire, and he collected up fifteen-month-old Jackie into his arms as he did so, as she had been seated beside her mother.

Peter approached quietly and peered into the swaddle, finding a perfectly pink baby sleeping inside. Brand new, and entirely faultless. She was beautiful. Already, Peter could see a thin dusting of dark hair on her head. She would certainly be a stark contrast to her older sister, who sported a head of brilliant white blonde hair.

Peter leaned over and kissed Claire's forehead before he gently kissed the top of baby Maria's head. "Welcome, lovely Maria," Peter said softly. "Well done, Claire," he congratulated his sister.

Claire's blue eyes shone. "I feel terrible now that I kept everyone away," she told both Peter and Jack. "I was terrified that something bad would happen and I didn't want to be surrounded by everybody. But now that she's here and she's well, all I want to do is have everyone see her ... I want to have Mama see her." Claire then chuckled to herself before she said to Jack, "I would even listen to your mother lecture me about having not eaten enough lamb's kidneys or something to have ensured a son."

Jack laughed before he leaned over and captured Claire's lips in a chaste kiss. "You rest," he instructed. "Despite the elation, you are not ready to take on the world. I will write and tell everyone that Maria is here, and when you both are ready, we will visit. We would be going anyway for Susanna's wedding. We will make it an extended trip. A month or so with my mother, just what the doctor ordered."

Claire rolled her eyes. "Hush," she chided. Her eyes flicked back to Peter. "You will come, won't you?" she asked expectantly.

Peter pursed his lips. He had been invited to Susanna's wedding to Alex Whitfield, of course. The news of the engagement had reached London before the invitation had. Society's richest jewel betrothed to a negro. It had been quite the scandal on the brink of the Season. Not that any one of them cared. Peter had not met this Mr Whitfield, but he was certain that he had to have been quite the man to win Susanna's heart. He admired Susanna as he admired each of her brothers. They chose love, not rank, money or station. They simply chose love.

However much he admired them, and envied them at times, that did not mean that he had been planning on attending the wedding. "I do not know ... I have a rather awful lot to do, what with the new book –"

"Peter, you haven't been home since Christmas. What will your mother think of me? She will assume I am working you into an early grave," Jack jokingly chastised. "The hard work is done. It is up to the printers now to meet the order, and we will both keep in contact with Mr Jessop to ensure that everything is on track. You are coming home with us, and that's final."

Chapter 3

S usanna twirled excitedly, watching as the skirt of her dress fanned out from the high waistline. Of course, she was twirling in the dress that Belle had stitched out of cheap calico fabric as a practise, but she was twirling, nonetheless.

"I am certain I shall never own, nor wear anything near so fine as this gown that you are making for me, Belle," Susanna said excitedly.

It was Sunday, and so Belle had had the time to finish her practise gown in the daylight, as opposed to stitching by candlelight as she so often did. She did not attend church. Not because she did not want to, just because it was easier on the Ashwood villagers if she was not there. Belle did not like to draw attention, and she did so well enough as it was. Susanna had only recently returned home with her family and had come up to Belle's bedroom to see how she was progressing.

"Only I wish you would not spend your Sundays thus. It is the day of rest. I do feel rather guilty," Susanna added.

Belle wanted to laugh, though she composed herself so as not to make Susanna feel badly. Never, not once, in her nineteen years of life had she known so much as a day of light labour, let alone rest. But she liked this work. This work was fulfilling. This work made her happy, and happiness was something terrible foreign to Belle, and to others like her.

"Guilt is not a feeling I would want you to have when you are standing in what will be turned into your wedding gown," Belle replied thoughtfully.

Susanna flushed. She had such a lovely, healthy complexion, with full, rosy cheeks and beautiful blue eyes that suited her so well. Nothing about Susanna was startling or could make anyone who looked upon her uncomfortable. Though, she supposed, such was the prerogative of the white woman, and Susanna could not be blamed for that.

"Would you lift your arms up for me?" Belle requested, observing that the seams at the bust appeared a little tight.

Sure enough, when Susanna lifted her arms, a few of the loose stitches that Belle had sewn burst, indicating that it was a little too tight, and the measurement needed to be adjusted.

"Oh, dear," Susanna said bashfully, bringing her arms down immediately. "How terribly embarrassing. I suppose I must have put on a pound or two in the last few weeks. I suppose it is how well we are eating now that we are home."

Belle fetched her tape measure and retook Susanna's bust measurement, and just as she had suspected, there had been an inch gained. Belle was glad that the changes and rips happened on the practise garment and not on the real dress. She and Susanna had spent an ungodly amount of money on fabric ordered from a French catalogue that had arrived only a few days earlier. Belle had never touched anything so fine, and she was nervous to prick the silk with her needle, let alone rip seams and make adjustments.

"I am certain that if I avoid ... breakfast, perhaps? Do you think that would help me?" Susanna worried, suddenly taking herself over to the mirror to inspect her figure. She placed her hands either side of her ribcage and squeezed in.

The English style of gown, the high waisted fashion, were not designed to hug the feminine figure, Belle had observed. There was a practicality about the style, and she enjoyed that the high waist disguised her own figure, or lack thereof. Of course, Belle had nothing whatsoever to her own bust measurement, but the flare of her skirt did not directly advertise that her waist and hips could belong to a twelve-year-old child.

Susanna, on the other hand, had a beautifully feminine figure. Soft and slender, yet rounded and womanly where she needed to be. Were it not a sin, Belle would have envied her. Perhaps she was a sinner, and she did, indeed, envy her.

"Don't you dare," Belle insisted. "I have never heard of such a thing as to refuse food."

Belle watched as the colour drained from Susanna's face and an expression of shame appeared there. "Oh, Belle," she gasped. "Oh, please, forgive me. How terribly tactless of me."

Belle had not meant to make Susanna feel badly, though she had clearly succeeded. It was a simple reaction. She could not fathom someone refusing food and choosing to go hungry. Hunger was a terrible pain, though it was not the worst that she had experienced.

"I change the dress to fit you, and not the other way around. You are healthy, and you look every bit the joyful bride. Never choose hunger."

Susanna bit down on her bottom lip before she smiled, pulling Belle into a tight hug. Belle hated that she needed to close her eyes and actively stop herself from flinching. Susanna was not a man, and she was her friend. Belle was not at all unsafe, and yet she loathed that her immediate reaction to touch that she was not prepared for was fear.

Belle somehow managed to conceal her panic, as Susanna did not pull away until it was naturally time to. "I won't," promised Susanna. "It was silly of me to suggest it."

Belle finished taking Susanna's measurements again, double checking to ensure that her numbers were correct before she began to sew using the expensive fabric. She and Susanna then spent the next hour poring over Belle's design drawings for the gown, editing and making any little adjustments before Belle began cutting.

While doing this, Belle quite forgot about her momentary panic when Susanna had hugged her, and her feeling of excitement returned. This was what she loved to do. She felt talented.

"Belle, this is going to be the most beautiful dress," Susanna crooned for the tenth time. "I wish you would make everyone gowns. You ought to have your own catalogue or something. People would pay an awful lot of money for a wedding gown like this. And not only wedding gowns, but ball gowns and debutante gowns as well."

A catalogue? Belle thought about the catalogue that she had Susanna had gone through to select fabric. What would it be like to have such a book filled with her own designs?

Well, it would be a dream, just as having her own shop was a dream. Belle had no desire to be disappointed when she was already achieving much more than she could have ever thought by working in Mr Andrews' grocery shop. It was kind of Susanna to think that people would buy from her, but Belle knew the truth. The hard evidence was in the very fact that she needed to give Mr Andrews sixty-five percent of her earnings. She could never survive on her own. No-one would come. No-one would buy from a black woman.

But Belle did not say that to Susanna. Despite being nearly five years her senior, Susanna was still naïve about some things, and Belle rather enjoyed this about her. She wished that she could possess some of Susanna's optimistic inno-cence.

"Thank you," was all she said in reply.

At that moment, both women heard the sound of hors-es outside, and their attention turned to the window. The horse's hooves were followed by the sound of carriage wheels turning over on the gravel road up to the house.

"Oh, is it Jack?" Susanna asked excitedly, as she scrambled away from the mirror and over to the window. She leaned on the windowsill and peered outside.

Two weeks earlier the Beresfords had received the news that Jack, whom Belle knew to be the sibling aged in between Susanna and Adam, and his wife, Claire, had been blessed with the arrival of a second daughter, Maria. The family was expected to travel to Ashwood when both mother and child were well enough, and the family were waiting in anticipation.

"Is it?" Belle queried, following Susanna over to the window. She looked out and saw that a carriage was travelling up the road, being pulled along by four large horses.

"I don't know," replied Susanna, frowning. "I don't remember Jack's carriage, and they all look the same anyway." Her fingers drummed against the wood of the windowsill. "I hope it is. I am desperate to see the baby. I want to know if she looks like me, too."

"Too?" Belle thought back to meeting the little blonde daughter of Jack and Claire when they had visited Ashwood back in April. She supposed Susanna was right, considering neither one of her parents were fair at all.

"Oh, yes," confirmed Susanna. "Jackie is just darling, isn't she? She has my hair and everything. Jackie and Maria ... oh, I cannot tell you how pleased I am for my brother. He is such a proud father. Both of my brothers are. And both blessed with two girls each. It makes me smile, even if it does worry my mother."

Belle had learned several new English words through the dowager duchess, Cecily, as well as several apparent remedies that she was otherwise unaware of. She had learned of a sweetbread, and that apparently if an expectant mother ingested one, she was bound to have a son. Cecily had apparently been mistaken with a few other concoctions in the past but was quite confident about this one.

Belle was quite certain that she would never become a mother herself, but if she were to be, she could not imagine wanting to determine the sex of her child. Girl or boy, it did not matter.

"Oh, it's stopped!" said Susanna excitedly, as she slapped Belle's arm, albeit lightly.

Still, the unexpected touch made Belle jump, and her heart quicken. Susanna, however, thankfully didn't notice.

Together, they watched as footmen surrounded the carriage, which was carrying several trunks atop it in luggage. The steps were let down, and the first person climbed out.

Tall, handsome, and wearing an impossibly proud smile as he carried his small, blonde, toddler daughter on his hip, was Jack Beresford.

Susanna beamed gleefully. "It is them! How delightful! Let me catch a glimpse of the baby before we go down."

Jack used his free hand to carefully guide his wife out from the carriage. Claire was wearing a mint shade of green with a matching spencer coat, dressed suitably for travelling in the summer. In her arms, she carried a swaddled infant, whose face could not be seen from above. Claire moved delicately, almost gingerly, appropriate for a woman who had given birth recently.

"Can you see anything?" asked Susanna as she craned her neck. "I cannot. Come, let's go down."

"Is there someone else coming?" Belle asked, as both Jack and Claire looked back into the carriage and waited.

Sure enough, a second man exited the carriage, almost bouncing out of it with the youth in his legs. He did look young, though Belle could not predict his age. He was tall, to be certain, as he stood nearly equal to Jack, and he was dressed just as finely as the few gentlemen that Belle had seen since arriving in England. He was not as lean as the other gentlemen though. Not that he was large, but the men that Belle had seen tended to be on the slim side. This man looked strong, broad in the shoulders, large in the arms and legs, as though he lugged sacks of flour in between signing important documents. But he did look lovely ... handsome, in a sweet way. Belle decided immediately that she liked that sort of handsome, and she had never, not once, thought of a man as sweet.

It was startling to realise that, as Belle's first thought that not been threat. This was enough to frighten her back behind her guard.

"Oh, it's Peter!" Susanna cheered. "Why, I haven't seen him since my Season last year. Grace will be pleased, and so will Mrs Denham."

"Who is Peter?" Belle asked softly. Threat, she reminded herself. A strange man, any man, could be a threat. This man was about to be staying under the same roof as her. She needed to prepare herself.

"Peter Denham," replied Susanna. "He is Grace's younger brother, though he works in London with Jack as a publisher."

Belle had been aware of one of Grace's brothers. She had met seventeen-year-old Jem Denham on several occasions. She had known of another brother, but she had not learned his name. Peter Denham, this strange man, was Grace's brother. Belle knew in her head that this meant he was trusted by this family. Every man that she had met within the Beresford family was safe. Peter should be safe, too.

Should.

Belle could not trust that. She wouldn't let herself trust that.

Chapter 4

"Claire!" cried Grace, who promptly flew down the stairs to receive her sister and the new baby inside the Ashwood House foyer.

Peter did his best to avoid the footmen who were in the midst of carrying in the trunks belonging to the travellers, and in doing so, inadvertently looked up at the magnificent ceiling that stretched two floors above. One could never fully prepare themselves for setting foot in a house such as this, and considering their modest upbringing, he wondered if Grace had ever properly become used to it.

His eldest sister, he observed, did look very well, and every bit a young duchess, right down to the glittering earbobs which hung from her lobes. Grace kissed Claire's cheek before she delicately placed a hand on little Maria's head, softly cooing over the precious infant.

"Oh, what a treasure!" she gushed,

Both Jack and Claire were terribly proud. Neither one of them had stopped smiling in the two weeks since Maria had been born. Peter did not think that he had ever seen two people who were more pleased with their brood than Jack and Claire.

"And that hair! Denham features, do you think? Or is that Jack's colouring?" Grace wondered.

"Of course, it is Jack's colouring," Claire said confidently. "Maria is his double. I cannot see anyone else."

"I think you are right," Grace agreed, before she looked up at the rest of the party and gave them all an apologetic expression. "Do forgive my rudeness."

"It is allowed when there is precious cargo," Jack teased as he received his sister-in-law, kissing her cheek.

Grace kissed Jackie's cheeks and fussed over her a little before she arrived at Peter and pulled her brother in for a tight hug. Peter had to lean down to kiss Grace's cheek, as Grace murmured, "You have gotten taller."

Peter chuckled. "Perhaps you have shrunk."

"It has been too long," she continued. "You work too hard. Do not forget about us in quiet, old Hertfordshire, while you build your empire in town."

"I could never," Peter assured her. Despite living in London, and loving the work that he did, the natural thoughts that passed through his mind as they travelled through the Hertfordshire countryside was that this was home. No matter where he lived, Ashwood would always be home.

"Jack! Claire!"

A blonde woman streaked down the stairs so quickly she might have been a blur as Susanna appeared before them with the biggest expression of anticipation on her face. Oddly, she was dressed in a rather dull, shade of beige. The dress itself was pretty, but the fabric appeared quite out of character for someone as usually fashionable as Susanna was.

But Susanna had changed in between now and the time that Peter had last seen her, and he supposed her choices of clothing had perhaps changed, too. She was a little darker in her complexion, with a dusting of freckles across her nose, indicative of someone who spent a great deal of time outdoors. What shone the most, perhaps, was her radiance. She was happy, and the Susanna that Peter had last known in London was terribly frustrated with her lot in life. Despite the rather arduous adventure that she had gone through, she did not seem to regret any of it, and Peter was glad for her.

Susanna was the next one to fuss over the baby, and soon the entire household became aware of Jack and Claire's arrival, as Adam and Cecily descended upon them as well. The moment Cecily appeared, nobody else could claim the baby. Maria was in her grandmother's arms for the foreseeable future.

Peter was received warmly by them all as well, and heard several reprimands about how hard he worked, and how he needed to visit more often, to which Jack defended him fervently. Peter was grateful for his partner.

"Congratulations, by the way, Susanna," Peter said, when he finally came to speak to her in and amongst the chaos of the reunited family. "I was so pleased to hear that everything worked out as it did for you and Mr Whitfield."

Susanna knitted her fingers together and held them in front of her as her cheeks flushed a little. "So am I," she replied. "Thank you, Peter. It is so nice to see you again. I cannot believe it has been so long. Are you happy in London? I hope Jack isn't working you too hard."

Peter grinned. "I must look like I am afraid of hard work or something," he mused. "Really, what I do now is less physically strenuous than what I used to do, and nobody seemed to worry about me beating on an anvil all day," Peter joked.

Susanna rolled her eyes as she laughed. "I suppose that is the beauty of having a family who love you. They worry about us incessantly, worry about our decisions and choices, and they are desperate to protect us when we go abroad, to London, or to the Caribbean." She teased a knowing smile. "But you are happy?" she checked.

Peter nodded. "Very," he promised. "When do I get to meet your Mr Whitfield?" he queried curiously.

"Oh, Alex will be along for dinner soon. Everyone comes for Sunday dinner." She suddenly gasped as she gripped the skirt of her beige dress. "Oh, I need to change! This is my wedding gown!"

Peter frowned. He would never pretend to be an expert in women's fashions, but certainly Susanna could have found something a little nicer to wear for her wedding than a gown that looked like it had been made out of a beige flour sack. "Your dress is lovely," he managed to compliment.

Susanna stared at Peter, as though he had grown an extra head, before she laughed. "Oh, this is not my wedding gown, it is just Belle's practise dress. But still, Alex cannot see me in the design. It is meant to be a surprise!" Susanna promptly turned on her heel and scampered back up the stairs.

How expensive it must be to pay for a wardrobe if one had to make practise examples of dresses before real ones, Peter mused. Belle, which sounded like a French name, must have been the woman making Susanna's wedding gown.

Evening soon dawned on the Ashwood estate and the additional members to the Beresford party soon arrived for dinner. Peter was animatedly received by his elder sister, Kate, and her husband, Jim, his younger brother, Jem, as well as his mother, Mrs Denham.

When he saw his mother walking towards him, supported by her cane owing to her lame leg from that injury year ago, Peter did feel a large pang of guilt for not visiting more often. How quickly time flew while he worked in London. It was hard to believe he had not been home in eight months or so.

"You are taller!" cried Mrs Denham, who had tears in her eyes.

"Grace said the same thing," Peter chuckled as he kissed his mother's cheek.

"Are you eating well enough? If you are having growth spurts you must be eating enough to support yourself! Just look at Jem! Look at how tall he is now. Practically eating me out of house and home, he is!"

Peter grinned at his brother, who looked quite sheepish. True enough, Jem looked to be about a foot taller than he was at Christmas. He looked a little gangly, as he was only seventeen, as though his weight had not yet caught up with him. Peter shook Jem's hand, before he hugged his little brother.

"Are you well?" Jem asked.

"Yes, you?"

Again, Jem appeared a little sheepish, which Peter thought was odd. It really could only mean one thing. "Anyone on your mind, Jemmy?" Peter asked quietly.

"Christ! Not in front of Mother," Jem hissed, hitting Peter in the shoulder, and dragging him a few steps away from everybody else.

"I asked you quietly! What did you want me to do? Communicate via thought?" Peter retorted. "Go on then. Who is she?" he urged.

Peter could not quite believe his eyes as Jem appeared to blush at the question. Lord, who was this girl, indeed. Jem seemed to be quite smitten.

"Don't get too excited," Jem said dismissively. "She doesn't exactly know I exist." He shrugged his shoulders, attempting to put on a bit of bravado to mask his disappointment.

"Who is she? Have you even spoken to her?"

Jem shook his head after a moment. "Well, no ..."

"How is the poor girl supposed to know of your existence if you have not even spoken to her?" Peter challenged.

"I have a plan!" Jem insisted. "I am going to ask her to dance at the Winter Assembly ... and if everything goes the way I plan in my head she will fall madly in love with me and think I'm the best-looking lad she's ever seen." Jem shrugged his shoulders, masking his bashfulness.

Peter grinned. Now he was desperately curious. "Who is she? Have I met her? What's her name?"

"No, you don't know her. She and her mother only recently moved to the area. Her name is –"

"What are you two boys whispering about?" Mrs Denham asked, interrupting the conversation.

Peter and Jem exchanged a glance, and Peter could see that Jem's mind was as empty as his own when it came to thinking up a lie. Thankfully, Peter's brother was primed to drop him in it.

"Peter's after a wife, Mother," Jem announced. "Got his eyes peeled for a fancy dame in London!"

Peter had a sudden urge to take his mother's cane and bash his brother over the head with it.

Mrs Denham's eyes lit up. "Oh, really?" she cried. "Well, how wonderful! I suppose town is filled with lovely girls at the moment, what with it being the Season and all. Do you have anyone in mind? There are certainly some lovely girls in Ashwood who would make fine wives, to be certain."

"No, Mother, I can assure you that I do not have my eye on anyone. I am the farthest thing from attached at the minute and I cannot foresee my situation changing anytime soon." Peter glared at Jem, who did look thoroughly amused and impressed with himself.

Were Peter a vengeful person, he might be tempted to go to that assembly just to drop Jem in it with whomever this mystery girl was. But he wasn't. Jem was lucky. That certainly did not mean that Peter wouldn't whack him one if he got the chance.

Before dinner, Peter was introduced to Alex Whitfield, who was perhaps the largest man that he had ever seen. He could have been a strongman in a circus performance, he was so large. Susanna looked quite the fairy beside him, but she did look so desperately happy. As did he. It was easy to see in the expression on Alex's face that he was quite devoted to his fiancée. Peter had never seen a black man before, at least not that he could recall. But he did read, and he did know of what went on about the world. What was worse was that he did know of how they were looked down upon because of their race. One only had to hear of some of the words that were used against Alex when his engagement to Susanna had been announced. And those were the words that had reached London. Peter was ashamed to think of what had been said in his own village.

But Alex Whitfield stood proudly in and amongst a room of genteel, white people, and Peter admired him.

Peter was also introduced to Madame Amélie Archambeau, Alex's mother. He had heard much about her from his mother's letters, as Amélie resided with her in the village. Her English was quite broken, but by all accounts, improved from when she had first arrived in England, and her son was quite attentive in translating much of the conversation into French for her.

"Where is Belle?"

Peter overheard Alex asks Susanna the question, and Peter recalled Susanna making the reference to Belle earlier. Was the dressmaker expected?

"Upstairs," Susanna replied. "I tried to coax her down, but she did not want to intrude. She thinks it's a family affair, and I couldn't convince her otherwise. I think she is just being a little timid."

Alex whispered something in Susanna's hear, to which she nodded, before promptly going over to her mother.

"– sweetbreads, I tell you!" Peter heard Cecily say as he tuned into the conversation that she was having with Claire, Jack and Grace. "I read about it. Apparently, stewed or roasted, they are excellent sources of the internal ingredients needed to have a son!"

"Codswallop!" Jack declared. "Where on earth did you read that, Mother? I think you must have imagined it."

"I did not!" Cecily retorted. She was still rocking baby Maria in her arms. "I read it in the newspaper."

"If she actually read that in a newspaper, I shall eat my hat," Jack said, rolling his eyes. "I am not going to feed my wife sweetbreads, whatever the bloody hell they are, and neither shall Adam. A son will come when he wants to. Don't you approve of Maria?"

Cecily gasped a most offended gasp. "Approve of her? How dare you! How could I not approve of my precious Maria?" Cecily cuddled her granddaughter to her chest. "Honestly, Jack. I don't know where you get your ideas from."

"Probably the same place you do when you read about sweetbreads," Jack muttered, to which Claire stifled a laugh, disguising it poorly as a cough.

"Mama," Susanna interrupted, before she ducked down to whisper something in her mother's ear, no doubt passing on whatever Alex's message had been.

"Susanna, take the baby," Cecily instructed, passing Susanna Maria. "I shall have her back, mind!" Cecily then rose from the settee where she had been sitting and marched out of the room and towards the stairs with purpose.

Not a minute later, Mr Cole, the butler, arrived to announce that dinner was being served in the dining room. The large family party began to make their way from the drawing room to the dining room, where the impossibly long table was laden with crockery, silverware, glasses, and tureens of fruit.

Peter found his name on a place card written in a neat hand as he took his seat. To his left sat his mother, which he knew had to be calculated on Mrs Denham's part, and to his right, the chair was empty. The place card read: Belle Desjardins.

"Dez-jar-dinz," Peter struggled to read under his breath. The dressmaker upstairs, anyway, was going to be on his right. Across from him sat Jem, who had already helped himself to a pear, which Peter was certain was meant to be decorative.

"So, darling, are you quite certain there have not been any young ladies that have turned your head recently?" Mrs Denham pressed.

"No, Mother –" but before Peter could finish articulating his response, the dining room door was opened for Cecily, and another young woman.

Peter's mouth opened as he quickly became entranced. Never before had he seen a woman like her before. How beautiful, she was, but that word did not seem strong enough.

Her skin was what had struck him first, such a cool, dark complexion that appeared smooth and flawless. Her small, delicate hands were clasped together nervously against the flat plane of her belly.

Everything about her seemed small and delicate. She did not stand very tall at all, reaching only Cecily's shoulder in height. She was thin and dainty, as though a strong wind would blow her over.

Her head was bowed slightly, and her eyes were down, and Peter longed for her to look up. Her hair was ebony in colour and curled in tight spirals. While she had the majority of her hair pinned away from her delicate face, several shorter curls framed her forehead and temples. Her cheekbones and jawline were angular, but her full lips, her nose, and the apples of her cheek perfectly softened her features.

From where he was sitting, Peter could see that she had a set of dark, thick lashes that shielded her eyes. Look up, he willed.

And she did.

Peter did not know what he had been expecting, but he had not been expecting those eyes. She took in the room with eyes of molten gold, a colour that he had never before seen on another person. But Peter quickly decided that they suited her perfectly, and they made her the most beautiful woman he had ever seen.

Chapter 5

Peter rose from his chair, as did every other man in the room as Cecily entered with the young lady who could only be Belle Desjardins. Once they were introduced, Peter knew that he needed to ask her how exactly to pronounce her family name. That was, of course, if he would have the sense in his head to form words. Peter had never spoken to a woman like her before. Really, he could count on one hand the number of women, excluding those of whom he was related to, that he had had a proper conversation with.

On second thought, could he really count the female authors that he had met? Peter had never really considered them romantic prospects and –

Romantic prospects?!

Peter choked. Shockingly audibly. He had sucked in a breath so violent after the thought had crossed his mind that anyone in the dining room might have thought that he had a vol-au-vent stuck in his windpipe. Much to his humiliation, his mother jumped up beside him, shaky as she was on her feet, and began whacking him in the back to help him cough up whatever he was choking on.

His pride, it seemed. And it came up just perfectly well and spilled onto the floor with the rest of his dignity.

It probably took Peter some ten seconds to compose himself, but it felt like an hour, and to his embarrassment, all eyes were on him, including the golden orbs belonging to Miss Desjardins.

"Do excuse me," Peter managed to mutter, before he bowed his head to both ladies and prayed for the attention to leave him.

Cecily pursed her lips, and in knowing what he did about the dowager duchess, Peter would have wagered that she would have wanted to utter some quip about him needing his mother to cut his food for him, but she did not. At least, not this time. And he thanked God for that.

"Do excuse Belle's tardiness, everyone," Cecily finally said. "She is working tirelessly on Susanna's gown and had to be forcibly pulled away to eat." She laughed. "One would think we are starving you by the look of you, dear."

The attention had left Peter, which allowed him to draw his focus back to Miss Desjardins. If she looked nervous before, then she looked dreadfully embarrassed now. Her shoulders had stiffened and her eyes and lowered once more, and they did so the moment Cecily had joked about her eating.

She was very thin, but she did not look unhealthy. One only had to look at the smooth brilliance of her skin to see that she was exactly how she was supposed to be.

"I am sorry for being late."

She had looked up again, only for a moment, to address the room. Her voice was soft, gentle, and heavily accented.

French, Peter could only presume. Her English could be understood perfectly well, but each word sounded different when uttered by her.

"Nonsense," dismissed Grace with a wave of her hand. She rose from her chair to collect Belle as Cecily took her seat at the end of the table, where she was immediately attended to by a footman who filled her wine glass.

Grace wove her arm through Belle's, and Peter noticed her stiffen a little again with nerves. Why was she nervous? Had she not known Grace for months?

"Belle, you, of course, remember my brother-in-law, Jack Beresford, and his wife, my sister, Claire," Grace said, reacquainting her with the couple.

Jack, who was still standing, along with the rest of the men, bowed his head. "How do you do, Belle?"

Peter hoped that he would become acquainted well enough with Belle to use her Christian name. He did not want to shame her, or embarrass himself, by stumbling over her surname.

"It is lovely to see you again," said Claire, smiling in a friendly manner.

"I am well, thank you," replied Belle quietly, managing a small smile.

She looked uncomfortable. Peter really couldn't understand why she would be uncomfortable in a room full of people, aside from the three guests, that she had known for such a long while. He was the one who had just choked in front of the room. If anything, telling her that, he hoped, would make her feel a little more at ease. He wanted her to feel at ease.

Grace then led Belle around to Peter's side of the table, and to the empty chair beside him. "And please allow me to introduce you to my brother, Peter Denham. Peter, meet our friend, Belle Desjardins."

Desjardins. Peter repeated the name ten times over in his head in quick succession as he formulated his next sentence. He was an intelligent young man. Why did he feel like he had nothing but dust in his brain? It certainly felt that way when she opened her eyes and looked up at him, those golden irises were burning a hole on his mind that was quickly leaving it empty.

"I am d-diluted to make your acquaintance, Miss Desjardins." Peter bit down on his tongue, certain that he had pronounced her name correctly, but ... had he really just said that he was –

"Diluted?" Belle frowned. "I don't know this word."

There was a God.

And He clearly had a wicked sense of humour as Jem, the abominable brat that he was, burst into a fit of laughter from across the table.

Belle artfully removed her arm from Grace's and sat down in the chair that the footman had pulled out for her. Once she was seated, the men could once more as well.

Peter glared daggers at his brother, and once he was seated, he threw out his foot under the table in hope and was pleased when his boot made contact with what had to be Jem's shin.

Jem yelped, and quickly shut his mouth.

Once Belle was seated, Peter noticed that she seemed to make herself as small as possible. Or perhaps he was a little unused to a woman who was as little as she was. By his estimation, she would not have been more than … perhaps fifty-seven or fifty-eight inches tall. She could easily be dwarfed by the grand dining room chair.

Delighted. Delighted. Peter repeated that word over and over in his head, as he prepared to rectify the beginning of their acquaintance. But as soon as he was ready to open his mouth, his mother claimed his attention.

God bless her, but he really did not want to be speaking about his business at that moment, a fact in itself that shocked him completely. All he could think about was the woman beside him probably thinking that he was a bloody fool who did not know how to speak properly.

Mrs Denham thankfully moved onto conversation with Claire after the first course, and Peter could finally turn his attention back to Belle. She had not spoken a word voluntarily. He had heard her respond to questions when she was asked, but she did not offer anything new to the conversation. She seemed very submissive, subservient, and timid in nature.

"I do beg your pardon, Miss Desjardins," Peter said finally, and, thankfully, correctly. "What I meant to say earlier was that I am delighted to make your acquaintance."

He was looking at her profile exactly, and he could hardly believe his eyes at the perfect lines that were her face. Her full lips parted as she gently turned her head to face him.

Her eyes were lowered first, before she carefully looked up at him. "Thank you," she replied.

Peter's heart fell a little. He would never want to be rude, but it seemed like quite a rehearsed answer. Though, through listening to her while being engaged in conversation with his mother, a lot of her answers had appeared rehearsed. She didn't volunteer information. She did not contribute or ask her own questions –

"What does that word mean?"

Peter blinked, dumbfounded.

"I don't know it." Belle pursed her lips as she waited for him to answer.

Belle had asked him a question. And once again, every bit of knowledge that Peter possessed had promptly fallen out of his head. He was the first person that she had engaged with, and he was about to look like an utter fool in front of her for the second, or third time that evening.

Think Peter, he commanded of himself. He noticed that Belle had not touched her wine through the first, second, or the current course. "Are you going to drink your wine?" he asked, and Belle shook her head. "Would you pass me your glass?" The moment he asked the question, Peter thought better of it, and added, "I shall do it, not to worry."

But Belle had already begun to reach for her glass as Peter went to collect it. In doing this, Peter brushed the back of Belle's hand with his own, and anyone might have assumed that his hand was a scalding iron by the way that Belle pulled her own away and hid it under the table.

Peter froze, staring at her, a little startled, as he watched her shoulders rise and fall quite rapidly as she looked like she was ... panicking. Belle's eyes were lowered, and she looked to be whispering something to herself. Was this reaction all because he had touched her, albeit so briefly?

Belle did not like to be touched. It made her panic. Peter made this connection immediately when recalling how she had stiffened when Grace had taken her arm. And Peter suddenly felt very ashamed for questioning her, and for causing such a reaction himself.

Peter seized Belle's wine glass and collected his own water glass. His actions captured her attention, though her shoulders were still rising and falling quickly. Peter poured the remaining water from his glass into Belle's wine glass and watched as the deep red liquid softened to a dark pink.

"To dilute means to thin a solution with water," Peter explained. "Do you see?"

"I see," Belle whispered. "I understand this word."

And her shoulders eased. Peter smiled; he couldn't help it. He hoped that his little experiment had helped to calm her in some way. For his own pride, he was pleased that it had worked, and that he hadn't spilled the wine everywhere.

Peter wanted to apologise to her. Furthermore, he wanted to ask her what frightened her so. But now was neither the time nor the place, at least for the latter. And for the former, he did not want to draw attention to her. Belle did not seem like the sort of young lady who enjoyed any sort of attention.

But Peter did not want their conversation to end. Belle had already turned back to her own meal and had cut a piece of asparagus to put into her mouth. His eyes fell upon her place card and he had an idea.

"I find it a little fascinating that family names often have meanings. My own, Denham, for example, means village or valley, or something along those lines." Peter knew that his own name, really, was terribly dull. "Does your family name have a particular meaning?" he asked.

"Yes," Belle confirmed, her voice a little steadier. "I believe, in English, it means 'gardens', like outside with flowers."

Peter could not mask his smile. He found it very endearing that Belle had explained what a garden was to him. "How beautiful. And it is certainly very interesting. Is it occupational? Was your father a gardener, perhaps?"

"I do not know," Belle replied softly. "It is not my family name, as you say. I was found in a garden."

And whatever confidence that Peter had found to continue the conversation vanished as he had once again spoiled things with his own ignorance and folly. What sort of idiot asked a young lady such as Belle about her father without first knowing her situation? She was clearly a girl who had not known a gentle hand, and Peter was not helping the situation.

"I am sorry," Peter apologised immediately. "Please, forgive me. I do not know what I was thinking."

Belle was found in a garden. What a start to her life. The very knowledge of it affected Peter in quite an alarming way, and he could only begin to imagine how her life had progressed from there. He, of course, could discern the lack of a gentle hand. What trouble, what danger, what cruelty had she known?

All she had endured had led her to this, to this night, seated beside a blabbering boy who did not know the first thing about talking to a woman.

"Monsieur Denham," Belle said, capturing his attention immediately. She was looking at him, her head a little cocked to the side as she appraised him.

This very appraisal made Peter straighten his posture immediately.

"Sûr."

Chapter 6

Belle had come to conclusion that Peter Denham was safe alarmingly quickly. Most alarmingly. It was frightening to think of any man as safe, let alone a man of whom she had barely begun to know. But in listening to him talk, Belle could hear the innocence in his voice.

It was odd to consider a man innocent, but she did. The innocence in Peter's voice told Belle that he had never hurt anyone. Peter had never harmed or used anyone. Peter had never taken advantage or exploited anyone. He had certainly never abused anyone. There was decency in innocence, and Belle admired it remarkably. Remarkably enough to declare this man as safe.

He was simply a young man, a baby-faced young man, who seemed to want to talk to her, with no ulterior motive, and certainly no evil intentions. Belle had known evil. She had experienced evil. She had an intimate knowledge of evil. She had a talent for seeing it in the eyes of men, and it was talent she was disgusted by. But it was a talent that protected her, nonetheless.

But there was no evil in the blue depths of Peter Denham's eyes. His eyes were like oceans, so mixed with they with the hues of sky and cerulean. And innocent. Belle thought that 'innocent' ought to be a shade of blue, too.

But then begged the question. Why would a good, decent young man, like Peter Denham, have any desire to speak with her at all? Did he not know who she was? Did he not know what she had been? Perhaps he did not. Perhaps he was blissfully ignorant.

What he certainly was not, however, was blind, and he clearly could see the differences between them. But, like his family, Peter Denham did not possess the common prejudice that she had known too many white men to possess.

And such knowledge only increased the safety that Belle saw in Peter.

"What does that mean?" Peter asked curiously. "I am afraid my French is ... well, I never received any French instruction."

Belle frowned a little. He seemed conscious, self-conscious of this fact. Was French language tuition common? A quick glance around the table and only Susanna and the duchess, Cecily, had been able to communicate in French with Belle. The others all could not. "My English is equally diluted."

Peter smiled, and then his grinned. He had a terrifically broad smile that took up nearly half his face. Even the skin beside his eyes crinkled, and Belle enjoyed that. His smile was just another innocent characteristic. Only innocent people could smile as happily as Peter could.

Belle did not know if she was capable of a smile like that. Her smiles, her real smiles, had been stolen from her a long time ago.

"Was that a joke, Miss Desjardins?" Peter's brows rose.

Belle nonchalantly speared a sprout with her fork and popped it into her mouth. She enjoyed English food. She enjoyed any food. Food was precious. But she did wish sometimes that the cook would choose another method of preparing vegetables than boiling them. The sprouts were a little grey.

"You have a sense of humour, I think," Peter observed.

Belle could not help but smile coyly. Perhaps she did.

Before Peter could speak to her again, his attention was commanded by the duke, who proceeded to ask both he and Jack Beresford curious questions about their upcoming publication.

The duchess, and Peter's, younger brother, Jem Denham, was smiling at Belle. A knowing, almost teasing smile, as she began to attempt to understand the next topic of conversation.

Belle did not know very much about books. Quite obviously, she had never held one in her hands until very recently, and even now, she was not a confident reader.

Belle could read, though it would often take her time to work out the words, and sometimes they would become too complex for her. She had never read a book in its entirety because it was simply too difficult. Now that she could speak English passably, Susanna's lessons had stopped, and Belle was far too bashful to ask for Susanna's help again, especially as she was wrapped up in planning her wedding. Teaching Belle how to read properly would not be a priority.

Belle had not even begun to contemplate writing. The very thought made her feel utterly stupid. She could write her own name, and simple words, the words that she had memorised, but her penmanship was dreadful, and she hated to think of the mistakes there would be in her spelling.

Susanna had been the one to send away for the fabric for her gown. Belle had managed to escape writing that letter. She hated to think of what would happen the next time that she would need to place an order.

Unlike Belle, Peter seemed very intelligent. Incredibly so. Belle could often be lost in English conversations, particularly when a topic was being discussed that she did not understand. But she knew that Peter was discussing his business, and he spoke with confidence and conviction, two traits that she did admire. To work in publishing and books, Peter must have been clever, and he must have been an excellent reader.

An innocent, decent man such as he would never call Belle stupid, but Belle wondered if he would think it if he knew how little she could do when it came to reading and writing.

"I need the hems taken down on that one," instructed Mrs Nancy Jones as she laid down a dress on Belle's table. "Two inches at least. My Helen has grown so much this summer. Same for this dress." She added a blue, gingham dress to the pile. "There's a button needs fixing on this coat, and my husband's breeches need a little letting out. Helen is not the only one who had been doing some growing this summer." Mrs Jones tutted. "As much as you can on those." She patted the dark breeches. "I must say, I was very sceptical about having one of you negroes in the village, but it is so useful to have a seamstress. Saves me so much time not having to mend things myself."

Belle did not take offense. It was quite useless wasting time and her emotion on being offended over little comments like that. Even in her backwards way, she did think that Mrs Jones had meant to pay her a compliment. This was her home now, and Belle needed to be amenable, non-threatening, and as small and unnoticeable as possible.

"Those will not be a problem, Mrs Jones," she replied. "They will be finished by the end of the week."

"Good. I shall return on Friday then." Mrs Jones turned around and began to browse for her groceries, adding items to her now empty basket. Mr Andrews was quick to attend to her and advise her on the latest stock from London.

Belle placed Mrs Jones' items in the little production line that she had made for herself, as she picked up the socks that she had been darning before. In the back of her mind, she could hear Mr Andrews fussing over Mrs Jones, and he was quick to sell her a few extra bits that she no doubt did not need. Nevertheless, she left the shop quite happily, just as a new customer entered.

Belle did not look up right away. She did not like to. It was an act of submission, a way to make the white people feel comfortable, especially around someone who possessed a stare like Belle. She would never be caught staring. To stare was to offend, and to offend a white person was dangerous.

Mr Andrews confirmed the identity of the new customer, and this made Belle lose all her reason.

"Peter Denham!" he cried.

Belle nearly dropped the sock that was in her hand as she looked up, and sure enough, Peter was standing in the entryway, dressed for the day. He removed his top hat and a lock of his dark hair swept across his forehead.

"Mr Andrews, how do you do?" Peter and Mr Andrews seemed to know each other well, though Belle presumed that most people who had grown up in the Ashwood village would have a good knowledge of one another.

"Well, well," replied Mr Andrews. "It has certainly been a little while since you deemed it necessary to descend upon our sleepy little village. Is London too diverting?"

Peter chuckled politely. "Very diverting," he confirmed. "My business keeps me busy. I have returned to Ashwood, of course, for Lady Susanna's wedding to Mr Whitfield. As well as to celebrate the birth of my new niece. Did you hear?"

"Oh, yes." Mr Andrews nodded his head. "The dowager duchess has been very quick to spread the good news about. Many congratulations, of course." He then sighed seriously. "Now, this wedding business ..." Mr Andrews pursed his lips. "What are your thoughts?"

Belle had managed to track and translate this conversation quite well, and it was not hard to guess just what Mr Andrews was thinking, and just what he wanted Peter to say.

But Peter would not disparage Alex and Susanna. Peter did not think with prejudice or cruelty. Belle had seen it in his eyes.

"I could not be happier for the bride or the bridegroom," Peter replied shortly. "As I am certain you are very pleased about the large order Mrs Reynolds will have placed with you for the wedding breakfast."

Mr Andrews chuckled, and clapped Peter on the shoulder. Belle physically flinched on his behalf. "But, of course! Aren't we all pleased? A wedding is such a joyful occasion."

"Certainly," nodded Peter. He subtly glanced in Belle's direction, but he did little to acknowledge her. "Now we are on the subject, how is business, Mr Andrews?"

"Oh, you know, there are good days and bad days." Mr Andrews shrugged. "I manage."

Peter frowned and seemed to appear genuinely sympathetic. Belle, on the other hand, had never known Mr Andrews to have a bad day, at least not since she had been working at her table. He seemed to have an endless collection of coins rattling in his pocket.

"I've had to take on Mr Whitfield's little friend," Mr Andrews continued, nodding to Belle. "Not to worry about speaking before her. I find her English comes and goes. Having her here does deter some of the customers away." Adding in a low voice, he said, "The compensation from her little table is necessary."

Belle did not react. Of course, she did not. She would never. Curiously, though, Peter did not react either. He did not appear angry, or amused, or anything. His expression was blank.

"You do know that managing the finances is exactly what I do for Lord Jack at Beresford Press. I have a head for figures, and it would be no trouble at all to have a look over your ledger. I would be happy to help you find room to improve your profit."

Belle tried to concentrate, but there were a few words in what Peter had just said that she did not understand, but from what she could discern, Peter was trying to help Mr Andrews. Peter was good and kind, and maybe Mr Andrews was his friend.

"You're too kind, young Peter," Mr Andrews complimented. "Go on then. I'll fetch them for you." He disappeared up the stairs that led up to the apartment he kept for himself above the store.

Now that they were alone, Peter turned his head towards Belle, saying nothing, but winking at her, ever so subtly. What did that mean?

Belle forced herself to keep darning, to keep up the pretence that she was not listening or trying to follow along with what they were discussing. Mr Andrews returned only a few minutes later with a thick, leather-bound book.

Peter seemed to be quite in his element as he opened the ledger and combed through whatever was written in there. He laughed with Mr Andrews about certain things in the book, and Peter produced his own pen and paper as he began to take notes.

From the way his pen danced across the paper, Belle could tell that Peter had beautiful penmanship.

"I can see here that this is where Miss Desjardins began working in the shop," Peter commented, reading whatever was written in the book. "You have additional income here, I see. Your compensation?"

"Yes," confirmed Mr Andrews. "My sixty-five percent."

"I see." Peter nodded slowly as he began to take notes. He continued to flip the pages and scrawl.

This was certainly the longest time that Belle had ever taken to darn a sock as she had to keep forcing herself to pay attention. Except for the fact that she desperately wanted to know what was going on.

Peter kept going through the ledger as Mr Andrews attended to the customers who entered the shop, charming them and selling them his goods.

Belle did not know how long it had been, but it had certainly felt like hours by the time that Peter closed the ledger. Meanwhile, she was still tending to the same sock. Luckily for her, Mr Andrews knew nothing about darning.

"I have to disagree with you, Mr Andrews," Peter finally announced as he returned his pen to his breast pocket.

"Disagree with me?" repeated Mr Andrews. "Whatever for? About what?"

"The presence of Miss Desjardins deterring customers. That is what you said, did you not? It seems that the reality of the situation is quite the opposite, and I think you know that."

Mr Andrews tensed. Belle recognised the signs of anger immediately, and she placed her sewing down gently. She would be ready to run. What on earth was Peter thinking?

"You have taken sixty-five percent of her income from her ... when I heard that from my sister this morning, I could hardly believe it." Peter shook his head. "Since Miss Desjardins has been working in this shop, you have never been more profitable, and that is without counting what you take from her. My guess would be your profits are coming from opportunistic buyers; buyers who come to drop of their mending and end up purchasing something that they do not necessarily need. Am I right?"

Mr Andrews said nothing, save for his eyes narrowing.

"Were Miss Desjardins to take her business elsewhere, you would stand to lose the substantial profit you have been enjoying of late," continued Peter.

Peter was arguing for her. Belle could not quite believe it. She would have been honoured if she were not so afraid. Only a fool angered a white man, and she prayed Peter was not in any danger. He was innocent.

"No other shop would take her," snapped Mr Andrews.

"Are you willing to wager your profits on that assumption?" Peter challenged.

Mr Andrews bit his tongue.

"I did not think so. What will be happening henceforth is a new bargain. Miss Desjardins will pay you two shillings per week in rent for the space she is occupying in your shop. In return, she will keep one hundred percent of her own income."

Two shillings? Belle's heart quickened. All she would need to pay was two shillings and she could keep the rest? Did Peter understand what this would mean for her? He had to, or else why would he be here?

"That's a dirty trick, Peter Denham," sneered Mr Andrews.

"It's not a dirty trick," countered Peter. "It's honest business, which I highly suggest you practise. Miss Desjardins has the favour of the Beresfords. They care that she has a good deal."

Mr Andrews snatched the ledger off of the counter and clutched it tightly. "I will expect my two shillings promptly." With that, he returned to the stairs and disappeared up into the apartment above.

Peter then immediately approached Belle, looking upon her with what appeared to be apprehension. Belle was still seated and had to crane her neck to look up at the very tall Peter Denham.

"Forgive me," he begged. "I could not help myself. I spoke the truth. I learned of your situation this morning from Grace."

For a fleeting moment, Belle wondered why her situation, or anything about her at all, would have come up in conversation between Peter and the duchess.

"When I heard, I had to rectify it. This deal is fair, I promise you. This is what I do for business. I am good with numbers, and –"

"Thank you," Belle said gratefully, interrupting him. She rose to her feet, though that did not do much to rectify the differences in their heights. "You helped me. Thank you. But ... he is angry now." Belle could not erase the fear that had now settled in the pit of her stomach. What would happen when Peter left? Would ... would he ...?

"Miss Desjardins ... Belle," Peter said firmly. "I just highlighted your value to him. He knows exactly what your talents are worth to his business. Everything will be alright."

Chapter 7

That morning, Peter had discovered that he did not possess the virtue of subtlety. Such was the case when he began inquiring with Grace after Belle. He, along with the rest of his family and the dinner guests, had stayed the night at Ashwood House. Peter had been expecting, hoping, to meet Belle again at breakfast, but alas, she had already left for her work in the Ashwood village.

It was then that he had learned of the ridiculous deal she had fallen victim to in order to earn a wage in the village, and it angered Peter greatly that anyone could view such a deal as fair. It certainly was not fair.

Peter was utterly unsure of the spell that Belle had cast over him the night before at dinner, but something had changed within him. Standing before her, as he was now in the grocer, Peter felt completely bewitched. He had never experienced such feelings before. His attention had never been captured like this before.

Of course, he had noticed pretty women before, but then, he supposed, Peter had never seen a lady as beautiful as Belle. He had never seen a woman like her before ever. It was as though he'd had no idea that women could be so lovely before he laid eyes upon her.

But beauty, to be certain, was merely skin deep, and what commanded Peter's attention was note solely Belle's striking face. Peter wanted to know her nature, her mind, her thoughts. She wielded an almighty shield to keep herself safe. He felt a yearning from deep within to gain her trust. He wanted her trust, and he wanted her faith. He could see that these gifts would indeed be challenging to earn from one who had no doubt suffered as she had.

Peter had dreamt of it the night before. The very thought fuelled an anger inside of him that he had never known was there. But in looking upon Belle, in seeing the fear in her eyes at the very notion that Mr Andrews was angry, Peter knew that he could never be irresponsible with emotions like anger.

She possessed a heartbreaking amount of fear for someone so young. Peter believed they were probably a similar age to one another, and he felt rather selfish at really never knowing true fear.

Inconvenience and frustration, to be sure, but never fear.

Peter wanted to earn Belle's trust. Such a gift would be an honour.

Mr Andrews stomped back into the shop and glowered at Peter. He would regret his slight deception only in the way that it might impede on the service his mother received, but he would never regret securing Belle a fair deal.

Regardless of the fact that Peter had assured Belle that Mr Andrews now understood her value, Belle had tensed now that he had returned from the flat upstairs. She was looking past Peter now, watching Mr Andrews carefully, almost as though she was ready to run at any moment.

What sort of evil had she known in her young life?

"Will you show me what you are doing?" Peter asked, re-capturing Belle's attention.

She blinked a few times, before her golden eyes settled back upon him. Would Peter ever get used to those irises? He did not know. How striking they were against the beautiful, cool brown of her skin.

Peter decided that he was going to remain in the shop for as long as Belle was today, though he did not want to offer to stay with her, to wait with her, or to protect her. He did not want Belle to focus on the fact that she was afraid, but Peter did not want to leave her when she was feeling frightened.

"Men ... do not like ... to know ... to sew." Belle stammered a little, stumbling over her words, and perhaps choosing a few that did not entirely make sense together as her accent became more pronounced through her apprehension.

But Peter did understand what she meant. And quite self-ishly, he was glad that he was not the one stumbling over his words, though he did acknowledge that Belle's tongue tiredness was not because of infatuation.

Peter gestured to the buttons on his coat, and he smiled reassuringly. "My coat has buttons. Oughtn't I know how to sew one back on should I lose it?"

Belle swallowed nervously. "No," she replied, her voice steadying. "You should pay me to do it."

Peter laughed. Genuinely. He could see as her shoulders relaxed marginally that she had made a joke, and he appreciated how challenging that had to be in a language that was not her mother tongue. He could also appreciate how challenging it had to be to joke when she had been feeling so frightened. But then, Peter hoped, that he had somehow helped to ease her fear.

But Belle relented, and for the remainder of the day, Peter sat behind her and watched her work. She finished darning a sock, and before this day, Peter had never before realised what had happened between the times he had worn holes in his socks, and his mother had returned them to him as good as new. Belle then moved on to hemming the skirt of a dress, and he watched in almost hypnotised fascination as her tiny hands moved so delicately with the needle.

Belle did not speak to him as she worked. Peter was determined not to distract her. He was simply there so that her shoulders could remain relaxed.

Though after a few hours of watching Belle diligently sew, Peter was quite certain that his hands, which really looked like a link of sausages in comparison to Belle's, were quite unsuited to such delicate work. Belle's hands moved with expertise and experience as she formed one perfect stitch after the other.

Customers came and went, and Mr Andrews returned into his charming self. Purchases were made, and Belle received more work from people bringing her their garments for alterations, as well as people coming to collect the clothing that she had finished.

Belle was a passive proprietor. That was what Peter observed. She kept her eyes low and her voice demure. Peter did not intervene on her behalf, even when customers, neighbours of whom he had known he whole life, barked orders at her as though she was a servant and not a businesswoman. Quietly, Peter willed Belle to do this herself.

Though this was how she had seemed for much of the dinner the night before as well. Belle did not tend to make eye contact. She did not speak until she was spoken to. She did not fight. But instead, she wielded her shield and she protected herself the only way she knew how.

Belle did not fight, and Peter could only assume that was learned, ingrained behaviour. From where ...? He hated to imagine.

The final customer through the door that day was Alex, who greeted a prickly Mr Andrews before turning towards Belle's table. His dark eyes widened when he saw Peter seated behind Belle. His head cocked to the side a little before his eyes narrowed.

Peter felt his stomach tighten. Why did he suddenly feel as though he was the one in danger?

Alex approached the table, removing his hat, and Belle took his arrival as time to conclude her work for the day. Alex then uttered something to Belle in French, his eyes flashing to Peter briefly, and Belle replied in the same tongue.

Peter couldn't help but feel as though they were speaking about him, and he wished he could understand.

"How do you do, Mr Denham?" greeted Alex, finally.

Peter stood, smiling awkwardly. "Well," he replied. "And you, Mr Whitfield?"

"Well," Alex returned. "I have come to escort Belle home."

Peter could sense his dismissal in Alex's tone, as well as an air of distrust. Which, Peter granted, was fair. They did not know each other well, and it was clear that Alex cared for Belle a great deal. He was protective of her, as though she were his younger sister.

Peter was momentarily distracted by the sound of coins, and he watched as Belle collected two shillings from her money tin before she took a deep breath and approached Mr Andrews. She walked stiffly, yet quickly, and she kept her eyes low as she placed the money on the counter for him.

Mr Andrews did not say or do anything to acknowledge her, save for snatching the coins as soon as her hand was away from them. Belle darted back to her table to collect her money tin, before she nodded to Alex.

Peter could not help but feel a little disappointed in this arrangement. Yet another surprise for him, considering he had only laid eyes upon this woman last night. But he at least thought he might have a chance to speak with her a little more had he been allowed to walk her back home. But it seemed this was not to be.

Peter realised that walking alone with a man was probably not going to earn Belle's trust. Alex, he understood, was different.

The three of them left the grocer and stepped out onto the street. Peter felt a sense of regret knowing that this was when he was going to have to leave her. When could he reasonably see her again? He could not very well sit behind her all day tomorrow, could he?

Alex said something to Belle, again in French. Belle nodded, before she looked to Peter rather shyly.

"Thank you," she said softly, yet gratefully. Her gratitude was layered, and Peter understood that she was thanking him for several reasons, some of which she could not articulate. After thanking him, however, she turned, and began to walk on ahead in the direction of the road that would take her up to Ashwood House.

"Are you not going to escort her?" Peter asked Alex, his brows furrowed. "If you will not, then I would be happy to."

"I told her to start walking, and that I would catch up in a moment," said Alex coolly.

"Ah," realised Peter, nodding his head once. The feeling of apprehension reappeared in his stomach.

Alex straightened his posture, making his already impossibly broad shoulders seemed wider and stronger. Her was an incredibly large man, with the sort of brawn that Peter had never before seen on another man. Really, with the flick of his finger, he would be quite capable of knocking Peter off of his feet, and he was not a small man either!

"What are you doing?" Alex demanded to know, his teeth clenching. "I do not care that you are a relative of Susanna. I care very little about you in this moment. What are you doing near Belle?"

But before Peter could even form a response, Alex interrupted.

His accent was not as thick as Belle's, as he had clearly been speaking English for longer, however in anger, the French became more obvious. "She is not a plaything ... not a conquest or a game you can play. Belle has suffered more in her young life than you could ever conjure up in your worst nightmares," Alex seethed in a hushed voice through his barred teeth. "If you are wanting a woman to ..." Alex did not finish the sentence, but he had implied the ending well enough. "Belle is not the one. She will not be used or toyed with. Not a hair on her head will be harmed so long as I am living. I made that promise to her, and I will keep it. I will say it again, Peter Denham. I do not care that you are a relative of Susanna's. If you are even thinking about hurting Belle, I suggest you run very far from me."

"I would never hurt her," replied Peter defensively. "I would never hurt any woman. I have three sisters, Mr Whitfield, and a mother. I am not the sort of man who plays with women," he said distastefully. "The whole reason I came here today was because I wanted the very best for Miss Desjardins! I negotiated her a better deal, to allow her to keep her income, and I stayed behind so that she did not feel afraid to be alone with Mr Andrews."

Alex exhaled, nodding once slowly.

"I understand her experiences –"

"You don't understand," interrupted Alex, though he did not do so rudely. In fact, his tone was sad. "You don't understand what she has endured. I can to a point, but not even I know, not even I can fully understand."

Peter accepted that, and he regretted his choice of words. Of course, he could not understand. But that did not mean that he did not want to. "I would never hurt her," Peter said again. "It is the very last thing I would ever want to do."

Chapter 8

"**W**as he making you uneasy?" Alex asked Belle as soon as he caught up with her. "He told me that he had come to the grocer today to help you but –"

"Mr Denham did help me," Belle said, interrupting him. Looking up at Alex, Belle could see the concern in his dark eyes, and the deep line of worry across his forehead. "He is kind." Safe, she thought.

Alex's brow softened a little. "Kind he may be, but that does not mean that you need him coming near you. I know you prefer distance. You need only say the word and I will ensure that he gives you a wide berth."

Belle understood Alex's need to protect her. Perhaps it was intense. Perhaps it was a little over the top. But it would only seem that way to an outsider. Alex had looked upon, and looked after, Belle this way ever since they had been sold together in the British Virgin Islands. She could see in his eyes that he still had not forgiven himself for allowing that wretched, vile man to lay his hands on Belle, to attempt to violate her as only an entitled villain could. Alex had saved Belle that day, but not before she had prayed to God to kill her to spare her from such a fate. Alex would rather die than given another man, any man, the opportunity to harm Belle again, even if he was perfectly harmless.

It would be easy, Belle thought, to give Alex her permission to make Peter Denham stay away from her. She had begun to tip-toe into a sort of life that could make her happy here in Ashwood. She was safe with the Beresfords. She had a way to earn her own income. She had food, shelter, freedom. What more could she want? What else was there to a fulfilled life? She had wanted nothing more than these things for years.

Never had she even considered the thought of a suitor, if that was even what a man like Mr Denham could be. Perhaps she was entirely wrong, but Alex seemed to think there was reason to believe it. Belle had never considered anything of the sort because she had never known a man to be capable of loving anything, let alone a woman. She had never seen love before.

That was, of course, until she had seen it with her own eyes. First with Alex and Susanna, and then the duke and duchess. And then, most recently, between the duke's brother and his wife. It certainly existed, and there seemed to be men who were indeed capable of holding onto a woman without harming her.

But to even imagine herself in such a situation was impossible. It was impossible. It would never happen. Could never happen. If there weren't so many obvious reasons as to why it could not happen, there was the sudden fear that had bubbled up into her throat as she imagined herself in the position of one those women.

Beholden to a man. Belonging to a man. To be at a man's mercy.

The very notion was terrifying and unimaginable. Belle envisioned pain, violence, and fear. She could feel the pain, as though bruises had already covered her body. Instinctively, Belle wrapped her arms around herself in an effort to calm herself.

Belle thought of Peter Denham. She forced her thoughts away from her fears, and she thought solely of him, of the man who had fought a battle for her today and won. The man who was the reason why she was carrying her own income home. The man who was safe. She had felt that he was safe. She knew in her bones that he was safe.

Belle was no fool. She knew exactly why he had sat behind her in the shop all day. He had sensed her fear, but he had not pressed her about it, nor had he expected anything in return from her. He had sat there, all day, just because Belle did not want to be alone with Mr Andrews. And she had been too much of a coward to even thank him, let alone to talk to him while he was there. She was glad, at least, that she had found her tongue outside before she had parted from him.

"I don't want you to turn him away," Belle told Alex, quite shocked at the words that were coming out of her own mouth.

All Belle knew was that everything frightened her. She could find fear everywhere. She still was terrified of men, and more so of what they were capable.

But she was not afraid of Peter Denham. And for once in her life, she was relieved to feel something other than fear.

"Are you sure?" Alex checked softly. "I know he is a relation of the family, and you needn't be fearful of offending anyone. They all would understand."

"It's alright," promised Belle. "What ... what exactly do you think Mr Denham has in mind?" she asked. The fear turned her stomach again suddenly. Belle had not expected it. Even if she believed Peter to be safe, her own mind could twist it into something to be scared of. Belle suddenly wished she had not asked the question.

Alex surprised Belle by offering a small, reassuring smile. "Despite my own fears, I suppose you would call them, I don't believe a cruel thought has ever passed through Peter Denham's mind. I think the poor boy is sweet on you. That is what I think he has in mind."

"Sweet on me?" Belle repeated. "Why?" She had not meant to sound so in disbelief, but she could not help it. Anyone could understand why the idea would seem a little ridiculous.

Alex laughed a breathy chuckle. "Well, I have come to understand that to some people, good people, appearance is simply that," he murmured. "Good people do not see skin like ours and think less. Good people take the time to appreciate us for what is on the outside, but what is also within."

Belle did know that to be true. Once again, she had seen it. "Susanna is good people."

Alex grinned as he nodded. "Susanna is very good people. And perhaps, just maybe, Peter Denham is good people, too."

Peter Denham did not visit Belle again that week. She was not frightened to be alone with Mr Andrews in the grocer.

She knew that he had been right when he had when he had claimed that Mr Andrews now knew her worth. But the very fact that he had not been to visit her did make her wonder whether or not Alex had reneged on their agreement and he had instructed Peter to stay away from her.

But, of course, this was not true. Belle, instead, came to the conclusion that perhaps Alex had been wrong, and that perhaps Peter wasn't sweet on her. Really, this made sense. This was practical. And it did not bother or disappoint her one iota.

Belle made peace with the fact that she had entertained the thought for a silly moment, and that was that. There was a reason why she never considered such things for herself, and it was a compelling reason at that. Belle did not like to remind herself of it, but it was always there.

So, she carried on, like she had been doing long before Peter Denham had arrived in Ashwood.

Belle had begun to work on Susanna's dress using the real fabric. While she had sewn a thousand garments in her time, she felt inept when she handled such expensive fabric. She was terrified of pricking her finger and getting blood on the silk. Or accidentally lighting it on fire. Or throwing it out a window. She was unsure how the latter might happen, but Belle was still conscious of keeping the windows latched just in case.

The following Sunday, as the family left for church, Belle sat up in her bedroom. She always prayed on Sundays. She prayed every day, but especially on Sundays. She sang, too. She sang the hymns that she had learned as a child, and she said her thank yous for her blessings, as there were indeed blessings in and amongst the fires.

It did fill the pit of her stomach with guilt that she did not attend church like everyone else on a Sunday, but what could be done? Even though the Beresfords were good people, like Alex had described Susanna, that did not mean that everyone else in the village felt comfortable enough to accept her skin for what it was.

Really, Belle thought, it would be very un-Christian of her to deliberately make people uncomfortable in a church. Even if, perhaps, the more Christian act would be for the people of Ashwood to love thy neighbour.

After Belle had said her prayers, she returned to working on Susanna's dress. As much as it had been unnerving, Belle had cut the pieces to size, and she had sewn together the shell of the dress through the week. It looked very simple without the embellishments that Belle had designed. Today, Belle was making the petal sleeves.

As she was midway through sewing the first sleeve, Belle was startled by a sudden knock at the door.

"Come in, please," Belle called, gently placing her work on the table as a housemaid entered the room.

"Excuse me, Miss Desjardins, but you have a visitor."

Belle's brows rose. A visitor for her? On a Sunday, no less. She had never had a visitor before. She did not have any acquaintances in order for them to visit. Everyone she would consider an acquaintance or friend either lived in this house, or they would be at church.

"Really? Who is it?"

"Peter Denham, miss," replied the maid. "He is waiting down in the drawing room."

Belle was suddenly so thankful that she had emptied her hands of her sewing, for she would have certainly pricked her finger in that moment and ruined Susanna's sleeve. Belle certainly hoped, for the maid's sake, that her expression was neutral. "Thank you," she said. "I will come down right away." Why on earth was Peter visiting her? Should he not be at church? He was expected this evening for dinner, anyway. Why had he come now?

As she walked down the hallway and descended the staircase, Alex's words floated back into her mind. "He is not sweet on me," Belle hissed under her breath, in French, too, just in case she was overheard. "He cannot be sweet on me."

A footman was waiting by the drawing room, and as soon as she approached, the door was opened for her.

The drawing room was bright, owing to the large windows letting in the morning sun. It was immaculate, yet empty, save for the well-dressed gentleman waiting by the fireplace. He had been leaning against the mantle and had straightened his posture just as soon as Belle had walked into the room.

He did look well. Belle really liked that despite the fact that he dressed in the fine robes of a gentleman, his youthful face humanised him. She liked that dearly. Peter certainly wore his Sunday best. His dark hair was combed neatly, and his jaw was clean shaven. His blue eyes found hers immediately.

To Belle's surprise, there seemed to be genuine concern in his gaze.

"SOUP!" Peter suddenly shouted, in a very strange attempt at a greeting.

Belle almost was uncertain that she had heard him properly. She translated the word in her head, and he seemed to have shouted at her about soup. Did he mean the food? Why would he be talking about soup?

Peter's cheeks flushed red a little bit as he shook his head. "Forgive me," he murmured bashfully. "Oh!" Peter then bowed his head to her, as though he had forgotten the act in his odd declaration about soup. His cheeks reddened further. "Oh, Lord," he muttered under his breath. "What's a bet God's on my side and she's got no idea I just shouted at her about soup instead of bidding her good morning?" Peter murmured to himself.

Belle couldn't help but smile. She liked this. She liked that he was bashful. She liked that he had seemingly made an error. It added to the safe. It built up the safe. It reaffirmed the safe.

"What kind of soup?" Belle asked. She smiled, enjoying the feeling, and enjoying the fact that Peter's embarrassment worsened. She didn't understand why he was embarrassed, but she liked that he was.

Peter ran a hand back through his head and laughed awkwardly. "So, you did understand that?"

Belle nodded, still smiling. "What kind of soup?" she asked again.

Peter took a breath, settled himself, and then bowed his head again. "Good morning, Miss Desjardins."

Belle curtseyed in return. "Good morning, Mr Denham," she replied. But she would not relent. "What kind of soup? Or does soup mean something else in English and not the food?"

"No, no, you are right. I yelled at you about the food." Peter rolled his eyes at himself. "Thank God my brother did not witness that, or I would never hear the end of it." He was still embarrassed.

Belle had not seen Peter since the Monday before, the very day when Alex had indicated to her Peter's possible intentions. In the six days since, she had convinced herself that Alex was wrong. Walking down the stairs moments ago, Belle had done so once again.

And yet, here she stood, smiling in a way she had not done so in ... ever ... because it pleased her in a way that she did not understand that this man was bashful in front of her.

"My mother has pea and ham soup on the stove for luncheon after church. When you were not there, I worried that you were ill and I meant to go home and fetch you a bowl ... but, as you see, I came straight here instead and completely forgot the soup. Hence why the moment I saw you, I shouted at you about soup." Peter shook his head. "Please forget I ever did that."

Peter had noticed that she was not in attendance at church. He had worried for her health. And he had meant to fetch her food. Belle slowly made sense over what he had just said in her head, ensuring that she had understood him exactly.

Peter cared. Belle understood that well enough. What she also understood was that she liked that he cared. But then came the problem, the fear, the worry, as to why she had never considered such a man for herself. No matter how she liked that Peter cared, Belle still could never –

"Are you well?" Peter asked, concerned, as he interrupted Belle's train of thought. "Or are you ill? Have I pulled you out of bed? Please forgive me if I have. You don't look ill, thankfully. You look remarkably ordinary." The moment the word escaped Peter's mouth, he turned away from her and rested his head against the mantle.

Ordinary. Ordinaire, Belle translated for herself. Well, she supposed ordinary was not frightful, or dreadful, or unsightly.

She jumped when Peter banged his head against the mantle. "I have a mind to walk out, and then walk back in again, and pray that a bloody miracle happens, and you forget this whole conversation. What is wrong with me?" Peter asked himself.

He was embarrassed again. Belle smiled.

"You are anything but ordinary," Peter promised her as he pulled at the cravat at his neck. "Why am I sweating?" he asked himself again. "Why did I just announce that I am sweating?"

Belle giggled, and immediately covered her mouth with her hand.

Peter's blue eyes narrowed. "I am going to leave now, before I embarrass myself any further." Peter collected his hat, which he had placed down on one of the end tables, and placed it atop his head.

Belle suddenly felt disappointment. "I am sorry for laughing."

Peter shook his head. "I would laugh at me, too. You wouldn't know that I am considered to be the brains of my siblings." Before Peter could start towards the door, he asked again, "Are you ill? That is what I came here to find out. Do you need anything?"

"I am perfectly well," she replied softly. "And I am sorry, really. I shouldn't laugh. It is cruel of me to laugh when you have come to bestow a kindness."

"I suppose you do owe me an apology, seeing as it is your fault that I am making a fool of myself," Peter agreed, some of his bashfulness disappearing as a nice smile appeared on his face.

"My fault?" repeated Belle. "How?"

But Peter did not answer. "Why do you not go with my sister to church?" he asked curiously. "I know it is none of my business, so please tell me to mind it if you like."

Belle's smile faded as her mind went to thoughts of good people ... and people who were good in other ways. Belle did not want to deny the issue. Perhaps her brutally honest answer would help her to know for certain whether or not Peter was sweet on her. "I do not go to church because I make people uncomfortable," she told him. "I make people uncomfortable wherever I go. I have done all my life."

"Hang them."

Peter's answer came so suddenly and so forcefully that it made Belle take a step backwards. Hang them. Did that mean she shouldn't mind them? The anger in Peter's tone told her that she was right.

"There are small minded idiots in every corner of this world … or, at least what I have seen of it. You are far more worldly than I. Hang them and their stupid opinions."

Belle certainly wished it could be so simple.

Peter seemed to sense this, as his voice softened when he spoke next. "I cannot imagine how that must feel, to worry, or to know, that you are making someone uncomfortable. I am so sorry you have had to experience this in my village, amongst the people of whom I have grown up with."

Belle had not realised that her eyes had begun to well up before a tear spilled over her eyelid and tricked down her cheek. Peter seemed to notice this immediately and approached her for the first time as he fetched a handkerchief from his pocket and offered it to her.

Belle accepted it with a quiet thank you and quickly wiped her eyes.

"What do you mean this has happened all your life? Surely there has been a time … maybe I am terribly naïve, but surely there was a time when you did not have to worry about what ignorant people thought," Peter wondered out loud. "Again, please tell me to mind my own business. I am leaving, you know. I fully intend to go and stew in embarrassment for the remainder of the day." His tone told her that he was trying to make her smile again.

But Belle wanted to tell him. She had revealed something about herself, and she was entirely uncertain whether she had done it purposefully or not. Belle had been very careful with the details that she had shared. Not even Alex knew the country from whence she hailed. But she had shared a detail about herself with Peter, and he had noticed it.

And then, Belle found herself sharing. "Where I come from, there are people who practise other religions. I don't know if you've ever heard of Obeah or Vodou ..." Peter shook his head. "They are peaceful people, but outsiders, many of the people I knew, were afraid of them, often accusing them of being witches or demons. They saw me the same way. They said God cursed me." Belle could not quite believe that the words were coming out of her mouth.

But Peter listened diligently, his brows furrowing. "God cursed you? How?"

Belle looked up at Peter, knowing that he could see the reason on her face. With her hands, Belle gently placed her fingertips underneath her eyes. "God cursed me with witches' eyes. Demon eyes. Evil eyes. Devil eyes. They saw me as unnatural. So, you understand? I have spent my whole life making people uncomfortable."

"And so you look down," Peter uttered softly.

Had he noticed that also? Belle couldn't help but drop her eyes.

"Stop," Peter instructed. "Look at me." Belle obeyed. "I think you'll find that the colour gold, in the religious sense, embodies the divine. God didn't curse you, Belle. In fact, I think it's clear that you were touched by an angel."

Chapter 9

Belle found it difficult to stop thinking of Peter's words for the remainder of the evening. How often was one told that they had been touched by an angel?

She, for one, certainly never had. For one who had spent so long feeling as though something was dreadfully wrong with her, feeling as though she had been cursed or damned, to have someone so kind, so innocent, say such beautiful words to her meant everything and more. In fact, Belle was quite certain that no one had ever spoken more beautiful words to her. It was quite easy, really, to be certain of that. No one before Peter had ever spoken to her in such a way.

They were seated next to one another at dinner again that evening, and unlike last Sunday, Belle did not keep her eyes to her plate. She found herself continually looking to her side at Peter. And when she did, she found his eyes, too.

And then he would smile at her.

Belle did not think that she had ever seen such a nice smile on a man before. She liked Peter's smile because there was no malice, no motive, and no wickedness. It was kindness, comfort, reassurance. His smile settled her and calmed her

…

... and it reminded her every time that Peter thought that she had been touched by an angel.

Lord, every time those words passed through her mind, she felt her stomach twist up in the sorts of knots that she had never experienced before. It wasn't hunger. She was used to hunger pains. It was a different feeling altogether. And it wasn't unpleasant. In fact, it excited her in a rather unexpected way.

And that, in itself, was frightening.

"I like that you are looking up. I like that you are looking at me." Peter spoke in a low voice so that only Belle could hear.

And when she did hear, she smiled. But she did look down bashfully.

"No, no, no," Peter pleaded in a whisper. "Don't you dare look down."

Taking a quick breath, Belle obeyed, and she returned her gaze to his.

"Angel," he murmured, his smile tugging at his lips.

Belle's stomach twisted even further as this wholly unfamiliar feeling spread up into her chest.

Though Peter did not remain smooth and subtle for long. While still looking at Belle, he reached out for his wine glass, albeit a little casually, for he knocked it over onto the white linen of the table runner which began to quickly absorb the red liquid. In Peter's surprise, and subsequent reflexive reaction, he knocked over Belle's water glass as he reached for his own. The water tipped into the bowl of soup that Belle had been midway through consuming. The sounds of crystal and china clinking and clattering interrupted the table's conversations, and Belle watched as Peter's cheeks turned pink and an expression of embarrassment returned to his face.

"My sincerest apologies," Peter stammered as he finally righted the glasses without tipping anything else over. He used the napkin that had been on his lap to dab away at the stained runner. "I have made an absolute mess of this," he muttered, chastising himself.

"It was my mother-in-law's dining linen, Peter. No matter," said Cecily dismissively. She then charged her glass. "It gives me quite the good excuse to finally be rid of it."

"I could never be so wasteful," Grace replied. "Honestly, a little vinegar and a good scrub with some soap and water and that stain will be gone."

Belle could have sworn that she heard the dowager duchess mutter something that sounded like, "spoilsport," under her breath, though Belle had no idea what that word meant.

Peter sat back down, very red-faced, and Belle was reminded again that she enjoyed when he was embarrassed, even if she did not always understand why. Of course, she did understand in this instance. She did feel badly that she liked his embarrassment, because he was clearly uncomfortable, but it further cemented her good opinion of him.

"Honestly, Peter, why so clumsy? Distracted by something, were you?" Peter's brother, Jem, was teasing his brother.

Jem seemed to get a lot of enjoyment out of his brother's situation, and Belle then felt quite poorly for feeling something similar. Jem then flicked his blue eyes to Belle, and he grinned devilishly at her. He then winked.

Peter glared at his brother. "Jem," he practically growled.

"Almost like your mind was somewhere else entirely," Jem continued mockingly, his voice rising so as to draw attention.

"What on earth are you going on about, Jemmy?" Claire asked in a tiresome expression. Claire was seated beside Jem on the opposite side of the table and had been distracted from her conversation by Jem's rise in tone.

"Jem was just about to tell us all about the mystery girl who has taken his fancy!" Peter announced to the table.

His announcement caused all colour to drain from Jem's face as he was put right back in his place. Jem sat back in his chair and nodded in defeat, though it was not at all enough to end the conversation.

"Mystery girl?"

"Who?"

"What girl?"

All three questions were asked by Peter and Jem's older sisters, the interest of them all having been captured by Peter's statement. Belle watched in utter fascination.

"Mystery girl? Jem?" prompted Mrs Denham. "What girl? Aren't you too young for a girl?"

"Mother, I am seventeen, not five," grumbled Jem.

"Pray, forgive me," retorted Mrs Denham facetiously. "What girl?" she pressed. "Do I know her? Of course, I must know her. For whom do you know that I do not?" Mrs Denham tapped her fingers on the table as she thought. "Annie Wilkins?" she asked. "She is a pretty, young thing. What about Jane Allsopp? Is it her? Though, I did have a mind to reacquaint her with Peter during this visit because I think they would do so well together."

"Jane Allsopp?" Cecily replied, raising her brow. "Why, I do agree. Very pretty, very amiable. No fortune, of course, but her father is a gentleman. She would do very nicely for you, Peter."

Belle found herself getting a little lost along the way as the conversation darted across the dining room table. But what she had managed to comprehend was that both Peter's mother and the dowager duchess had a bride in mind for him.

The knots in her stomach, which had been pleasurable in their anticipatory nature, suddenly twisted in an unholy way, and Belle felt the pain suddenly rise up into her throat. This news should not bother her. It was not at all right that it bothered her.

Really, this was the way of the world. It was right. Was she mad? What was Belle even thinking entertaining such unfamiliar giddiness? It was not for her. It could never be for her. There were some things that she would never be able to have, and Peter Denham was certainly one of them.

She looked at Peter again, only this time he was not looking at her. He appeared to be quite angrily glaring at his mother. What Peter didn't know, or understand, was that he deserved someone like Jane Allsopp, whomever she was. Belle predicted that she was a beautiful, innocent, delicate flower of a girl, who would no doubt make Peter a dutiful wife, and be a doting mother to their children.

There was one thing for certain that Belle could never do. She could never have children. She wasn't capable.

Thump.

Belle froze. It was as though she had felt a physical punch to the chest as the thought had crossed her mind. She had not pondered her own barren state in a long time, and even when she had, it had never pained her. In fact, she had always thought of her inability to bear children to be a blessing. For why would she ever want to bring a child into the life that she had once led?

But in this moment, it was the first time that she had ever thought about since being free.

And she felt pain. Great pain. She looked to Peter, and she felt pain within her. Stop it, stop it! Belle commanded of herself. She could not fool herself into believing that she was someone that she was not after receiving some kind words and the attention of a good, safe man. Belle knew exactly who she was.

Peter did not.

Peter did not deserve to be burdened by Belle. He deserved perfect, innocent Jane Allsopp, or someone like her.

"I thank you kindly to cease the matchmaking," Peter snapped at his mother. "We were talking of Jem, who, indeed, has a very real lady on his mind."

Peter's reminder had refocussed Mrs Denham, and she looked back to her youngest son. "Jemmy, tell me who she is," she encouraged. "Are you courting? How could you not tell me that you are courting!"

"Jane Allsopp," Jem replied with a wry smile, "though I will take back my claim on her as Peter is so clearly meant for her." Jem was very clearly lying, but Belle could not force herself to be curious in that moment.

The conversation surrounding Jem continued, with many around the table trying to encourage him to reveal the identity of the girl who had captured his attention. But Belle could not concentrate. All she could force herself to do was to eat as much of each course as she could manage, her eyes, one again, keeping to her plate.

"It is all in good fun," Peter finally uttered to Belle when the attention drifted to another conversation. "They mean well. Where Jane Allsopp is concerned, well ... I do not think I have spoken to her since ... perhaps the Winter Assembly last year?" he thought back. "Regardless, there is not any sort of understanding ... just in case you were wondering."

Belle didn't answer.

Peter spoke again after waiting through Belle's silence. "Though, of course, you were not wondering. Why would you be?"

"No, I wasn't," Belle murmured softly.

"Right," replied Peter, rather awkwardly. "Exactly right. Exactly what I thought." There was disappointment in his voice. She heard him take a breath, before he asked, "Won't you look at me? You were before, please."

Belle kept her gaze down. What did she hope to achieve? What could she delude herself into thinking could happen? Belle knew exactly what could happen. Nothing.

Lord, she could imagine the spectacle in this village if Peter were to ever stand up with a black woman, such as her. But that was not the problem. Belle wished that was the problem.

Peter knew nothing about Belle. No one did. Not one person in this room knew anything about her save for her name, and she had done that on purpose. She had wanted to keep her past, and everything that had happened to her, locked away in a place that nobody could find. Only there was one particular nightmare that would never end. But it was her nightmare, and she had survived this long. She would keep surviving, because this was her burden. Not Peter's.

"I am not feeling well," Belle suddenly said, rising from the table. "Please, excuse me." Without waiting to answer any of the questions that suddenly arose from the diners, Belle fled from the dining room.

Belle had locked herself in her bedroom for the remainder of the evening, and had thrown herself into her sewing, allowing Susanna's wedding dress to consume her thoughts.

Thankfully, she was not disturbed, save for Susanna who came to check on her before retiring. Belle was able to send her away with an assurance that she would be well once she slept.

But Belle lay awake, staring up at the canopy ceiling of her bed. She felt such pain in her stomach, an ache that would not dissipate. Was this affection? It felt horrible.

Belle felt horrible for the disappointment she had heard in Peter's voice.

She felt horrible for enjoying his embarrassment.

She felt horrible for inviting any of his attention with her looks and smiles.

She felt horrible for herself, in knowing that she could never have any of it. And this all twisted up inside her, making her insides ache, making her belly ache like it had never done before. What on earth was this?

It was pain. Real pain. Not phantom pain. Something inside of her really was painful.

"Oh!"

Belle cried, and she sat bolt right up in bed as she felt something ... something odd between her legs. What on earth ...? In a panic, Belle scrambled to light the lamp that had been dimmed beside her bed, and she threw back the bedclothes. Holding the lamp to the sheet, she shuffled back to see whatever it was.

Blood.

Belle screamed. She was bleeding. That pain was real. She was bleeding. Oh Lord, she was dying. Why now? Why now would God grant her wish? Why now when she was free? Why not then? Why not kill her the thousand other times that she had asked? Why now?

Belle scrambled out of bed in a panic, realising that her nightdress was similarly stained with blood as her sheets were. Her heart thundered in her chest as she forced herself to think coherently. She needed to get help. She may have wished for death before, but she did not want to die now. Belle ran to the door. She was bleeding, but she could still run, and she practically pulled it off of its hinges.

Nobody came to her aid when she screamed as she was the lone guest in her wing. She sprinted down what felt like a mile of hallway before she came to the family's quarters. When Belle came to Susanna's bedroom door, she burst inside, not bothering to knock.

The noise of Belle's entrance shocked Susanna awake, and she sat up in bed with a cry of fright.

"Susanna, help me!" Belle begged.

Susanna quickly realised that it was Belle who had entered, and she scrambled out of bed. She raced over to her and put her arm around Belle in support. Not even this touch, which would have ordinarily made Belle jump, could affect her when she was in such a panic.

"Belle, what is it? What's wrong?" Susanna asked desperately.

"Please, a doctor. I need a doctor, one who will treat me," Belle pleaded. "I'm bleeding, look! I'm dying!" Belle held the lamp down and showed Susanna the blood stains on her nightdress.

To Belle's horror, the fright completely disappeared off of Susanna's face, and a smile of reassurance appeared. "Oh, Belle," she said calmly. "What on earth are you worrying about? You are not dying. It is just your courses."

Belle's stomach clenched. "My courses? What is that? I don't understand that word. Help me!" she stressed.

"Shh," hushed Susanna. "Be calm. Wait a moment and I will fetch something to help you." Susanna left Belle's side and went to the bottom drawer in her bedside table. She pulled out some clean rags and then proceeded to explain to Belle what she needed to do with them, sending her behind the dressing screen with a clean night dress to change into as well.

As Belle dressed, she did not feel any less panicked.

"How do you not know what your courses are?" Susanna asked when Belle reappeared. "Your monthly courses. You bleed every month. Every woman does."

Belle vociferously shook her head. "No, no, I do not bleed," she said firmly. "Not like this. I do not understand courses."

Susanna thought for a moment. "Avoir ses règles," she explained.

Belle froze. No. It couldn't be. "Les règles?" she whispered, before looking down at her belly. Instinctively she clutched it. She still felt a great deal of pain.

"You have never bled before?" Susanna asked again, clearly confused.

Belle was just as perplexed. "I did, a long time ago, when I was a young girl. For a little while. But they stopped, and they never came back. I thought ... I thought that they were gone."

Susanna smiled. "I think we all wish they would go away at some time or another, but I remember Mama telling me when mine first appeared that to bleed was a celebration of one's fertility. You'll be alright, Belle. It is normal. I don't really understand why your courses stopped, but at least you know you are not dying, you silly thing!" She chuckled. "You really ought to get some sleep," she encouraged.

Fertility. Belle knew that word. And it seemed impossible.

Chapter 10

Peter had put his foot in it. Well, perhaps it was not he himself that had put his foot in it, but the conversation at the table had resulted in Belle retreating right back into her shell.

He was quite put out about it. For a brief moment, he had seen her smiles, her eyes ... those beautiful eyes. Her shoulders were not so rigid, and she had relaxed a little, and Peter wanted to believe that he and his terribly awkward behaviour had contributed to that.

Receiving those looks and smiles felt precious to Peter. In a short acquaintance, he had come to understand that those were rarities, and not bestowed on just anyone. In perhaps a rather naïve way, he believed that she might have cared for him a little.

And it was not until he had witnessed Belle's rapid retreat that Peter realised just how attached he was to her. Immediately, Peter felt the disappointment and frustration at being denied something that he had so quickly come to enjoy and take pleasure in.

Peter really did not know what to do. He did not have much experience at all with women. He did not know the right things to say, or how to behave in a way that wasn't embarrassing. Of course, he never intended to embarrass himself on purpose ... it just seemed to happen that way.

"Do you intend to call on Jane Allsopp today, or shall I?"

Peter's thoughts were interrupted by his brother sitting down at the table. Jem was grinning at him as he collected a slice of bread to butter. When Peter did not respond with a teasing remark of his own, Jem's grin faded, and was replaced by a much more sympathetic expression.

"I wasn't really planning on calling on her, you know," he then said in a hopeful tone. "She is all yours."

Peter shook his head. It was his family's conversation surrounding Jane Allsopp that had caused Belle's change.

"I am just joshing, you know," Jem continued. "I didn't mean to offend. She'll be lucky to have you." After he finished buttering his bread, he made quite a mess as he spooned a large helping of the Haitian marmalade that Amélie had made. Alex had brought some fruit back to England with him and planned to cultivate what he could on his land in a greenhouse that he was constructing.

"I don't really know how that is meant to happen," replied Peter. "I really don't know what I am doing, and ..." Peter didn't finish his sentence. He was going to say that he did not know if Belle cared for him at all. Would she smile at him if she did not? No, that was selfish. Peter understood that he was not owed romantic feelings.

Peter also understood that it was foolish to chalk Belle's emotions down to silly gossip surrounding village girls.

Belle's mind, and her heart, were not vapid little streams, but deep oceans.

Jem folded his bread in half and nearly inhaled the whole thing in one mouthful. As he chewed, he gave his brother a sympathetic look. "My instinct is to tease you, but I fear that would be hypocritical as I have an equal amount ... or perhaps ever less ... of experience with women. At least you know the object of your affection cares for you. My girl does not even know that I exist."

"How do you figure that?" asked Peter.

Jem helped himself to another slice of bread. "Well, just as it is obvious that you care about Miss Desjardins, she does not have the talent of concealing her own feelings. I saw the way she was smiling at you, Peter. Again, be thankful she knows you exist."

Peter had foolishly gotten his hopes up for a moment, but he felt the disappointment sink in his stomach once more. He loved her smiles, but that didn't mean she cared romantically. She did not have to.

Oh, he was confused. And his confidence was shot. He didn't know what to do.

"Who is this mystery girl you are so devoted to?" Peter asked, changing the subject. "And why is she oblivious to your existence?"

Jem had just polished off his second marmalade lathered piece of bread and began on a third.

Jem, who was usually in such good humour, reddened in his cheeks briefly. "If you breathe a word to Mother about this, I will kill you in your sleep."

Peter was strangely glad to be thinking about something other than his own awkwardness. "You have my word."

"Her name is Cressie. Cressida Martin. She and her mother arrived in Ashwood only recently ... and my God, Peter." Jem actually banged his head against the table, causing the crockery to rattle.

"That pretty, eh?"

"Beautiful," Jem mumbled against the table. Looking up, he continued, "I am going to speak to her at the Winter Assembly, though. I am determined. Gives me a good two months to muster up the courage."

Cressie Martin. Peter did not know the name, nor the face to put to it, but he supposed he had not lived in Ashwood for some time. Despite that, it was clear that Jem was quite lost to her. He could not recall his younger brother ever being quite so lost to a young woman before. Peter wondered if he appeared to look quite so lovesick, too.

"Is she really so intimidating?" wondered Peter.

Jem looked quite helpless. "I just don't want to make a fool of myself in front of her."

Peter's mind immediately went to all the instances when he had quite literally made a total fool of himself in front of Belle. How was it possible that there was so many incidents in so few meetings? How hopeless was he?

"Perhaps that is where you might offer me advice, brother," continued Jem. "You, after all, were the one to spill wine everywhere and yet Miss Desjardins still had smiles for you."

"She did, didn't she," agreed Peter quietly. His confidence was definitely dashed. His hopes were not up. But Peter needed to adjust his expectations. Things were not going to be simple, quick and easy.

Simple, quick and easy reminded him of the courtship that Jim Ellis had pursued with his elder sister, Kate. It could not have been more than a few weeks, a month at most, between their courtship starting and an engagement being announced. It had been simple between them. And while he did not begrudge his sister at all, Kate and Belle were really worlds apart.

Half a globe, in fact.

Expecting smooth sailing was certainly a fool's errand.

This realisation did offer Peter some comfort and clarity. Something had happened that had spooked Belle. He needed to learn what it was that frightened her so that he could prevent it from happening again. This would become easier once he got to know her better. He only hoped she would allow it.

Because Peter really did want to know her. Once again, with how focussed he was on the anguish of not knowing the meaning of the sort of smiles she gave him, did Peter realise just how attached he already was to Belle. What on earth would he feel like after a few more meetings?

"You really care for her, don't you, Peter?" murmured Jem softly.

Peter looked up. "I can't explain it," he said simply. "Something inside of me was stirred when I saw her, and now I cannot stop thinking about her. The fact that she was quiet when she left the dinner table abruptly, and that I have not seen her since, makes me feel a sort of anxious anguish."

Jem shook his head as he threw back the remainder of his tea. "Women," he huffed. "But we have got to keep trying, don't we?"

"Yes, we do."

Peter was not able to stay away or wait for an invitation. No formal invitations were ever really sent out from Ashwood House as it was understood that the family was always welcome to call whenever they wanted.

Peter did manage to leave it a day, so as not to appear overbearing, before he entered Mr Andrews' grocer on Tuesday morning. His breath did catch as he caught sight of Belle sitting at the back of the shop, her attention focussed on the shirt that she was sewing. Mr Andrews' attention was occupied by a customer, so there was no one to interrupt Peter as he immediately started towards Belle.

It struck him how she appeared so small when she sat behind her table. She was not a tall woman by any stretch of the imagination, and she was certainly very slender and delicate. But most women when they were seated sat up straight, with their shoulders widened with a sense of pride in their posture. Belle's shoulders curled inwards, as did every part of her torso, as though she was determined to take up as little space as she could.

Peter deduced that this was a learned habit alongside the tendency to look down.

As he approached, Belle's eyes looked up briefly, before her instinct returned her gaze to the floor. When she realised just who it was who approached, she looked up again in surprise.

Her golden eyes warmed, and her lips upturned in a smile for the briefest of moments before her expression became neutral. Peter was not mistaken. She was happy to see him, or at least she had been.

"Good morning, Miss Desjardins," greeted Peter softly as he bowed his head respectfully.

Belle gently set her sewing down on the table and rose from her chair. "Good morning, Mr Denham," she said in reply, her voice calm.

She had spoken to him. This was a start. He had seen a smile. All was not lost. He did not have ridiculously unreasonable hopes, but he could not deny that a little hope still bubbled underneath the surface. It was not fair to put any undue expectation onto Belle. If Peter cared for her, then he needed to respect her and her limits.

"I wanted to ask after your health," Peter announced. "You left the table quite suddenly and I wanted to ensure that you were well." His tongue was not tied, his words were not unclear, and he had not made a fool of himself yet. There was nothing hazardous in his immediate environment to trip over, either.

Belle appeared to soften momentarily, before her neutral gaze returned, almost as though she was conditioning herself to appear this way. What on earth was going on inside her head?

"I am well, thank you, Mr Denham," Belle replied. "Just a little −" Belle paused as she frowned in thought. Her hand gestured to her stomach. "J'avais un peu mal au ventre," she explained, though she appeared quite frustrated with herself.

Peter did not understand what she had said, but he could deduce there was some ill in her stomach as that was where she was pointing.

"In English, I don't know," she said apologetically. "I don't know all the words, I'm sorry."

"You certainly need not apologise," Peter assured her. "You can speak two languages. Your tongue is far superior to mine." As soon as the words had escaped his mouth, Peter began to overthink them. Lord, he hoped that was not inappropriate or a strange thing to say. Of course, he had managed to give her a compliment in an awkward way. "You are well, though?" he said, quickly moving the subject along.

And as soon as he did, Belle's facial expression returned to the neutral that she was making an effort to maintain. It almost was a look of cool indifference. Belle was forcing herself to appear this way, it was clear.

What was also clear to Peter, however, was that Belle was not very good at keeping in character. She had already broken it several times. But that did not answer the question of why she was determined to appear indifferent to him.

"Yes, I am well," she replied coolly.

Peter longed to know what was going through Belle's mind. She held his gaze, even if her shoulders were rolled forward in a submissive way, but her eyes did not warm. They were hard in a way that indicated to Peter that she was concentrating on something. Whatever she was thinking, she was thinking it hard.

What was clear though was that Belle's natural instinct was not indifference. Her natural instinct has been displayed for a brief moment when he had approached her table. Her eyes had warmed, and she had smiled. She was not indifferent, even if she was determined to be.

Peter thought back to the conversation he had had with Jem over breakfast the morning before. He had to keep trying. This attachment was certainly not going anywhere.

Chapter 11

After two weeks of diligent and delicate sewing, Susanna's gown was completed just in time for the wedding. It was perfect. It was a masterpiece. Belle wished she had some sort of way to capture the memory of what would be the most beautiful garment she would ever create.

Throwing herself into the making of Susanna's wedding gown had been a godsend to distract herself from the burgeoning feelings in her heart towards Peter Denham, but it had also been an important reminder of what Belle really wanted to make out of her life.

As much as she appreciated making a wage at the grocer, and as much as she was grateful for the work from the people of Ashwood, Belle's dreams were bigger than that. She had talent. She knew it in her soul. Belle had the ability to create magnificent things, and it was honestly saddening to think that Susanna's wedding gown would be the first and last creation of that kind for her.

Belle had dreams. But so did many of the people whom she had known in Saint-Martin. Dreams were not achievable for people like them. Belle had already done the unthinkable. She had escaped. She was free. She was a free woman of colour.

All of her dreams, every one of her wishes and prayers, had already been used up. To ask more of God was selfish and unreasonable ... and so very unrealistic.

"Susanna ..." uttered Cecily breathlessly as she clapped her hands over her mouth.

Belle couldn't help the fluttering of pride she felt at seeing tears in the dowager duchess' eyes. Belle had never before seen such emotion in her.

Susanna beamed as she ran her hands over the skirt of her gown. She was stunning. The most beautiful bride there ever was. Not that Belle had been privy to many weddings, but she was quite certain that there had never been such a bride as Susanna Beresford before.

Susanna's golden hair was styled intricately under her veil. Her soft, feminine figure simply melted into the wedding gown. The dress, itself, was a beautiful champagne silk colour with a net of white lace over top. The short, layered puff sleeves were perfect for an early autumnal wedding. Belle had embroidered Haitian hibiscus flowers in silver thread over the lace, a labour that had taken her hours upon hours, nearly making her fingers bleed. But the result was worth it. The silk and embroidered lace continued through the marvellous train of the gown, giving the bride and air of grandeur and drama, as she was certain to be the centre of all focus when she entered the church.

"Belle, what you have managed to do ..." gasped Grace. "Why, I have never seen anything so meticulously beautiful. You are an artist."

Belle felt deeply prideful. "Thank you," she said appreciatively.

"It is, without a doubt, the gown of my dreams ... and the flowers, Belle!" gushed Susanna as she traced over one of the hibiscus flowers with her index finger. "It is perfect. Thank you, my friend."

Belle smiled. "You are welcome ... my friend." To speak those words meant a lot to her.

"How are we to get through this day without crying?" Grace asked exasperatedly as she fanned her face.

"We're not!" declared Claire as she dabbed her eyes with a handkerchief.

"Don't you start, or I will!" Susanna begged.

But then Cecily let out a sound that Belle had never heard before. It was a sob, and she quickly pulled her daughter into her arms and hugged her tightly. "How can I part with you? How can I do it?" she asked emotionally. "How could you leave me?"

"Mama, I am moving but a mile down the road," Susanna said assuredly. Nevertheless, she returned her mother's hug tightly, and Belle could see the emotion there.

It was a sight that Belle felt privileged to be witness to, for she had never had something like this herself. She had felt this all the months she had been in residence at Ashwood House. This was family. They were a family. They loved one another. There were weddings and birthdays, Sunday suppers, occasions in which they gathered and celebrated one another. To have such a family would be, without a doubt, a treasure to Belle.

But like her other dreams, she knew it was not attainable.

"It might as well be a hundred miles," retorted Cecily. "You will no longer be in the next bedroom." She pulled back and cupped her daughter's face. She sniffed, before smiling through her tears. "Who will support me in my efforts to make Grace eat better when she is with child so that she may have a son?"

Susanna, Grace, Claire, and finally Cecily laughed, and Belle felt that she had certainly misunderstood whatever the joke was. Sometimes humour was lost on her with the language difficulties.

"I never supported that nonsense in the first place. You can be certain that I will be here as much as you like ... as an ally to Grace, of course."

Cecily shook her head as she kissed Susanna's cheek. "I love you. I am so proud of you. And how I will miss you, a mile or not."

"I love you, Mama," returned Susanna, her voice cracking.

"I wish your father was here to see you, dear Susanna," Cecily then murmured softly. "He would be so proud to give you away."

The mention of her father caused Susanna's eyes to well up, but she smiled still.

Their attentions were all captured by the sound of a gentle knock on the door.

"Are we all decent? May the gentlemen enter?" sounded a voice from behind the door.

"Yes!" called Susanna. "Come in."

The door opened and Adam and Jack entered, both dressed in their finest tails and looking very dashing, indeed. But their eyes were only for their sister.

"You look wonderful, Susanna," complimented Adam sincerely.

Jack stood at his wife's side, resting his arm around her waist as he agreed with his brother. "Amazing what can be done when one isn't racing to the altar."

Claire turned quite the colour of a tomato as she slapped Jack's chest, eliciting a chuckle from him. He then kissed her temple.

"You're a vision, Susanna," Jack then said seriously. "I wish you nothing but the purest happiness."

"Come along then, everyone," urged Adam. "We've a bride to give away."

The church was filled. The entire village, the Beresfords' London acquaintances, and dozens upon dozens of people whom Peter did not recognise had filled each and every one of the pews. Peter had never before seen the Ashwood church so populated.

Alex stood at the altar looking quite uncomfortable. Ordinarily, Peter presumed, bridegrooms would be standing in anxious anticipation of their intended's arrival. Though Alex was, sadly, standing up on a stage in perfect view of the gawking crowd. Peter was certain that there was more than one guest who had accepted the invitation to view the spectacle and to spread the word about the most scandalous match that would probably ever be made.

A beautiful heiress, the daughter and sister of a duke, to wed a black freedman. Peter honestly hated to imagine what the papers in London were saying about now, and he was relieved that he was not currently there to see them.

But their life would not be in London. Their life would be on their land. And this spectacle would die down when they grew bored of waiting for Alex and Susanna to attempt to enter to society together. They would not. Their life was to be far greater.

That was how they loved each other.

It did not make Peter envy. But it did make Peter wish. It had been two weeks since Belle had made whatever decision it was inside her head to be indifferent to him, and his visits to the grocer, and his presence at Sunday dinners, had not convinced her away from this mindset.

He willed himself to have patience and to be compassionate. But he missed her. He missed her, and yet he had never really gotten the chance to know her. How could one miss something that they'd never had? It only further convinced Peter that there was something special to be uncovered.

"It's very lovely, isn't it?" Mrs Denham whispered to Peter. "Alex's garb. Madame Amélie made it herself. It is traditional, I understand."

At first glance by the length of the garment, Alex looked to be wearing a black nightshirt. Though anyone could see it was much finer. The front of the shirt was decorated with golden swirls of embroidery. It was entirely symmetrical on both sides and was certainly magnificent.

The doors to the church opened and, naturally, every head in the church turned back. Cecily entered first on the arm of Jack. She looked incredibly dignified as mother of the bride, and anyone who had might have dared whisper something about Cecily's soon-to-be son in law certainly kept their lips shut.

Behind Cecily and Jack came Grace and Claire, before finally their four nieces toddled in as Susanna's bridesmaids. Perrie, as the eldest, was responsible for pulling along the frilly, lacy wagon in which Maria was laying. Both Lily and Jackie waddled in alongside the wagon.

But Belle was nowhere to be seen.

"Oh, my precious angels," whispered Mrs Denham in a gush.

Peter heard a door to the side of church open and close gently. He turned toward the noise and that was when he spotted Belle sneaking into the church in hopes that she would not be noticed. But how dismally she had failed when she looked as she did.

She wore blue, a beautiful coral blue that he had never seen her in before. The cool brown of her skin looked absolutely stunning with the colour that she had chosen. The bodice of the dress hugged her small frame just so, and the skirt moved with her elegantly. Her dark, curly hair was pulled back away from her face, and underneath a white bonnet with a ribbon that matched her gown exactly. A few of her tight curls still framed her face which, Peter could not be certain, but which appeared today to look slightly rounder, as though her cheeks were a little fuller and he had not noticed.

"Oh," said Mrs Denham breathlessly. "Oh, she is just so beautiful."

"Yes, she is," murmured Peter in reply, not taking his eyes off of Belle as she quickly took a seat on the end of the front pew beside Amélie.

But it was the harmonium starting that made Peter realise his mother had been referring to Susanna, who had just entered the church on the arm of Adam.

The ceremony was lovely, if not a little long, as Susanna had surprised her now husband by repeating her vows to him first in English, and then in French. But no one, not even the naysayers, the gawkers, or the gossipmongers, could deny that Alex and Susanna loved love one another, and Peter did not know how anyone could not wish them happiness.

The wedding breakfast was elaborate and magnificent, and no expense was spared. Peter did not think that he had ever seen so much decadent food in his life.

With Susanna on his arm, Alex appeared to be much more relaxed as they roamed the room, receiving the congratulatory wishes from their guests, both genuine and the saccharine sweet, before they were claimed by Alex's father, Captain Whitfield, who had returned in time to attend the wedding.

The jovial music was playing, dancing had begun, and the ballroom was certainly abuzz with laughter, conversations, and gossip, of course.

Peter had not yet been able to speak to Belle. They had been seated at different tables for the meal, and until recently, Susanna had been bringing Belle around the ballroom introducing her to people as the brilliant craftswoman who created the wedding gown.

Belle looked entirely self-conscious. And, of course, she kept her eyes low whenever she could. Peter wanted to believe that her bashfulness stemmed from modesty over Susanna's praise, but he knew it was far more deep-rooted than that.

How he wanted to ask her about it. How he wanted to know her mind, her heart, and exactly how and why she felt the way she did. How he wanted to be someone she could trust, to be someone with whom she felt comfortable confiding in.

"Doesn't Lady Susanna look divine?"

"That dress! I know. It is positively stunning. What I would give to wear something that ethereal when I marry."

The women gushing behind Peter sounded like so many others he had overheard in the ballroom. Peter hoped that Belle could hear it, too. They loved her work.

"I really struggle to believe that she could have made something like that. I heard she's a seamstress in the village. She mends buttons."

Peter's ears pricked up. The tone of the women had changed, and they were talking about Belle.

"I heard that, too," agreed the other woman. "She's not a very remarkable one of them, is she? At least the husband is somewhat striking in a way. She's so ... scrawny ... and I never imagined anyone's skin could be so ... black."

"Oh, you needn't be so polite with me, Margaret," giggled her friend. "My father's known quite a few blackies in London. They are all frightful to look at, he says. If he knew I was here at this wedding, he would certainly disinherit me, but I could not deny the chance to see the shambles that is now Lady Susanna's reputation. Of course, it would have been better, made sense, you know, for the blackies to marry each other. But with Susanna taking him, it leaves so many more gentleman in town searching."

"You're right," agreed Margaret, laughing. "Well, she might be a fright to look at, but her sewing is not. Wouldn't it be a treat if Papa could buy her for me? A dress slave to sew me gowns like that, oh! What a dream."

Something inside of Peter snapped and he rounded on the two women rather quickly, so quickly, in fact, that his sudden presence startled them.

"How dare you?" he snapped furiously, his tone making the women jump. "How dare you stand there and giggle and tease and make jokes about something so vilely inhuman?" he seethed. "What does that say about you? What little women does that make you? Does it make you feel prettier in the frocks you are wearing to degrade an innocent young woman because of the colour of her skin? Or are you so jealous of her and her talent that you feel the need to find false faults within her? Whatever the truth, it is utterly pathetic. You should be ashamed of yourselves. Belle Desjardins is quite certainly ten times the woman either of you are." Peter did not stutter. He scolded as though he was a man twenty years older than he was, and he could have kept going.

But the two women were white as ghosts, as their eyes suddenly looked past him. Peter looked around to find a pair of golden eyes standing not five feet from him, witnessing the entire exchange. Belle's features were softened with surprise, her lips parted as though she wanted to say something, but no words came.

As Peter was distracted, the two women scurried away, leaving him with Belle.

"I hope you did not hear any of that," Peter uttered.

"I did not hear them," Belle said softly. "But I heard you. I can imagine what they said. But I heard what you said, how you spoke for me."

The indifference was gone. The hard shell that she had hidden herself away in had vanished, and Peter felt like for the first time he was seeing into her. There were no shields in front of her golden eyes. They were molten oceans of feeling. And she was looking at him.

There were dozens of things that Peter could have said, or that he would have liked to have said. But only one came to mind in that moment. He held out his hand and asked, "Will you dance with me?"

Peter knew with this gesture that he had asked a lot more of Belle than for just a dance. He was asking her to brave something that frightened her. She didn't like to be touched. He had witnessed this unease. But, in this moment, he watched in awe and delight as Belle's small hand floated through the air before settling in his. The moment he had her, he closed his hand around hers, and he looked deeply in her eyes.

Belle's eyes were still so open. She was not hiding, at least not from him, and Peter could see how frightened she was at such a gesture. But she had done it. She had trusted him. That was all he wanted.

Chapter 12

Such was the chant that was flowing through Belle's mind in that moment. Her heart was thundering. Her limbs were shaking. It was as though her body was determined to be afraid, but her mind wasn't. Belle didn't want to be afraid of Peter, and she knew in the deepest parts of her soul that she didn't need to be. Such certainty was another sort of terrifying.

Belle was too busy in that moment reminding herself that Peter was safe to remember that she had meant to avoid him. In fact, she was not at all certain how she had come to be in such close proximity with him, but she was glad that she had done. To hear what he had said in her defence filled her with a sort of security that she had never felt before.

Thoughts of any sort of residual or underlying prejudices, anxieties or doubts about her appearance and what it would mean to stand up with her, all vanished. Belle knew that Peter was proud to stand up with her, and he would put anyone who had anything nasty to say in their place. Belle had not heard what those women had been saying about her, but she had heard it all before. She did not need to imagine. But nobody had ever spoken for her like that before.

Not even Belle, herself, had spoken for herself like that before.

Looking up at Peter, whose gaze was focussed ahead as he led them through the crowd to the dance floor, made her want to cry. All resolve to spare him from the burdens she carried had vanished, and Belle knew that she would punish herself for it later.

But she wanted to dance with Peter. She wanted to dance with him like normal young women danced with young men. She wanted to be spun about a dance floor and pretend like her nightmares were not realities, and that her burdens did not exist, and that she might have what Susanna had been blessed with today.

But there was something else inside of her burgeoning. It was like the truth was more at the forefront of her mind than it had ever been before. It was bubbling to her lips and she wanted to speak. She had been very careful to keep much of herself a secret from everyone.

Nobody knew even from whence she came, and yet she felt the first secret spill out of her mouth with no sense of control at all.

Just as Peter delicately left her in the line of ladies and took his place opposite her in the line of gentlemen, Belle uttered, "Saint-Martin."

Peter's brows furrowed slightly at her confession. "I beg your pardon?"

The music started and Belle realised suddenly that she had quite no idea of the steps. Her eyes widened as she froze. But Peter stepped forward and claimed Belle with an elegant sense of gallantry. He claimed her hand and placed his other on the small of her back. Belle took a breath as she reached up her other arm to place her hand on his shoulder. She allowed him to lead as they broke away from the line of dancers.

"I wanted to dance a waltz anyway," he murmured with a wry smile.

Peter had saved her. It was a different kind of saving, but it was one that she enjoyed. It was one that she was certain that she could quite easily get swept up in if she allowed herself. But Belle was quickly learning that her resolve was far weaker than it ought to have been.

She really took no notice of the other dancers as she kept her eyes on Peter, but out of the corner of her eye, she could see that several other couples had paired off as they had and were dancing together rather than in the line.

"Saint-Martin?" he prompted quietly as they turned. "Is that what you said?"

Belle nodded. She had certainly said it. She had practically shot the information at him as thought it had desperately escaped the confines of its prison inside of her mind.

"It where I was born," she returned. "It is where I am from."

Belle wondered how the colour blue could ever be seen as warm, but it was when she looked into Peter's eyes. They were warm and caring and safe. What pleasurable oceans they would be to get lost in.

"You have come a long way, haven't you?" he said softly.

Belle could hear the layers to that observation, and she knew what he was meaning, and Peter really had no idea.

The musicians continued to play their romantic strings as Peter effortlessly led Belle, who really was like a newborn fawn with her inexperience. But no matter what she looked like, Belle was entirely swept up in the moment, and she experienced a kind of peace for those three minutes. It was the sort of piece that one could only dream of.

The hand that held hers was clasped around her tightly, and the other on the small of her back, with only a few layers of fabric separating it from the scars that so many like her bore, held her close.

And she didn't look down, nor away, nor anywhere that was not his gaze.

Those three minutes were perfect.

But they ended when the music did, and Peter released her, though he did not step away, as he applauded the musicians like everyone else. Belle snapped herself out of her trance as she took in the ballroom for the first time, and she, too, clapped. There was certainly more than one pair of eyes on them. Dozens in fact. Eyes that were curious, eyes that were disapproving, and there were certainly eyes that were green.

Belle's immediate, instinctive thought was that they ought not to be jealous, for nothing could ever come of this. But that pain, the pain that had been plaguing her stomach these last weeks, reared its ugly head, and Belle seemed to move a few inches closer to Peter without even realising it.

Belle didn't want to say goodbye. She didn't want to move away. Would there be anything that anyone could say in this moment to make her want to do the right thing? What she wanted to do was talk, and be heard, and be listened to, and be understood. She wanted somebody to know her. Was that allowed? Was she allowed one good person to know who she was?

Peter looked back to Belle, and he smiled when he found her eyes, which had not left him. His smile was one that quickly set her at ease. It was the wide one that she liked.

"People will ask you questions now," Belle commented nervously, "now that you have stood up with me." She did not mean for it to sound like a warning, but then she realised that perhaps that was sensible.

"What answers shall I give them?" Peter replied.

Belle really didn't know. Her conviction was nowhere to be found tonight. But there was something that she would need to guard, and she would now have him guard it, too. "Tell them what you will," she murmured. "But please, please don't tell them where I have come from."

Peter smile vanished as he peered at her intently. "And break your trust? Never," he promised.

Belle's heart swelled. She might have cried. She might have cried for the beauty of the night, and for the beauty that was Peter, and for the beauty of what might have been. But she knew that when this night was over, she would cry for her reality.

"I want to talk to you," Belle continued softly, "if you will listen to me."

Peter nodded, a sympathetic expression on his face, as he offered Belle his arm once more. She did not hesitate in taking it. Peter led her once more through the crowd, taking no notice of the stares of the onlookers. Belle was not at all certain where his family were, but she was quite sure that they would be looking on at Peter and his companion also.

Peter expertly led Belle down a hallway in Ashwood House, and the sound of the instruments muffled. Shortly after, he seemed to find what he was looking for as he found a set of doors that opened out onto a small stone balcony that overlooked the gardens below. The air was fresh with a slight bite to it as the brief English summer faded. Belle almost found it laughable that this weather was considered summer.

Regardless of their little sun, there was great beauty here, and Belle would not have wanted to be anywhere else. Belle leaned against the stone banister and Peter casually sat on top of it, a foot or two away from her. His hands rested on his knees as he waited, never pushing.

"I am sorry that I have been ..." Belle's mind went blank as she tried to search for the word in English. "Dédaigneux ... do you know this word?" She frowned.

Peter subtly shook his head, but he did not speak.

Belle thought hard, searching amongst all the vocabulary she had memorised. "Not talking," she continued. "Not talking. Rude. You are nothing but kind and I must be horrible to you sometimes."

"You are not rude. I have never thought you rude," Peter assured her quietly. "I don't want you to apologise for things that are not your fault. You wanted to talk to me. What did you want to tell me?"

What did Belle want to tell Peter? She wanted someone to know everything, and to tell her that it would be alright. She wanted to be comforted like a child was after a bad dream, and to be promised that her fears weren't real.

"There was a hurricane last year." Belle hadn't thought of where to begin, but she had begun somewhere. It certainly wasn't the beginning of her story, but it was already more than she had told anyone. "It was a bad one, and people were not careful, they made mistakes."

Belle could vividly remember the chaos that was the preparations for the storm. People running about, shouting orders, and neglecting things like locks and keys.

"I had waited for a long time," years, in fact, "to have a chance to escape. People had tried before me. But they were hunted. With the hurricane I had a chance to escape, a chance not to be followed, and I took it."

Just speaking the world, reliving the memory, made Belle's heart thunder in her chest at such a pace that it made her feel nauseous. She leant down on her elbows, nestling her forehead in the palms of her hands as she closed her eyes and breathed.

"You were so very brave," uttered Peter delicately.

Belle could hear that he was on tenterhooks. He didn't know the right thing to say, or if what he had said was the right thing. But he was trying.

"I knew it was a possibility that I could have died in that storm, and I was willing to die rather than go back. I wished for death so many times." As she opened her eyes, she caught a glimpse of Peter flinching at her words. Belle immediately bit down on her lip.

"I'm sorry," he apologised immediately. "I'm so sorry you ever had to feel that way."

Belle had lost count of the number of times she had prayed for death. Every time it happened, every time he came near, every time any one of the unsafe men came near, she wished to die, to leave her abused body behind.

"I didn't know where I was going, but I wanted to get as far away from Saint-Martin as possible. I stowed away on a ship and I made it to a country called Portugal."

The very fact that she had reached Portugal, that she had put so many miles between her and that life, made Belle believe that the danger was over. She was free. It was over. She couldn't be hurt anymore.

"My freedom was brief, and my fate was cruel." Belle shuddered as the memories came flooding back, the ones that she had tucked away into a place where they could only haunt her in her nightmares.

Belle heard Peter step down off of the banister. "May I touch you?" he asked tenderly. "May I hold you?"

Belle couldn't look at him. If she did, she knew that she would cry and lose all resolve. But she nodded. Thinking these thoughts, she felt unsafe. She wanted safe.

She felt Peter's arm around her then, resting gently on her upper arm, rubbing it softly, comfortingly.

As she vividly remembered being discovered, captured, corralled and herded like an animal by the smugglers who had found her in Portugal, she focussed her energy on the sensation of Peter's arm around her. What they did to her in that alleyway ...

Belle turned into Peter's chest and she cried, no longer able to hold it in, or hold her resolve together. Peter immediately wrapped his arms around her tightly. The tightness of his embrace was what she needed to feel as though she was not about to fall apart of go everywhere at once. She needed it to feel safe. She needed him to feel safe.

Belle didn't know for how long she cried. "They caught me," she whispered after a long time. "And they ... they hurt me." Her voice was shaky and broken.

Peter's already tight embrace grew even more so.

"And when they were done, they put me back in chains on a ship with others they had caught and stolen." To be back on a ship after she had tasted freedom briefly had been devastating. Everything had been devastating, but bright lights had been difficult to find in her life, and to have one snuffed so quickly and so cruelly, had broken her. The smugglers had taken what little she had left and had broken it.

The men she had known, every one of them to that point, had used her and ruined her and had taken whatever they had wanted from her.

It was a little while later that Alex had been captured as well and brought down into the hold, and Belle, for the first time, met a man who would not take anything from her.

Belle couldn't share anything more. Not right now. While she had not said the words, she had insinuated, and Peter now knew what had happened to her. Rather, Peter now knew one of the days in Belle's life that haunted her nightmares. What would he think? "It was my fault that time," she whispered. "I was alone. I wasn't careful. I –"

"It was not your fault," Peter interjected forcefully. He leaned away from her only so that he could angle his face down, before lifting her chin so that she could look at him. As soon as she saw the conviction in his eyes, she lost whatever composure she had found. "What evil men do is never the fault of their victims. You bear no guilt. You owe nothing. Lord –" he hissed, and swore under his breath, "– it is not your fault," he emphasised again. But he softened, and he lifted his hand to gently brush away one of her tears with the back of his knuckle. "You don't have to be afraid. I promise you that nobody will ever hurt you again. You are safe. It will be alright."

Peter had uttered those words that Belle had wanted to hear. But it didn't settle her in the way that she had hoped. And she knew it was because everything wouldn't be alright. How could it be?

Chapter 13

Peter couldn't show his anger. He couldn't show Belle one ounce of the fury that was pulsating through him. He had never felt anything like it before. He had never had cause to feel so inhuman, so furious that he might have ripped the heads off of the men that Belle had spoken of.

And what angered him, and what hurt even more, was that the assault she spoke of, it was but one day in her life. She had told him of her escape from Saint-Martin, but she had not detailed about what, or whom, she had escaped from. She had spent years enslaved on that land. Only God knew what had happened to her there.

And God had watched.

If there was any justice in this world, He would smite down every last one of the evil blackguards who had dared violate Belle, and any other woman who had the misfortune of coming across them.

Peter didn't want to be furious at God. He couldn't be furious in this moment.

When Peter looked into Belle's beautiful, golden eyes, he saw such a frightened, delicate young woman who desperately wanted safety. And by confiding in him, by telling Peter her tale, Belle was trusting him to be a safe harbour for her. The momentousness of this moment for Belle was not lost on him, even in and amongst his anger.

Peter decided then and there that he would never show Belle anger. No matter what happened, what became of them, he would never be like any of the villains that she had happened across in the years of her life that had led her to be here.

Before now, Peter had never had cause to be an angry man, and that had made him well practised in gentleness. He was a gentle man, and perhaps that was one of the reasons as to why Belle had trusted him.

And he doubted that she had ever trusted anyone like this before.

"I wish that I wasn't afraid," Belle whispered, almost as though it was a confession. "I want so badly to be brave."

Peter felt her trembling against him, and he was at a loss as to know what to do save for holding her tightly. "You are brave," he uttered back quietly. Lord, how could she think she was not? Peter could not even begin to imagine what Belle had survived, what she had fought through. And he hoped one day that she would enlighten him. "You are a survivor, a fighter. I can see it in you."

Belle's trembling grew worse, and Peter worried that he had said the wrong thing. Before he could apologise, she murmured, "There were so many times when I wished that I would not survive. Is that not a mortal sin?"

Her words were like a dagger to his heart as the gravity of her confession dawned on him. Lord, he wanted to hold her and never let go. He held her in his arms now and in this moment, Peter knew she was safe. He never wanted that to change. "No," retorted Peter fiercely. He rubbed Belle's arms comfortingly. "That is being human, and it is not a mortal sin."

But Belle still trembled.

"What can I do?" Peter asked anxiously. "How can I make you feel safe?"

Belle almost startled him with the speed in which her eyes found his. Her golden eyes were glassy, and her lids were swollen, but she looked into him. "You are safe," she whispered. "I know that I am safe when I am with you."

Peter prayed that knowledge brought some comfort to her.

Because he was, without a doubt, falling head over heels in love with her.

Peter smelled the forge before he saw it. He would forever recognise the scent of a forge no matter where he went. The smoke triggered a decade's worth of memories for him.

Owing to the fact that he had only been a boy of ten when his father had died, Peter had little hope for securing an apprenticeship as their family did not have the money. And Mrs Denham certainly never could have afforded to send Peter onto university, no matter how clever he was.

Peter had been realistic as a young teenager. No matter how well he had done at school, further education was impossible. He was the man of the house, no matter his age, and it should not have been up to his mother and his eldest sister to earn an income to support the family.

Luckily for the Denhams, the Ashwood blacksmith, Jim Ellis, had quickly fallen in love with Mrs Denham's second daughter, and Kate had persuaded her new husband to take Peter on as an apprentice for a fraction of the cost.

Peter remembered feeling excited, relieved, glad even, when he had secured his apprenticeship. He had always been an eager student, and he was keen to learn this new skill. He knew that it meant his family's future security.

Jim had been an excellent mentor and an even better friend. Peter had quite looked up to his brother-in-law as a father figure for a long time.

And while Peter had all but mastered the blacksmith trade, he could not deny that his ambition was still there underneath the surface. He had brains in his head and determination in his heart and he needed to go. While Peter would never regret leaving his apprenticeship and going into business with Jack, he would always carry guilt for leaving Jim.

He was the one man, really, who knew Peter best. They had spent years in each other's company, beating away at an anvil and talking about life.

When the forge came into view, Peter could hear Jim's hammer, and he did smile. Peter had caught up with Jim at family suppers and gatherings, and he had, of course, been at the wedding the day before, but Peter had not been back to the forge.

Jim placed his hammer down when he saw Peter walking towards him, and he removed his gloves and placed them down on the anvil. Jim was a strong, burly man who was built like an ox. The work had had a similar effect on Peter's body, though he was a few inches shy of Jim's height, and about a foot less on his shoulder width.

"Mornin'," Jim greeted, giving Peter a grin as he walked out onto the street. "What brings you down here?"

"I thought I'd come to see the forge," replied Peter. "It's been a long while."

Jim embraced Peter as an old friend, and he jovially slapped him on the back. "There's no shortage of work if you're wanting to do a few jobs for me," he joked as he beckoned Peter inside.

The forge hadn't changed much at all, and for a moment Peter felt like he was fifteen years old again and coming to work, about ready to pick up where he had left off the day before.

"That horse needs shoeing, if you don't mind." Jim nodded towards the open stalls at the back of the forge to where a chestnut coloured horse was waiting.

Peter had shoed dozens of horses in his time. He wondered if he still had the touch. The tools were still where they'd always been, and he collected what he needed. He then walked over to the horse and opened the stall door, clicking his tongue and running his hand over her rump to let her know that he was there. She whinnied in response and Peter continued to calmly pet her.

Peter ran his hand down her first leg and squeezed the tendon above her ankle, before feeling her shift her weight onto her other three legs and allowing him to lift her hoof. Peter tucked his hip against the horse's hock and gaskin, before using the inside of his knee to pull the hoof out slightly and between his legs. Peter used a hammer, a clinch cutter, and a metal pull off to work the old shoe off before using a hoof pick to clean away the compacted debris.

Peter remembered the steps that Jim had taught him years ago and went to work. It might have taken him a little longer than it had used to, but eventually, the mare was as good as new.

"Good girl," Peter commended softly.

"I can't convince you to come back, can I?" Jim asked, coming up behind Peter to rub the side of the mare's neck.

Peter chuckled. "I'm sorry, you know."

"Ah," Jim shook his head, slapping Peter on the back. "I'm just joshing. I know your dreams are far beyond this place. You're just lucky I've now got a son of my own to pass it on to when I'm too old to wield a hammer."

"I'm that glad for you."

"I'm that glad for you, too," replied Jim, pride in his eyes. "Go on then," he then encouraged. "Out with it. I know you didn't just come down here for a peek at the scenery."

Peter laughed nervously. He had been through a whirlwind of emotions since the wedding the day before. But that was nothing compared to what Belle had been through. But in and amongst it all, he had realised that he was falling in love with her. Perhaps he already was in love with her. He wasn't certain. He had never been in love before. He had very little experience with these sorts of things. He didn't know what to do. He didn't know how to approach it. Peter certainly knew that he needed to be gentle, patient, and delicate, but how did he go about things like courting?

"Let me guess. She speaks French, she sews dresses, and her name starts with a 'B'," surmised Jim.

Peter sighed. "Am I that transparent?"

Jim chuckled. "Yes. But it means that you're an honest man. You really care for her, then?" His eyebrows rose.

Peter nodded. "I think I more than care for her," he confessed.

"She's a timid little mouse, isn't she?" Jim folded his arms across his chest.

It did not surprise Peter that this was Jim's assessment of Belle. He would guess that it was the probable assessment of many in the village who were used to seeing Belle with her head down, not speaking unless spoken to directly. Timid, maybe, but she was so much more than that.

One had a right to be timid when they had been through what she had been through. But she was also talented and modest and humble. She also had a sense of humour, a very quick wit at that, to be able to joke in a language that was not her mother tongue. Peter knew that there was certainly much more to delight in if she allowed their acquaintance to continue.

"I really care about her," Peter said seriously. "I want to ... but I don't know how ... it is so much more complicated than normal courtships and I wouldn't know where to begin if this was normal."

Jim leaned back against the stall door and furrowed his brows. "How is it complicated?" he asked.

"I can't say," replied Peter. He would never betray Belle's confidence.

"It is because of her colour?"

Peter's eyes narrowed. "No," he snapped, in a tone he had never used with Jim before.

Jim put his hands up defensively. "Alright," he said quickly. "Alright, I was only asking. There'd be many a stupid man who would have a problem with her colour, but I know you are the farthest thing from stupid."

"I think she's beautiful," Peter uttered. "But she has endured so much, and I don't know how to ..."

Jim took a breath. "Love, courtship, marriage, it's all complicated. I don't think you would find a couple in fifty miles who would say everything had been easy, and that there had never been any trouble."

"You had it easy," countered Peter. "You and Kate worked out perfectly. You never had any trouble." The words escaped his mouth before he'd even realised what he was saying, and as soon as he'd said them, Peter could see more than one ghost in Jim's eyes.

"No, Peter," he murmured. "We haven't had it easy, and we are not free from trouble. It might have seemed that way in the beginning, and perhaps it was for a little while at the start of our marriage, but it hasn't been easy.

"Did you ever notice the five sycamore trees, the saplings I planted out back?" he asked quietly.

Peter nodded slowly. Kate loved those sycamore trees. She had always tended them diligently.

"Buried underneath them are five souls, five of our babies."

Peter felt his stomach fall out of his body and onto the floor. He felt like a right cad for ever assuming that Jim and Kate had had it easy, but how could he not have known? He had been here, in the house ... how could he not have known they were suffering?

"People hide their pain well, don't they?" Jim continued. "Kate masks her grief remarkably, but it's to me that she turns to for comfort, and that privilege isn't lost on me."

Peter felt keenly for his sister, but also for his friend. He was also so glad that they had finally been blessed with a healthy son. But Peter saw the parallels between himself and Jim. He hadn't been able to see it, but Kate had been suffering a terrible trauma, too. They both had.

"People who have suffered, or are suffering, will turn to the one they trust. Not because they need to do something remarkable, but for the person they have always been. I am not any different to the way I was the day I met Kate Denham. I have always been as I am, and I always will be. I am her constant. Healing takes time, but it does happen. Being there, being yourself, being her constant is what you need to do."

Chapter 14

"Two shillings, Mr Andrews, as is our agreement." Belle approached the counter with the coins and gently placed them before the shopkeeper. Mr Andrews nodded dismissively, but he did not verbally respond. Belle pursed her lips, before uttering, "I wish you a good night." She then fixed her cloak before leaving the shop and stepping out onto the street.

As soon as she was outside, Belle spotted Peter walking towards her from the direction of his mother's house. The moment he saw her, he smiled warmly, and Belle felt a rush of calm wash over her. It was certainly an intoxicating feeling, and one that dissuaded her more and more from keeping any sort of distance from Peter Denham.

"Might I escort you home?" he asked as soon as he was in earshot.

Belle nodded, feeling her cheeks heat.

Proudly, Peter offered Belle his arm, in full view of every person on the street, and watching from their windows. He did not mind at all to be seen with her, and that made Belle's heart swell.

"I wanted to tell you that I very much enjoyed our evening the other night," Peter said as they began walking. "Of course, it was not our night, I mean to say that I enjoyed the time that we spent together. Of course, I would never presume ... or assume ... or expect ... oh, what I am trying to say is –"

Belle could see that Peter was quickly becoming flustered and tongue-tied. She had understood the first part of his sentence, but as soon as he began to stammer words, he had lost her. She wondered that if he knew this, whether or not his embarrassment would ease. But, as she had already realised, Belle found enjoyment in Peter's bashfulness. "I enjoyed our evening, as well," she said, interrupting him.

To say that she enjoyed it was putting it most lightly. Belle had never experienced such comfort with a man before. She had never experienced any comfort with a man before. She was always on her guard. She had to be. But she did not need to be with Peter.

"You did?" Peter sounded relieved.

"I am safe with you. I promise I enjoyed it."

Peter's reached with his other hand to rest on hers affectionately, and only for a brief moment. He wouldn't push. She could see it in his eyes as she looked up at him while they walked.

"How was your day?" he then asked, relaxing his shoulders.

"Quiet," Belle replied. "Most days are quiet. People ..."

"People what?" prompted Peter.

"People tend not to speak to me," Belle explained. "Or if they do, it is ... oh, I do not know this word in English ... à contrecœur." It was indeed very begrudgingly when villagers would engage in conversation with her. In fact, Belle did not think she had ever had a conversation with a villager that was not in relation to a mending need of theirs. "I have told you before that I make people uncomfortable."

"And I have told you before to hang them," Peter retorted firmly, shaking his head in disappointment. "I do not know what à contrecœur means," he said, with an atrocious accent, "but I can infer."

"Your French accent is terrible."

Peter smirked, before chuckling. "Is that all you got out of what I said?" he asked, raising his eyebrows. "Do you hear me mocking your English accent?"

"It is à contrecœur," Belle persisted, smiling. "You must roll the r sound off of your tongue. It is soft, not harsh."

Peter played along. "À contrecœur," he said again, still as British as anything.

Belle boldly stopped him and reached up to his face, using her hand to squeeze his cheeks so that he looked like he was holding his breath. "Soft, gentle," she instructed. "French is a romantic language. It is not for harsh tones. Say it again. À contrecœur."

Peter did his best to speak through Belle's grip, which was stopping him from bastardising the word. It was not perfect, but it was better. But Belle was having fun, and she felt a brief thrill in teasing him.

"You're hopeless," she scolded, a smile on her face.

"Well, I'll have you know that we use a harsh h sound in England," returned Peter with a grin. "I do not know what 'opeless means," he said, imitating the way she said the word.

"Say it again," he challenged, looking down at her with an intense, yet playful gaze.

Staring up into his blue eyes, Belle lost a little of the nerve she had found as she felt her heartbeat quicken. Belle used every bit of her concentration to push the h sound out of her mouth as she stammered through the word, "Hopeless."

Peter's smile softened. "Maybe," he agreed, "but you certainly are not. I mean it though. Hang them. There will always be small minded people wherever you go. Wherever any of us go. Sadly, this country is filled with them. It is a very old country in that way. It is very hard for people to rise up in this society, and even more so for people who have journeyed from afar. But that doesn't mean that we can't dream." Peter took a breath. "Would you tell me what you dream of? What is it that you would want for yourself? If you could have anything, what would it be?"

Belle's mind went immediately to her answer to that question. She knew exactly what she wanted. She had prayed for it for years. And when her prayers were not answered, she had taken it upon herself to secure her own freedom. And even though she was thousands of miles away, she was not free. If she could have anything, it would be that.

But she sensed that Peter was asking after her fantasies, her wishes ... those unrealistic dreams that children have that never come true. Belle certainly had plenty of those as well, but one above all.

"If I were a white lady, I would want my own shop where I would make and sell gowns just like the one that I made for Susanna. I would be a modiste. Ladies would come from all around just to buy something of mine. Creating and sewing is ... it is really the only thing that I can do well." Belle could certainly see her dream in her head. She could picture her name on a shop sign. She could hear ladies declaring that their gowns were made by Belle Desjardins. But it all quickly vanished when Belle saw herself as the modiste, and not a fancy, fashionable white lady. "But dreams are just that, are they not? Dreams. Wishes. They are not possible."

"You certainly are unbelievably talented," complimented Peter. "I really know nothing of women's fashions, but even I could appreciate the craftsmanship that went into Susanna's wedding dress. Never abandon your dreams, Belle. I implore you. I hope that I may be living proof that nothing is impossible.

"I always loved school growing up. I was a bright student, and I certainly had always wanted to pursue my education. But my family, my siblings and I, we grew up very skint after the death of my father. And so, I became a blacksmith's apprentice. Did you know that?"

Belle shook her head.

"My poor mother, bless her, could never have afforded to send me to university, and so it would have been very easy to resign myself to the life of a blacksmith. I certainly have enormous respect for the trade. It is very physical, very exhausting work. But it was not my dream. Now, I know that I cannot compare my struggles to yours, and I understand that our circumstances are very different, but had I given up on my dream, I would never have fought for the opportunity and the role I now have at Beresford Press."

Belle could hear the passion in his voice, and she could see the justice in his eyes. He truly believed that she could have anything that she wanted. He was naïve in such a lovely way.

"If you ever feel your will to fight wane, I am more than happy to pick up the sword. I have made a few of them in my day, you know."

"You would do that for me?"

"I am quickly finding that I would do anything for you," Peter replied honestly.

A small gasp escaped Belle's lips. No, certainly she had misunderstood. Her English was not perfect. It could not even be considered very good. She had certainly not comprehended the meaning of his words.

"Maybe one day I will have my shop," mused Belle. "One can dream."

"Yes, they certainly can."

"What exactly is it that you do?"

Peter seemed glad, and very proud, to explain to Belle what it was exactly that he did for work in London. Some of the words were lost on her, but from what she gathered, Peter had a head for arithmetic, and he handled the finances of the business, the procurement of paper and ink, the payments to authors and distributions of their books, the wages of the printers ... everything. It sounded like arduous work meant for someone as clever as Peter.

Belle wished that she was clever. Another wish, another dream.

She certainly was not as clever as Peter. She knew for certain that he would never think less of her for her lack of education, but that did not make it feel any less shameful.

Women, people, who had experienced life as she had … well, it was common for masters to keep their enslaved possessions as illiterate as possible. It was one of the methods that discouraged escape attempts, and it kept them solely dependent on their masters.

"Would I be able to give you a present tomorrow?" Peter asked.

"A present?" repeated Belle, frowning. Whatever for?

"I would love to give you a copy of a book, the first Jack and I ever published. Perhaps it might sit on your bookshelf and serve as a reminder to never give up on your ambitions. Nevertheless, I would wager you would enjoy the story. Jack has terrific taste in literature, and he never chooses a disappointing manuscript."

Belle felt the blood drain from her face, and she was grateful that Peter could not see it. She appreciated the tender thought that had gone into his idea for a gift, but she would not be able to read it. It felt very embarrassing to think that Belle could not appreciate what it was that Peter did properly. And she was certainly far too embarrassed to confess this to him.

Belle forced herself to shake away the negative thoughts, and instead, she made herself focus on the kindness that Peter was trying to show her. He truly believed that she could achieve anything that she wanted to. While Belle knew that in reality, it was impossible, that did not mean that she was not grateful to Peter for such belief.

Where on earth had this man come from? Belle had known far too many white men. In fact, there was a time, not even that long ago, that she would have been happy to never know another one of them again. She didn't know they were capable of being so good, so kind, so gentle.

"I would love to have your book," Belle told him fervently.

There was, indeed, one dream of hers that she could achieve if she did not give up on it. Belle would properly learn to read.

Chapter 15

Belle knew enough of written English to recognise her name. She could read and write that well enough and was clever enough to know that her name was quite plastered all over the newspaper that the duke had had delivered to Ashwood House all the way from London.

"Thank the Lord that Susanna and Alex are away on their wedding journey," Grace murmured as she read over Adam's shoulder, taking in what the newspaper had to say.

The duke did, indeed, look very seriously displeased as he read. Belle did not think that she had ever seen the duke appear so serious and angry. How she wished that she could read the newspaper, too. Selfishly, she wanted to know what they had said about her. She wanted to know what they were writing. If her name was in conjunction with Susanna's, then Belle worried that it was not good. Surely, they were speaking negatively about a lady, such as Susanna, marrying a black freedman. Certainly, they would have a similar view on her black wedding gown designer.

"Ignorant twits, the lot of them," cursed Adam. "How dare they write of Susanna in such a way and cast Alex in such a poor light. What do they know? I have half a mind to set Mother on them all."

"Cecily does have a copy of the same newspaper up in her bedroom with her breakfast. I would wager she might be halfway to London by now," replied Grace. "You know what they are like in London. As soon as any of the gossip mongers catch a taste of a scandal, they run with it, spreading it about like wildfire without a care for the damage caused. They did the same thing when you married me, don't you recall?"

Adam's face, if it could be believed, fell even deeper into a furious expression. "Yes, I do remember what these bloody rags said about you, Grace," he said through gritted teeth.

Belle had become aware of the fact that before she had become Adam's wife, and the Duchess of Ashwood, Grace had been employed as a maid in this house. Learning that had been of great comfort to Belle, to know that there were truly good masters.

But clearly, as evidenced by the obviously negative story about Susanna and Alex in the newspaper, the London press had not received the news of a servant duchess well.

"It will die down just as soon as the newest scandal erupts," Grace assured her husband. "And while I would never wish for misfortune to befall anybody, it is inevitable that it will. When the press realise that they will not get any more of a story from Susanna and Alex, as they plan to make their lives quietly here, they will move on."

Belle knew that it was not right, that it was highly selfish and inappropriate, to ask the duke to read the newspaper aloud. She remained silent as she consumed her breakfast, while their small party was joined by Jack, who was dressed very casually in a light pair of breeches and a lazily buttoned shirt.

"And what a merry party we are this morning," Jack commented as he swiped a pear from the tureen of fruit before plopping down into a chair beside his brother. "Who died?"

"Our sister's reputation," muttered Adam as he folded the newspaper shut and discarded it on the table. He then reached for his cup of tea and drank the lot in one go.

Jack bit into his pear. "What fun is a good reputation anyway?" he asked, his mouth full. "I, myself, have a little experience with scandal."

"No, really?" asked Adam facetiously.

Jack smirked. "It's healthy to break the rules now and then. It keeps society on their toes. Pushes them in the right direction, you know?"

"I am glad that you are so optimistic," returned Adam.

"Susanna is happy," Jack said simply. "Who cares a wit what bloody Roger and his wife, Betsy, down in Cheapside have to say?" He laughed as he took another bite. "Scandals are always easier to bear when you have a loving partner by your side." Thoughtfully, he added, "As is life. Don't you agree, brother?"

Grace rubbed Adam's arm and he caught her hand with his and squeezed it. Such a simple display of regard affected Belle.

"Yes," agreed Adam. "You are right, Jack."

"Brilliant. Do me a favour, would you? Say that exact statement again, only this time in earshot of Mother."

Adam's irritation and fury melted away and he laughed, his mood eased by his brother. Belle admired such affection between the brothers. In fact, she admired the easy affection between the entire Beresford family, and their extended relatives in the Denhams. They all really loved one another.

Belle felt a yearning in her chest to belong to it. A large piece of her wanted to be a part of it, of it all.

When breakfast was concluded, and the Beresfords had moved on from the dining room to go about their days, Belle could not help herself as she swiped the discarded newspaper from the table.

The headline was printed in bold, black letters.

SCANDAL BLACKENS THE HOUSE OF ASHWOOD

As Belle walked into the village that morning, she tried her hardest to read what just the headline had to say. She could recognise the letters, and she recalled some of the sounds, but something in her head prevented her from comprehending what it meant. It did not help that there were many, many English words that she was still yet to learn, and she hoped that the reason she could not read even the mere headline was because of the English, and not because she was a fool.

As Belle sewed that morning, she abandoned the headline, and continued on trying to find words within the article that she could read.

And ... but ... wed ... can ... go ... from ...

The words were few and far between, and Belle began to grow increasingly frustrated with herself as she struggled to make any sense of it.

But her name, she recognised. Belle Desjardins. Belle Desjardins. Belle Desjardins. Her name was written five times throughout the article that she could count, and yet she had no idea what they were saying about her.

To be named so publicly was new, and quite possibly dangerous for Belle. And she didn't want to think of the danger.

Belle paid little attention to the chime of the bell as it rung over and over throughout the morning as Mr Andrews' customers came and went. Nobody ventured over to Belle's table and owing to the ease in which sewing came to her, she could mend and try to read at the same time.

It was not until half past ten that morning that someone did approach her table. Belle's eyes looked up, though not to the person's eyes. She never did that when a stranger approached her. But when she saw and recognised the way this customer walked, she did look up. It would have startled Belle a little longer that she could recognise Peter by the way he walked had she not been so eager to meet his gaze.

Peter was smiling at her, and Belle could not help but smile back at him. She felt a wave of ease settle over her, as though Peter's presence was a calming state of safety, and Belle's frustrations melted away, albeit temporarily.

"Good morning," he greeted in a soft, familiar tone.

"Good morning," she replied, her voice startlingly hoarse with surprise. She anxiously cleared her throat.

"I have brought you a gift," he said, sounding rather proud and excited as he produced a parcel wrapped in brown paper. "It is the one I spoke of yesterday."

Belle's frustrations had only been temporarily stopped. When she realised what Peter was holding out to her, she felt frustrated, and completely embarrassed. But despite feeling this way, Belle reminded herself to focus on the kindness that Peter was showing her. He was proud of himself, and he was gifting her the evidence of pursuing one's dreams. Peter wanted to share this with Belle, and she would not ruin it with her own faults and shortcomings.

Belle accepted the parcel with a smile and laid it down on the table in front of her. She could see on Peter's face that he was anxious for her to open it. Belle pulled on the string that was fastening the gift and carefully unfolded the paper, removing from it a small book that looked so new that not even the spine was creased.

"It is the first book that Jack and I ever published," Peter told her proudly. "If you open the cover, on the inside there," he waited for Belle to comply, "you can see the Beresford Press stamp." He grinned. "What's more, and what is very important to Jack, is that this book was written by a woman, and it was just as successful as if a man had written it. Jack plans on leaving his half of the publishing house to his daughter. Daughters now, I suppose. It is important to him that we normalise women in publishing and print, as he wants his girls to have the opportunity and the power to be businesswomen one day. I fully support the idea. If I ever had a daughter, I have my half to bequeath as well." Peter's cheeks suddenly flushed, and he suddenly grew bashful, scratching the side of his head awkwardly. "Not that I am ... suggesting ... or forcing ... or expecting ..." he trailed off.

Belle had always enjoyed Peter's bashfulness. While she did still enjoy it, her amusement was stunted by the very fact that she hadn't gotten lost in the English. She had understood his meaning, and she knew what he was trying to backtrack out of.

A child. Their child.

Belle could see in Peter's eyes that he was not backtracking for lack of want. He was doing it out of courtesy to her. Peter could see that in their future. God bless him, Peter seemed as though he was making plans for that in their future.

Peter believed that he had a future with Belle. Peter actually wanted a future with Belle. Could it be possible that Peter might love Belle one day?

She could not look away from him. She could not look away from his handsome, youthful, innocent face. Only a short time ago, Belle had believed that she was barren, destined to never have a child, but now she knew that was not the case. It was possible. She was able if God allowed it, and Belle knew that if she allowed herself to think on it for too long, then she would begin to mourn. Because even if she was able, she would never be able to bear Peter's child ... the one he wanted to leave his publishing house to.

Belle was attached to him in every way possible. He was right in front of her and her head was telling her to mourn him, to mourn the life that they could never have. This was why she had pulled away. This was why she had meant to stay away. She hadn't meant to grow attached. She hadn't meant to start falling in love.

But it had happened, slowly and quickly at the same time. Her heart had claimed a man that she could never have, and what a wicked, cruel fate that was.

Belle could never be married to Peter.

"I hope you like it," Peter finally said, still as bashful as ever. "I promise it is a good read. Jack never chooses anything less than."

Belle realised right in that moment that she wanted that future ... the one that Peter was quite possibly envisioning. But ...

Belle could never be married to Peter.

"Peter," whispered Belle, the truth on her lips. But even as she wanted to say it, another truth escaped. "I cannot read."

Peter's face fell, and Belle watched as he turned nine shades of purple. "Oh," he realised, completely embarrassed. "Oh, forgive me, Belle. Forgive my ignorance ... my complete lack of tact and care. Forgive me, please."

Belle started to tremble uncontrollably. Had she confessed this truth at any other moment, she would have felt humiliated, but that was not what she was feeling. She felt the heavy weight of devastation in her chest.

All because Belle could never be married to Peter.

"Please ... let me," Peter implored, carefully making his way around her table with his arms extended. He gently placed his arms around her, and Belle's traitorous body leaned into his embrace. "Hush, hush, please," he said softly. "You need not be ... ashamed ... if that is what you are feeling. There is no shame in this. If you would like ... if you would let me, I could help you."

Peter wanted to make it alright. Care and tenderness flooded his tone and Belle yearned for it. She yearned for it all.

But Belle could never be married to Peter.

How could she be when she was already married to someone else?

Chapter 16

The very thought of his name paralysed Belle. The memory of his face, in all its forms, haunted her nightmares. They had done since she was a small girl.

The earliest memory that Belle possessed was the very first time that he had displayed his monstrous, gluttonous, evil self. While he had only been a young man of sixteen, young Belle had been all of five years old.

He had called her his favourite. He had given her treats that the others didn't receive. It sickened Belle to her core to remember ever feeling any sort of gratitude to him, now knowing what he had been planning on doing. If she allowed her mind to wander, she could still feel the innocence in her heart leave her the very moment he had shut himself in a room with her.

After the first time, Belle didn't want his favour. She didn't want his gifts. She didn't want to be within a hundred miles of him. But her life was not her own. She had no power, no say, and no right to refuse. But she did.

Every time, she fought. Every time.

This behaviour only made him angry, and he grew utterly obsessive.

Belle had never understood the word 'insatiable' before being at the mercy of him. And she was powerless to stop him. Nobody would help her. Nobody could save her. How could they? When they, too, were at his mercy.

Belle had never understood his obsession. She had never known what she had done to appeal herself to him when she had only been a five-year-old child when he had set his sights on her.

The only way she could make any sort of sense of what had happened to her was that some people were innately evil, and would, indeed, face judgement for the pain that had been inflicted upon others. Every scar she bore, save for the sabre wound on her abdomen that she had received while hiding from the smugglers with Alex, had been as a direct result of his anger.

But the scars that were invisible to the naked eye, were perhaps the worst of all.

Belle couldn't bear to be touched. She was too afraid to look people in the eye. She was too frightened to speak for fear that she would say something out of turn. She never felt safe.

But things had begun to change since she had met Peter Denham. Belle had felt the sort of security that she had never imagined was possible. She had found a man with whom she felt safe, and she had known what it was like to be held with gentle hands. She had finally known a good man, the sort of man who could only be a figment of her imagination were he not a living, breathing, blue-eyed, handsome, gentle giant in front of her.

Belle had fallen in love. Real love. Not … not his kind. Really, she had not realised that she was falling until she was very really in it, in the very thick of it. And all Belle wanted to do was lose herself in it. She wanted to leap into Peter's arms and to ask him to take her somewhere they could be happy. She wanted to be married in the way she had seen while living in England. She wanted a family … and she thought now that there was a real possibility that she could become a mother.

And at the same time, Belle knew that none of that was a possibility. None of it could be. The dreams that had tried to eclipse her nightmares had failed, because she was still bound to the man who had shut her inside of a room when she was five years old. The same man who had done so repeatedly, over and over, brutally, evilly, sickeningly, until she had escaped at eighteen during a hurricane.

Belle had thought she understood being owned until the day her master had died. She had marked the fourteenth anniversary of the day she had been found as an infant only three days earlier. He had assumed his father's role as master and made it his intent to possess Belle in every way humanly possible.

He had taken her before a priest. She didn't understand why. She didn't know why he wanted to marry her. But again, the only way she could make sense of it was to believe that he desired to possess her before God as well.

Belle had cried, and refused, and she had begged for help, foolishly believing that she was safe in a church, and safe with a priest. But she hadn't been safe. She was never safe. And that priest had not been a man of God. He had watched him strike her down on the altar, and he had performed the ceremony as her cheek swelled, and her lip split open and bled right on the floor.

Belle understood the Devil to be known by many names. Satan. Lucifer. Beelzebub.

But in her nightmares, and her memories of hell, his name was Jean Leclerc.

Peter felt like a right fool. How on earth had he managed to miss something like this? How on earth had he allowed himself to humiliate Belle in such a way? Of course, he did not think any less of her for not being able to read, but he could see by the expression on her face that the confession ... well, it looked like it sickened her.

Peter hated that she felt such shame, and he hated that his oversight and his obliviousness had been the cause for her cool, dark skin to become ashen-like.

He wanted so desperately to be able to take her shame away from her. Didn't she understand that he could never think less of her?

"Do you need to sit down?" Peter asked tenderly.

Belle slowly nodded, and Peter helped her to the chair behind her table. Lord, she looked as though she had seen a ghost. What on earth had he done to her? Peter stashed the book inside of his coat pocket, wishing that he'd never given it to her. It was completely insensitive of him.

This action seemed to capture Belle's attention. Her golden eyes watched his hands, before she finally looked up at him. Would there every come a time when the colour did not bewitch him? "You do not want me to have the book?"

Her voice was startled, raspy, disturbed. Peter wanted to bang his head against her sewing table.

"Not if it is going to make you feel like this," Peter replied softly.

Belle blinked, a little of her colour returning. Her breaths seemed to even out, and she rested her hands on the table. "Your gift did not make me feel any sort of bad way, I promise. I ... I am honoured that you want to give it to me. If you still do, that is."

Peter was confused, and extremely hesitant. If the book had not elicited that reaction from her, then what had?

Slowly, he pulled the book back out from his coat pocket, and gently placed it down on the table, the cover brushing her fingertips. Belle immediately ran her hand over the cover, as though she was petting a cat, feeling the embossed letters of the title.

"I don't want to be a fool. I don't think I am," Belle murmured. "Susanna tried to teach me words on the journey to England. But it was very difficult. I learned to speak better, but reading ..." Belle swallowed. "It is very hard."

Peter couldn't imagine the confusion inside Belle's brain in learning to speak, read and write in a language that was not her mother tongue. How challenging it must have been for her teaching experience to be English. He wondered if reading would have come easier to Belle had she learned to read and write in French first.

"You are not a fool," Peter assured her. "Of course, you are not." Peter knew then that he most definitely took his ability to read and write for granted. He could not remember a time when he was illiterate, and it was truly criminal considered so many in this country were not afforded and education. "If you would let me, I'd like to teach you."

Perhaps ... just maybe ... she would eventually be able to write to him when he returned to London. His return was nearing, and thus their impending separation was nearing, too. Peter had been intending on asking her to correspond with him. Thank the Lord he had found this out before doing so, or else he would have really put his foot in it more than he had already.

A subtle, very small smile teased Belle's lips, and Peter thanked God for it. He had not permanently wounded her. "I am a slow learner," she whispered.

"I am a patient man, as I hope you already know," he returned.

Peter's stomach then suddenly dropped as he watched Belle's golden eyes become glassy. Tears. Why? What he had done? What had he said? What on earth was wrong with him? Why was he determined to harm this poor, beautiful girl?

But Belle composed herself quickly, and instead picked up the newspaper which had been folded on her table. Peter recognised it as one of the London papers, and realised that it must have been one of the newspapers that Adam sent for at Ashwood.

It was not long until he saw the sickeningly dark headline. SCANDAL BLACKENS THE HOUSE OF ASHWOOD Peter wanted to swear while tearing the rag to shreds. Oh, how he'd wager the editor of that paper cackled to himself at the double entendre he had created with such a word.

"Would you ... would you read me this?" Belle asked fragilely. "I know my name. I know it when I see it. My name is in this. Please, would you read it to me?"

Peter hated to think what this sort of article would say about Belle with a headline like that. He would have to think fast to soften the blow. Would it be cruel to lie to her, or would it be crueller to tell her the truth?

Peter took the newspaper from her, and he read over the article as quickly as he could.

It is the union that has shocked a nation. This past Saturday, on September 28 in the year of our Lord 1811, the Lady Susanna Beresford, only daughter to the late Duke of Ashwood, was married to a West Indian negro slave.

Peter hissed.

"What?" asked Belle. "What does it say?"

Peter's eyes flashed to her. "They are not particularly fond of Alex," he said truthfully.

Belle pursed her lips. "I can imagine. A marriage between two such people must be quite unheard of."

Peter read on, his stomach curdling as the writer referred to Susanna as chattel, and any children that they would have as mulattos.

The bride's association with enslaved negroes did not cease with her intended. West Indian slave woman, Belle Desjardins, was reported to have been the designer and craftswoman of Lady Susanna Beresford's wedding gown.

Witnesses of the marriage stated that Belle Desjardins' design was a modern and expensive creation that did well to disguise the designer's bondage roots. In what was a startling turn of events to many in attendance at the Hertfordshire event, Miss Desjardins showed a level of expertise in her craft that ensured the bride elevated that sorry state of affairs.

While she couldn't read this, Peter could protect her. Perhaps it would not be for forever, but it could be for now. He didn't want her to experience whatever she had been only a few minutes earlier. He couldn't see her face like that.

"Belle Desjardins was reported to have been the designer and craftswoman of Lady Susanna Beresford's wedding gown," Peter read, editing out the unnecessary drivel. "Witnesses of the marriage stated that Belle Desjardins' design was a modern and expensive creation that did well to highlight her skills as a modiste. Miss Desjardins showed a level of expertise in her craft that ensured the bride was fit for the occasion."

Peter couldn't read anymore. He could see Belle's name mentioned elsewhere in the article in conjunction with Alex's, as they were described yet again as slaves infiltrating their way into a prominent family. He did not have the ability to think quickly enough to make something up out of that sentence.

"London loved your dress," he said softly. That, at least, was not a lie. They had paid Belle a rather backwards compliment.

Belle smiled, this time a little more widely. "That was not all they had to say, was it?" she probed.

"You knew I was lying?" Peter frowned. "Why are you smiling?"

"My name was written five times. You read it only three. You are protecting me. There is a difference. How I wish ... I want ... I have always wanted to be protected."

Chapter 17

Belle jumped awake when she heard a booming crash. Her heart began to thunder in her chest as she felt the pure energy begin to course through her veins. She shuffled up to a seated position in her bed, pulling her blanket up to her chin as her body began to uncontrollably tremble.

No.

He couldn't be back already. He was supposed to be away for another week at least. The last lot of bruises and welts had barely begun to heal.

"BELLE, WHERE ARE YOU?" she heard his furious voice bellow. She also heard the thickness of his voice, as though it was lubricated with drink.

Belle was in the slave bunk with everyone else. When he was away, she slept in there, on the small, wooden cots with the scratchy blankets. Perhaps one would wonder as to why she preferred such meagre quarters when she had the option of sleeping in the master's house. But Belle could never sleep in that house. In the two years since Jean had forcibly married her, Belle had not slept for one minute in that house.

Belle heard the fearful whispers of the others who had been awoken by Jean's shouting. Though the darkness concealed their expressions, she knew that their faces would have looked quite frightened.

Belle couldn't remain silent. She couldn't hide now.

Though Belle had learned to remain silent. Sometimes she could be so quiet that people would often forget she was there. She learned to move soundlessly. Should an itch arise, she could think it away. She would never, ever speak unless she was directly spoken to.

It was how she survived.

But Jean was furious, and Belle's galloping heart knew what was coming. Jean had a fearsome temper. Jean could become angry if the crop was not being harvested quickly enough. Jean could become angry if a thread had come loose from the hem of his shirt.

He was angry tonight that his enslaved plaything of a wife was not where he had left her.

It must have been God who intervened on behalf of the others, as it was not Belle who got up out of the bed and put one foot in front of the other. Stepping out into the humid night, Belle was confronted first by the scene of ale. It permeated the air, and his clothes stunk.

Jean was a large man in every sense of the word. He overindulged on his favourite French cuisine and he was nearly as round as he was tall. But with his size brought strength, and one swipe from his meaty hand could knock her unconscious as he had many times before.

"There you are!" he sneered in a drunken slur. He gripped a lantern in one hand, and she saw his top lip upturn distastefully. Jean usually kept his sandy coloured hair combed neatly, but he looked quite dishevelled, and his shirt and breeches looked creased and crumpled.

Belle swallowed. It never got any easier. Sending her mind elsewhere did nothing to detract from the harrowing experience. She fought all she could, every time. She never wanted to give up. But she could never win. She was never strong enough to win. When Jean didn't want her to struggle, he could easily silence her with the swing of his fist.

Jean stepped forward and reached for her, intending to grab hold of her upper arm, but Belle instinctively jumped out of his reach.

"Little slut," hissed Jean, "probably been out here whoring yourself!" He lunged for her again, but this time he did not reach for her arm, instead grabbing hold of a fist-full of her hair. He yanked, and by some miracle he did not pull her hair out, instead Belle lost her footing and was dragged a few feet by the roots of her hair. Her scalp burned, and Belle let out an involuntary yelp of pain. Jean laughed.

He liked pain.

"Where has your mind wandered to, my dear?"

Belle jumped so violently that she felt as though she had left her body behind and she was now on the ceiling. She quite nearly fell backwards off of her chair as reality suddenly settled back in.

She was not in Saint-Martin. She was not sixteen and at the mercy of Jean. She was sitting at her table in Mr Andrews' grocer, and Peter's mother was standing before her, leaning on her cane while smiling at her.

Mrs Denham had a very kind and cheerful face, and Belle could see that she would have been very lovely in her younger years. Her three daughters had definitely inherited their mother's fairness. But she did not see much of Peter in her. The Denham siblings all had such blue eyes, and Belle deduced that Peter had inherited his handsome looks, and his blue eyes from his late father.

Belle suddenly gasped, it dawning on her that it was Peter's mother who was standing before her. What on earth was she doing here? A quick glance showed that she had not brought along any garments for alterations or mending. Certainly, she must have had something to say. But she was smiling ... so, she must not have had any grievances ... but how could that be? What must she be thinking?

Belle quickly stood up and pulled out her chair. "Would you like to sit, Madame?" she asked nervously.

"Oh, you are too kind. No, thank you, dear," Mrs Denham replied, shaking her head. "Are you alright? You appear as though you have seen a ghost."

Belle managed a small nod. "Fine, Madame," she lied.

Mrs Denham did not appear quite convinced, but she did not press the subject. "I have come to invite you to supper tonight," she announced. "I suggested to Peter that he invite you along, but he seemed to have some sort of silly notion that it would be putting you on the spot ... something about expectations ... pressure, I don't know. He's a worrier, my son. You are courting, are you not? Peter wouldn't say." Mrs Denham looked to Belle hopefully.

And that she was, hopeful. As though she wanted the answer to be "yes". Mrs Denham would be happy to have her son court Belle. Belle would have been happier about that thought were she not still recovering from where her mind had wandered.

How could she answer this woman? What could she say? Belle certainly knew what she wanted to say. But it was not the truth. And it could never be reality. Her stomach twisted with criminal guilt.

But Mrs Denham saved her before Belle had to answer. She sighed. "I suppose that is me putting you on the spot. You're a lady. These things will be announced properly when it is time, I know," she huffed. "But I will have you know, this village talks." She grinned. "And though he might try, Peter is certainly not practised in hiding his affection." Mrs Denham made a wistful noise and she looked over Belle's face, which at that moment was wearing a rather astonished expression. "My, my, you really are the most striking young woman. So, so pretty. But I am getting away from myself. My invitation! Supper tonight. Madame Amélie is preparing a Haitian dish. I really do not know any more than that, I am afraid."

"Is that a good idea?" Belle asked Mrs Denham quietly. "If people will talk ..." Belle could not even begin to contemplate her embarrassment if Mrs Denham and her family were subject to a slanderous article because she dined with them. It was bad enough that the Beresfords were newsworthy at the moment.

Peter is certainly not practised in hiding his affection.

That statement had not been lost on Belle. It warmed her soul in a way that it ought not to be warmed, and never had been before.

"Oh, pish posh," said Mrs Denham dismissively. But then she stopped herself. "I suppose that is simple for me to say, as I have no understanding of what it is like to be wearing your shoes, my dear. But I can assure you that everyone is welcome in my house, and I would so very like to have you to supper this evening. I shall see you, won't I?"

This woman had welcomed Alex's mother into her home and had given her a safe place to live. Belle wondered if Mrs Denham realised how rare she was. It would be a privilege to be welcomed into her home as well.

"Yes," confirmed Belle. "I would love to come."

Mrs Denham smiled warmly. "Wonderful," she replied. "I shall send Peter over to collect you later on. You take care now, dear."

"Thank you, Madame," Belle said gratefully.

Mrs Denham only continued to smile, before turning around and supporting her weight on her cane. She then proceeded to walk out of the grocer, struggling slightly with her pronounced limp.

Peter arrived several hours later with a rather distressed expression on his face. He did not even acknowledge that Mr Andrews was present before he hurried over to Belle's table.

"I am so sorry," he apologised as soon as he was before her. "When my mother told me what she had done I was furious. I didn't want her to put you on the spot. The last thing I wanted for you is to feel pressured or feel any sort of expectation from me, but my mother, bless her good intentions, just thinks I am being coy." Peter was frowning with concern, a line forming in between his brows.

Belle had been thinking about it for the remainder of the day, and the more she did, the more selfish she felt. Mrs Denham had asked her to dine with them because she believed that Belle was Peter's future intended. Mrs Denham believed that Belle would one day be a member of her family. She was planning on welcoming Belle into her home.

And if Belle attended, then she would no doubt be portraying herself as the biggest and worst fraud to ever cross the threshold. It was enough that she was not being honest with Peter. She was already tricking both him and herself into believing that there was a future between them. It would be criminal to involve Peter's family as well.

Looking up into Peter's eyes, she could see the turmoil, the stress and worry he was experiencing because of her, and out of concern for her. Lord, she loved him for it, but she knew that was wicked. It was wicked to be putting him through this. It was wicked to be fooling him in any sort of way. Peter Denham was a good, gentle, beautiful young man, and he deserved better.

Belle's eyes flooded with tears as she realised what she needed to do, what she had been delaying and ignoring for their entire acquaintance.

Peter's face fell even further. "Oh, I knew it," he murmured. "I am so sorry. She means well, she really does, but she has no control when it comes to matchmaking. I blame my sisters and their happy husbands for it." He tried to joke, to elicit a smile from her, but none came. "Belle ..." he said softly. "You needn't be upset. You do not need to come tonight. You know I would never force you to do anything that made you feel uncomfortable. Or at least I hope you know that."

How could God tease her in this way? How could He allow her to meet and know such a man only to force her to send him away?

"I need to tell you something," Belle confessed quietly, before eyeing Mr Andrews standing behind the counter watching their interaction with distasteful curiosity. "In private," she added in a whisper.

"Of course." Peter nodded.

Belle stood up from her table and abandoned her project. Peter allowed her to move past him and he followed along behind her. She offered a quiet word of departure to Mr Andrews that went unanswered before exiting the grocer and stepping out onto the street. She looked to her left and then to her right, wondering where they might speak without being overlooked or overheard.

"Come on," urged Peter, offering Belle his arm.

Belle knew it was wrong, but she could not help herself. She threaded her hand through his arm, allowing her hand to rest on the strong muscle there. He led her down the little alleyway between the grocer and the baker, navigating their way around boxes and rubbish that had been discarded there.

And then suddenly they were concealed behind a pile of wooden crates, the hum of the street still audible. Tears had already begun to roll down Belle's cheek as Peter released her, turning to face her.

"What can I do?" he asked her in earnest.

Belle used the sleeve of her dress to wipe her face, and Peter then anxiously retrieved and handkerchief from his pocket. She accepted it to wipe her other cheek.

"You have done everything," she promised him. "You have been so kind to me, so good ... just wonderful." Oh Lord, her chest. Her heart was about to beat through her ribs, ready to split her wide open. Belle could feel the pain building.

"Belle ..." Peter's voice was hesitant. She dared not meet his eyes.

"I have to tell you something," she said again, forcing her voice to be steady. "I have to tell you that I am sorry. I am sorry because I have ..." Oh, she could not think of the English word. Her brain was a mess and searching through her vocabulary was impossible. "I have been ... not honest. Not truthful." She took a shaky breath. "You are ... if I could have chosen ... I would want ... but I did not get to choose ... it was not my choice ... I was forced ... he made me ... I ... I ..."

"Belle," Peter said her name again, only this time his voice was firm. "Look at me, please."

Belle's glassy eyes found his when she lifted her chin. Once again, she was greeted by an ocean of warm concern.

"Take a moment," he said calmly, "find your words, and tell me. Tell me knowing that I would never be angry with you."

And there, in that moment, was when her heart split open.

Chapter 18

Peter did not know the right thing to say. He never seemed to. He always seemed to find some way to stumble over his words, or to say something odd, or something that he had not meant to. But he wanted to be better. He wanted to be better for Belle.

It affected him deeply to see her so frightened, so tortured by memories past, as she tried to speak about it. He wanted so badly to be able to say the right thing, and yet he couldn't find the words.

All he could do was assure her that whatever she had to say would not anger him. He had already made that commitment within himself to never show Belle anger, and he never would.

Peter wanted to hold her. He wanted to take her somewhere far quieter, far safer, than the rear of Mr Andrews' shop. He wished that they could be alone without the gossip mongers of this village having a field day.

With how he was feeling, the anguish, the concern, and the torment, it was as though his heart had begun to live outside of his own body. As though it had been placed with Belle without either of them realising until now.

"I know what you wish," Belle stammered after a long minute of silence. Her accent was heavier than ever as her voice was thick with emotion. "I know what you want. I know ... your maman told me ... but I know, too. I want it, too."

She was so torn, so conflicted, so tortured. Her eyes were molten, filled with fear, grief and regret.

Peter's first thoughts were that his mother had said something to frighten Belle, to pressure her without realising. But he quickly saw that Belle's reaction was quite beyond this. Her fear was remnant of when she had told him the story of her capture.

What was going on inside of her mind?

"Belle," said Peter again, using every ounce of his being to remain steady and calm. "Find your words. Just tell me, please."

Whatever it was, it was tearing her apart. She had to know that whatever she needed to tell him would not change anything. Nothing she had done, or ever could do, would change anything. That had become apparent quicker than anything. And he knew, sadly and infuriatingly, that it was highly likely whatever she needed to tell him had nothing to do with what she had done, but what had been done to her.

"I am already married."

The words tumbled out of Belle's mouth so quickly, and so heavily accented that Peter needed to stop for a moment to wonder if she had actually said them in French as he could not possibly have understood her properly. But after that moment, he realised that she had, indeed, spoken English, and she had confessed what he had heard.

Married. Married? How was this possible? How could she be married already? To whom? Where was this husband? Why was she not with –

Peter's irrational thoughts ceased immediately. Belle was not an unhappy wife seeking a torrid affair.

Belle was barely of age, and had suffered a monumental life of abuse, culminating in her escape, recapture, and liberation from that life. He only needed to read the terror in her eyes to know that her husband, whomever he was, could only be seen as a contributor to her torture.

Belle was looking up at him, her emotions and thoughts as plain as day on her face as she searched him for any reaction. Peter had only been silent for a moment, but it was a moment too long.

Peter could not think about what this news meant for him. To do so was entirely and criminally selfish. Belle had told him that she saw him as safe, and he would continue to be that harbour for her, remembering Jim's words of advice.

"You are safe with me," he murmured to her softly.

He watched as some, not all, but some of the tension eased in Belle's shoulders. She nodded and she took a deep breath.

"I am sorry," she whispered, her voice shaking. "It ... it happened five years ago, when I was fourteen ..."

Fourteen? For God's sake, she was but a child!

"... my master, he ... he made me ... he always made me ... I don't know why he wanted to marriage me ... but I ... I had to." Belle was losing her voice again, her firmness all but gone as her words shook and her accent clouded her pronunciation.

Years from now when Peter would look back on this moment, he would always wonder how he managed to stay calm, to be still. Because inside he was raging. Peter could feel his blood boiling. His brain was about to burst with the ire that was coursing through his body. Those details, those brief details about Belle's former life were harrowing and heartbreaking and knowing that she had been subjected to this killed him.

Her master, whomever he was, had forced her ... forced her into everything. Peter couldn't picture it lest he explode right there in that alley, which only increased his guilt as he knew Belle had to live with the memories.

Belle had been a fourteen-year-old girl ...

And here she stood at nineteen, frightened, shaking ... but alive, here as evidence of her perseverance and strength –

"I do not want you to be angry with me in knowing that you cannot ... that we cannot ... that I have lied ... that we must stop ... I am so sorry to hurt you ..." Belle interrupted Peter's thoughts with such ludicrous ones of her own.

Why was she worried about him?

But his question was answered by one look upon her face. Belle was worried about Peter because she cared about him.

Hang that man. Peter really wished that the law would hang him. Hang him and his hold over her. How dare he and his evil eclipse one more day of Belle's precious life.

"You are free," Peter told her fervently. "You are a free woman with your own will. You make your own choices. You chose to come here. You chose to settle in Ashwood. You chose to make your own income. You chose ... you chose to trust me, Belle. You are no longer belonging to any one person but yourself. You are answerable to no one, not even me. You are a world away from that life, and I pray, I pray that you are able to forge a new one for yourself that brings you fulfilment, joy and peace. Peace above all. And if you so deign me good enough to be welcomed into your life, then I shall consider it the greatest privilege of my own."

Belle's eyes widened and her full lips parted as she whispered, "I am free?" The way she said the words sounded more like a question.

And so, Peter would assure her. "You are free," he promised. "Whatever hold that was once upon you no longer exists."

Peter did not know if this was true. He was not a solicitor. He had very little knowledge of the legality of owning humans. Quite frankly, the idea of researching the subject made him sick to his stomach. Logically, he knew that it would be a little more complicated than just wishing oneself free. But Belle was safe here. She had been away from Saint-Martin for more than a year. That life was behind her. Her master was long gone, destined to be a figure who would slowly fade from Belle's memory as she replaced him with good ones.

If they got married one day, what did it matter if it was not entirely legal? Only they would know. And Belle would further have the protection of his name.

"I am free," Belle said again, this time with confidence, her voice sounding the steadiest it had during their entire conversation.

Peter smiled down at her. He then saw something flash through her eyes that seemed rather like gumption. It was certainly nerve as she placed her hands upon his chest and stood up on her toes, leaning up to ...

... to kiss him. Peter did not need to be told, or invited, twice. He immediately reciprocated, gently placing a hand on her waist, and other on her cheek as he leaned down towards her.

But before he could kiss her, he felt her freeze in his arms. Before he could release her, before he could calm her, Belle cried out, "No!" and was ten feet away from him, having ripped herself out of his arms.

She was gripping onto one of the empty wooden crates in the alley, panting, her eyes darting about as all manner of embarrassment and shame flashed across her face.

"Belle, it's alright," Peter promised her.

She dared not look at him. "I'm sorry. I'm sorry. I'm sorry," she repeated over and over. "I thought I could ... I thought ... I'm sorry. I'm sorry. Don't be angry."

The frustrated thought of 'When will she understand that I will never be angry with her?' crossed Peter's mind initially. But he then knew, and understood, that it had been ingrained into her to fear the reactions, the retaliation, the anger of men. He needed to change that.

Belle had tried to kiss him. She had tried to be vulnerable in a way that she was not yet ready to be. It meant the world to him that she had tried.

"I am not angry," Peter said gently, approaching her carefully. "I am not angry, I promise you."

Belle seemed to hear the sincerity in his voice, and she slowly turned her head to face him. She bit down on her bottom lip as she frowned sadly. "I am sorry," she whispered.

"Will you stop apologising, please?" he willed. "I am not angry, I promise."

Belle was quiet for a moment, before she finally nodded. "I believe you."

They stared at one another for a short moment, before Peter uttered once again, "You are free."

Those three words brought a smile to Belle's face, and after the anguish that he had seen upon her during this conversation, seeing that was blissful.

"Your maman invited me to supper," she said suddenly. "Perhaps ... perhaps I could go now. It would be alright to go now, would it not?"

Peter knew that Belle probably had no idea as to the level of enthusiasm that she would meet inside of his mother's house. But he could see that she had resisted going because she believed that she was not free to. Peter had succeeded in helping her to see that she did, indeed, have free will. If she wanted to exercise that free will to dine with his family, then so be it. He would shield her for the rest of his days.

"Let us go," said Peter, offering Belle his arm.

This time, without hesitation, she took it.

Chapter 19

Belle would never disrespect the Ashwood cook, but she had never eaten so well in her life than to have been in the presence of Alex's mother, Madame Amélie.

When Amélie had served Belle a generous helping of maka-woni au graten to start, she had uttered to Belle that "we eat well now". There was no reference to her size or weight, or a direct reference as to the reason for her once being so unhealthily thin. It was a simple statement of understanding between them. They ate well now. There was no reason why they did not. They were free women, and they ate well, just like everyone else.

And she certainly enjoyed the warm, baked sheets of maka-woni covered in cheese and sauces that tingled on her tongue.

Belle felt as comfortable as she could be at the dinner table, and she did notice that Mrs Denham was being kind to her. She could see that the compassionate woman was desperate to ask her questions, but she was careful not to focus attention on Belle. Instead, she scolded Jem about his table manners, and the fact that he was serving himself a second helping before anyone else had even finished their portion.

She eventually instructed Jem to clear the dishes away as Amélie prepared to serve the main dish. This led to Mrs Denham, Peter, and Belle being the only ones seated at the table. Mrs Denham could not hold herself back any longer.

"Belle," she began gently. "I am certain that you agree Amélie's cooking is divine. Jem will tell you that she is far more talented than I ever was." She laughed at herself. "Is it nice to eat something that reminds you of home?"

Belle knew that she had meant her question in a kind way. She could never presume Mrs Denham, or any of Peter's family members for that matter, would ever intend anything resembling maliciousness. But her question was ignorant, and that was through no fault of her own. She didn't know. She hadn't been taught.

Ordinarily, Belle would have answered with something obliging. She would never dare correct a white person. To survive was to oblige the white man. But Belle did not need to do that anymore. Belle was a free woman. Whatever hold that place, and those people, had ever had on her no longer existed.

Belle looked to Peter, and she found him watching her with patient, wondering eyes. He hadn't leapt to defend her. He hadn't gone to deflect or suppress the question. He was waiting for Belle to find her voice.

"I have never eaten this dish before," Belle replied, her voice surprisingly steady. "I had never been to Haiti before meeting Alex and Madame Amélie. I was born on an island called

Saint-Martin," she explained. Belle had been so, socareful to conceal such information about herself. To have such a confession roll off of her tongue almost frightened her.

Mrs Denham's eyes widened. "Oh, I had not realised! I am sorry," she apologised, sounding embarrassed.

Belle bit down on her tongue. She had certainly not meant to embarrass Peter's mother. She was very ill-prepared in knowing how to correct and educate a white person. "Please, do not apologise," Belle begged. "You have nothing to be sorry for. But to answer your question, yes, I am happy to eat this food. It is delicious," and certainly more flavourful than anything that could be called British food. But she, of course, did not say the latter thought. "However, it does not remind me of home. I ... I do not call where I was born 'home'. Truthfully, I do not know where my family came from. I was found abandoned as an infant. That is why my name is Belle Desjardins."

"What does your name mean, dear?" Mrs Denham asked quietly.

"Beauty of the Gardens," Peter answered automatically, seemingly recalling that fact from when Belle had translated her name for him in the beginning.

Mrs Denham's lips parted as her brows furrowed sadly. "Oh, my," she whispered.

"The people who laboured, who were enslaved upon Saint-Martin, and Haiti alike, were stolen from their homelands in Africa. That I know." Though she may have been born on Saint-Martin, there were many people who worked the plantations who had arrived on ships. Belle knew exactly what those ships were like. "Home, I have come to understand, is the place where one lives freely."

Jem returned to the table carrying a large dish of food that smelled divine. He protected his hands from the heat with a large, linen cloth. Once he had set it down in the middle, he plopped back down on his chair. Amélie returned to her chair as well, though she sat back down much more gracefully.

Amélie's comprehension of English was much improved, but she still preferred to speak in French. Belle understood this lack of confidence. To the table, she said, "Ma maison est avec les gens que j'aime."

Amélie had been listening, it seemed, and she understood Belle perfectly. Belle smiled at her. "She says, 'my home is with the people I love.'"

"I understand what you mean, Belle, and you, Amélie," Mrs Denham said then. "I believe I do not tie my home to a building, but to people. Were this house empty, I would not feel it was home. And I know in my heart that I have been spoiled with a level of autonomy that you have only begun to grasp yourself. Oh, really, I do not understand at all, do I?"

"But you want to, don't you?" asked Belle.

Mrs Denham took a breath, and she looked upon Belle with a respectful, sympathetic gaze. "I think that you are an extraordinary young woman, Belle," she uttered simply, "with a level of worldliness a woman like me could never hope to comprehend. But that is not an excuse not to try. If I have learned anything from Peter, it is that it is never too late to educate oneself, to better oneself."

Belle felt something swell in her chest that felt astonishingly like pride. Her smile broadened and she felt her cheeks warm. She was certain that she could have done a better job at explaining. She was certain that she could have done more to articulate what had happened. But was she ready to do that? She had barely begun to tell Peter what had happened to her. Despite this, Belle had spoken up to a white person for the very first time in her life. It was an achievement that she would not have been able to do not twenty-four hours earlier.

As Amélie went to dish up the main course of poulet aux noix, made possible by the cashew nuts that Alex had cultivated, Peter squeezed Belle's hand under the table.

Touch that she was not anticipating historically made Belle jump with fear. But she did not flinch at all away from his touch then. He smiled at her, and quietly murmured, "I'm proud of you."

The next fortnight saw a belated celebration for Perrie's fourth birthday, as well as Peter and Belle stepping out into the Ashwood village society with their defiant liaison.

Of course, the rumours had been circulating as rumours tended to do, but Peter had proudly escorted Belle to and from Mr Andrews' store each day. He dined at Ashwood House, and she was invited back to his mother's. And she attended the Ashwood parish church service for the first time since arriving in England. Belle did not think that Susanna's wedding could be counted.

The church was where the term 'defiant liaison' had been coined by tasteless gossips. The dowager duchess had been the one to declare those women as such directly to their faces.

To be so defended by the highest-ranking woman in the village next to Grace was deeply humbling for Belle. Home was where one lived freely, but it was also where one felt accepted as part of the family.

Ever since she had accepted that she was a free woman, she was slowly starting to accept the happiness that she could have with Peter. At times ... Belle felt that it was all too good to be true, as though something might happen to spoil everything. But that was the pessimist, the tortured girl inside of her talking. She still needed to learn to ignore her.

Then, she supposed, Peter leaving to return to London was spoiling things, and she felt very selfish for thinking that. Peter's life and his business were in London. He had been away for a long while and it was high time that he returned. He had explained to Belle that while he had been away his printers had been filling their order for their new book, "Confessions of a Lady". Peter had promised to send her a copy.

Regretfully, their reading and writing lessons had barely begun. Belle was still not at all confident, even if she felt as though her spoken English improved each day.

They sat together under the shade of an evergreen tree in Ashwood House's palatial garden. It was Sunday, and Peter had arrived with his family for dinner, before he and Belle had stolen away outside for a quiet moment alone. It would be their last before he, Jack, Claire, and their two daughters would depart for London the following morning.

"Would you like to travel to London one day?" Peter asked her quietly.

"Do you love it?"

Peter nodded. "Yes, I do."

Then Belle nodded, managing a smile. "Then yes, I would love to travel there someday." Someday seemed impossibly ambiguous. She didn't like it at all, and she was most definitely hiding behind her smile. It didn't seem fair that their defiant liaison was coming to an end. Of course, Belle knew that it was not final. But they would be thirty miles from one another. It was not as though he could walk to her door like he had been doing each morning. Peter would be returning to his life, and Belle was a little unsure of where she belonged.

Though they were both seated, Peter's tall torso meant that he was still a head above her in height. He looked down upon her with a caring, gentle smile. "You are touched by an angel, without a doubt," he murmured.

Belle's stomach fluttered as Peter reiterated perhaps his most meaningful compliment to her.

"If I am, then you must be as well," she countered softly.

"I will be back for the Winter Assembly," he told her. "It is an annual ball held here in Ashwood. Ordinarily I would miss it, but there is someone here I would like to dance with," he hinted. "And I did promise my brother I would be there for a little encouragement. He plans to woo a young lady." He chuckled. "But, in the meantime, would you do something for me?"

"Anything."

Peter pursed his lips. "I want you to write to me."

Belle felt the blood drain from her cheeks as she quickly looked away from Peter, focussing her eyes on a fountain in the distance so that they would not well up with embarrassment. Even though logically she need not be embarrassed, it was hard not to be when something that others did with ease was so challenging.

"Don't look away from me. My time left with your angel eyes is limited," he appealed, attempting to making her smile.

"I can't," she said quickly, her voice bordering on unsteady.

"Belle," Peter said again tenderly. "Please, please don't feel bashful with me. I believe I have made enough of a fool of myself since we both met that you need not feel embarrassed ever again."

Belle did not laugh. "I can't write," she said again, this time more firmly. "You know this. I couldn't read your letters either." At this confession, she buried her face in her hands with frustration. This was normal. Correspondence. It happened all the time. Every morning she watched as Adam, Grace, and Cecily received letters from friend, neighbours, and the like. Lord, she would love to be able to correspond with Peter, to maintain their connection through their separation.

"Belle, I would be happy to receive a word, a blot of ink, anything from you," Peter promised her. "Even if it is just a 'good day, Peter', so that I know you have not forgotten about me," he teased.

Belle looked up then, frowning. "Forget you?"

Peter smiled sincerely. "I know what you are capable of reading, and I will write accordingly," he told her. "I am not expecting essays, but I would like ... I would love for you to write me anything. Would you try, please?" he implored.

Belle's heart lurched as she quietly confessed, "But I do not know how to spell your name."

Peter suddenly appeared inspired as he took her hand and gently turned over her palm. Using his opposite index finger, he began to write, articulating as he did. "P ... E ... T ... E ... R."

Belle's skin tingled at the softness of his touch.

"Will you write me?" he asked again hopefully.

"I will try," promised Belle.

Chapter 20

"Our printers have worked tirelessly to ensure your first run of copies will be ready to distribute by the New Year, Miss Granger," Peter informed the excited author proudly.

As she had been during their last meeting, Miss Hattie Granger was dressed incognito as a widow, black veil and all. Her smile, however, would let anyone assume that she had loathed her husband.

"I am very confident about Mr Denham's projected sales numbers, Miss Granger," added Jack, who was casually leaning against Peter's desk. "Your book is one I would have both of my daughters read when they are old enough. I have already set one aside to purchase as a Christmas present for my wife."

Hattie clapped her hands together. "Oh, I am so pleased," she replied gleefully. "I cannot thank you gentleman enough for your encouragement and support. I never ... I never could have imagined that I would be able to find a publishing house willing to give me, as a woman, a chance."

Peter knew that with the right advertising, and money spent in the right places, plenty more women authors could be very successful, and it would be a wise decision for other publishers to be more diverse with their choices in manuscripts. There was a market out there if they were willing to look.

Jack, however, bought manuscripts on talent alone. He was building Beresford Press to be a place of opportunity, so that one day, Peter knew, he could have Jackie, or indeed Maria, work alongside him equally.

Peter couldn't help but wonder where he would be bequeathing his half of the business. Could he have his own child in the near future? Lord, if everything went to plan, he hoped so.

"You have a strong voice, Miss Granger," complimented Jack with a sincere smile. "Should this book do as well as Mr Denham predicts, then we will be very interested in what other manuscripts you have to offer. We will have the bound book sent to your address come January, and then Mr Denham will be in touch with regards to your royalty shares."

Hattie stood up from the chair opposite Peter's desk and nodded. "I am working on another manuscript," she replied.

"You shall bring it to me personally when you are finished," urged Jack.

Hattie thanked them both again, before pulling her black veil back down over her face and departing the office, leaving Peter and Jack alone.

"Jackie is clever," Jack stated confidently. "Very much so. She is terribly bright."

"Jack ... she is not yet two," Peter murmured, frowning. "I don't think you would do very well bringing her into the business just yet." He smirked.

Jack grinned. "No, no, that's not what I meant. I mean that whenever I read to her, she takes it all in. She listens intently, and she stares at me with her big, knowledgeable eyes. Of course, I have only been reading her children's stories ... you know, she likes Candide by Voltaire, she loved Robinson Crusoe, so that is how you know she is my child." He chuckled. "I really tested her with The Decline and Fall of the Roman Empire, but she did listen to that for a good twenty minutes before she fell asleep."

"Yes, they are all terrific examples of children's stories," confirmed Peter, rolling his eyes with a wry smile.

"Naturally," agreed Jack. "Which is why I think she will take in Miss Granger's story now. Oh, Peter, I cannot wait for my girls to be able to read themselves."

Peter was proud that his two nieces in Jackie and Maria would never want for education. He was confident that Jack would secure them every possible opportunity to be as educated as was allowed in this society. What would be as close to attending university would be what those girls would be provided with.

With the money he had saved since working for Jack, he knew that he would do all he could to ensure the futures of his own children. He did not think that Belle would ever object to a thorough education considering how hard she was working to learn herself.

His thoughts drifted to Belle so often throughout the days and weeks that he had been back in London. Peter's mind took him to Belle when he was sitting idly, and when he was working hard and needed to be focussed. He couldn't help it. He missed her terribly. This separation confirmed it for him. He didn't want to be parted from her. He wanted to be with her always. He could only pray that she missed him as much as he did her.

Peter could not write as much as he wanted to in the letters he sent back to Ashwood. Firstly, he did not want to overwhelm her with his feelings. And secondly, he had to be very careful with the words, and the volume of them, that he wrote. Peter sent back simple, brief letters that he knew Belle would be able to read without getting frustrated or embarrassed.

And she had kept her promise to him. He had received seven letters from Belle. One for every week he had been away. Peter had received the seventh letter that morning at breakfast and had carried it with him in his breast pocket to the publishing house so that he could pull it out and read it again.

"I cannot believe it is the end of November already," commented Jack, bringing Peter back out of his own thoughts. "Wind is biting, the sky is grey and low, weather is miserable. Nothing like England in the winter."

Peter laughed before he took a breath. "We ought to go through the invoices for the book advertising and the distribution plans for January. I will be able to correspond from

Ashwood, but these payments need to be made by the fifteenth and you will need to go to the bank –"

"Peter," interrupted Jack. "If you continue to stress like this, your hair will be grey before your twenty-first birthday. We went through this yesterday. I have my instructions. You are very thorough. I certainly know I wouldn't be able to run this publishing house without you. I know when the payments need to be made, I have all the correspondence, and I will go to the bank."

In order for Peter to return to Ashwood in time for the Winter Assembly, Jack was handling all of his responsibilities leading up to the release of Miss Granger's book. Peter, of course, had organised everything that he could, and had written Jack copious amounts of notes and instructions, but he was grateful to Jack for his generous offer.

Because of this, Jack was not able to take Claire home for the ball. They would not be travelling to Ashwood now until the week before Christmas.

"Before I dragged you home with us when Maria was born, you have not taken a day off since last Christmas," continued Jack. "You're welcome, by the way."

"For what?"

"For dragging you home. Had I not, then you would not be sneaking off with my wife to look at shop locations and newlywed flats." Jack smile smugly, folding his arms across his chest.

"Claire is such a gossip," hissed Peter.

"She is just excited for you. We both are."

Peter had turned to his elder sister for assistance when it came to his future plans. He intended on proposing. He was not certain when. He supposed that he would know when the moment was right. But he wanted to return to London in the new year engaged. Ideally. And if they were engaged, then he wanted to be prepared. He couldn't help himself. Peter knew that Belle dreamed of opening her own shop and seeing that he was becoming quite the savvy businessman, he had been scouting locations with his sister. He and Claire had happened to find one a few streets over that had a comfortable flat above it.

Peter needed to keep reminding himself, however, to not get too far ahead of himself. He knew that Belle could be easily overwhelmed and frightened, and he didn't want her to know any of this before the time was right.

Truthfully, he worried that the time would never be right. He worried that she wouldn't want any of this ... or him. It was difficult to gage her feelings from her letters, and he knew that was not her own fault. She was doing her best. But what he would give to speak with her. He would not have to wait very much longer.

When Jack returned to his office, Peter pulled out the letter that he had been keeping in his pocket.

Der Peter, Belle had written. Her penmanship improved with each letter she had posted. He could see how careful she was trying to be by the pressure she applied with each stroke of the pen.

I am wel.

I did so a jres for winta asemblee. I hop yoo lik it.

I wnt too see yoo hr soon.

I hop yoo ar wel.

Yor Belle.

As he read it over and over, he read between the lines. It was hard not to hope, not to get ahead of oneself when reading that. Despite it only being four lines, it had been the newsiest letter he had received from her. He couldn't imagine the time she had spent poring over that letter and trying her hardest to spell words that she had never written before.

He prayed that everything would be as it was when they were reunited. Even better than it was. Peter hoped that Belle would only grow in her confidence and trust with him, and he hoped that she would feel her safest when she was with him. It was too presumptuous to hope that she would allow him to kiss her, but Peter couldn't help but wish for that as well.

If everything went to plan, he would kiss her on the night of the ball, and if God, and fate, and everything in between, was on his side, he would propose to her as well.

Peter had never seen his younger brother so tense in his life. Jem looked like he was about to be sick as he stood before the mirror to make certain that his cravat was straight. Peter had certainly never seen Jem in a cravat before. Not even at any of their sisters' weddings had he deigned it necessary to don one.

But tonight, he had.

Jem combed his fingers through his dark hair, pulling at a few of his curls, before making a frustrated noise as they sprung back to where they wanted to be.

Jem was usually very cheerful, slightly mischievous and cheeky, and always was ready for fun. If it was at his elder brother's expense, then Jem was fine with that. But tonight, he didn't look like a cheeky boy. He looked like a nervous young man of seventeen, determined not to make a fool of himself.

Selfishly, watching Jem worry was a good distraction for Peter. He had arrived home that morning, and so he was yet to see Belle. She would be travelling to the ball with Grace and Adam, and so they would not be reunited until they met at the assembly hall where Peter planned on escorting her inside.

It also occurred to Peter that he still had no idea what this mystery girl of Jem's looked like. Jem, of course, had been very secretive, but Peter hadn't thought to ask around for news of any Cressie Martins ... though he never would have jeopardised Jem like that.

"My arms and legs look too long for my body," Jem complained, stretching out his arms in front of him. "I need to gain a stone for them to match. What if I trip her over?"

"So, what if you do?" Peter said encouragingly. "If she's an obliging young lady, she will not worry at all about it."

"I still don't want her thinking I'm a fool," muttered Jem half-heartedly. "I want to impress her. I want her to like me. I don't want her to see a stupid boy. I want to be a suitor."

Peter supressed an amused smile. He had definitely never seen his brother this way. "Jem, you are only seventeen. You are still a boy, really. You need not put this sort of pressure on yourself. Just be yourself. If she's a good judge of character, then she will see what a good egg you are."

"I feel like I only have one chance," replied Jem, sighing as he looked at his reflection before turning to his brother. "She'll be of age next summer. She'll be able to go to London like Susanna did ... her mother seems like the sort to do that sort of thing. Any man with half a brain would take one look at her and be lost."

Much like Jem, it seemed. "Do you actually know anything about her, save for what she looks like?" asked Peter, frowning. Jem was clearly infatuated with her appearance, but perhaps he was too immature to be making hasty decisions if he knew nothing deeper about her.

"That's what tonight is for," Jem retorted. "We'll get to know one another."

Peter would, indeed, need to keep one eye on his brother throughout the evening.

They were interrupted by a knock on the door, and their mother entered the bedroom. She was dressed in her best gown and looked very elegant indeed. Leaning on her cane, Mrs Denham sighed with pride. "Oh, my boys!" she cried. "How handsome you are! Peter, so dapper! And Jemmy! Oh, Jemmy, when did you grow up?"

"Mother, promise not to call me 'Jemmy' in earshot of anyone tonight," Jem begged. Before he turned to Peter and asked, "Do you think I ought to start going by 'Jeremy'? Is that not more grown up?"

Peter smirked. "I don't think I have ever uttered the name 'Jeremy' aloud until this moment. You don't even look like a Jeremy. You are Jem, I am afraid."

"You will always be my baby Jemmy!" Mrs Denham declared, making her way over to stand before Jem before looking up at him. "Even if you are taller than me, you are still my baby."

Jem pulled a face. "Get all the Jemmys out now. I will deny any relation to you if you call me that in public."

Mrs Denham laughed and pinched Jem's cheek. "What is the matter with you?"

Peter knew that he would have dropped his younger brother in it, just as Jem usually would were their roles reversed. But Peter was the gentler brother, and he knew Jem was feeling nervous. So, he decided to spare Jem instead.

"Come alone, Mother. We ought to be leaving now. We do not want to be late," he urged.

Amélie could not be convinced to attend the ball, so Peter, Jem, and Mrs Denham travelled by carriage alone to the Ashwood assembly hall. There were carriages, horses, and people everywhere, as was the tradition. People came from every neighbouring parish to attend the last ball of the year before the villages began to hibernate for winter.

When their carriage stopped, Peter opened the door and let down the step before the driver could. Grace was always so kind to send their servants to assist with the carriage, but Peter didn't like to be waited on.

He then helped his mother carefully out, before Jem followed, anxiously searching their surroundings with his eyes. Peter did the same, only he was searching for the Ashwood carriage.

"Come along, Cressie. Don't dawdle."

Peter's ears pricked up at the sound of a mother's hurrying tone, and the mention of that name. He turned around to see Jem was frozen in place as he watched a pair of women arrive without a carriage.

The elder, Mrs Martin, was a very elegantly dressed woman who walked with great pride and purpose. She was pale and delicate, and seemed to have passed on her fair looks to her daughter.

Miss Cressie Martin was certainly very beautiful, and Peter could understand Jem's infatuation. She was very fair, with light, golden hair and dainty, elfin features. She looked very young, younger than Jem, though he seemed to think that she was going to be of age by next summer, so she had to be sixteen or seventeen years old. Either way, she seemed nervous and apprehensive, just as Jem was. By the expression on her mother's face, it seemed as though they had recently quarrelled.

Peter would have wagered that Jem would have followed along after her like a puppy dog were Mrs Denham not holding on to his arm. His eyes had not left her, though Cressie had not noticed him staring.

"Here they come," announced Mrs Denham. "What good timing that was."

Sure enough, the illuminated windows of the grand Ashwood carriage could be seen travelling down the road, pulled along by four of their horses. Peter felt his stomach tighten in anticipation. Lord, it had been so long, and he had missed her so. He was anxious for even a glimpse.

The Ashwood driver slowed the horses to a stop before the footman jumped down from the rear of the carriage to open the door and let down the step. Adam climbed out of the carriage first, before assisting his mother, Grace, and finally Belle down.

Peter's breath caught in his throat when he saw her standing there, all nervousness and excitement. She was breathtaking. She had written to him that she had sewn her dress, and she was once again displaying her talents. Her dress was lilac in colour and flowed down her delicate frame in soft cascades of silk. The bodice was embellished with white roses at the shoulders, where she had gathered the silk to create elegant sleeves that appeared as though they were merely draped around her upper arms. The cool, dark skin of her décolletage was bare and beautiful, as was her face. It was free from any of the powders and pomades that women usually applied, leaving her natural beauty to exude through her excitement. Belle's curly hair was pulled back, save for a few spirals framing her face, with a ribbon that matched the colour of her dress. Her ensemble was completed with white elbow gloves, of which she was currently pinching and twisting the fingers with anticipation.

Belle's golden eyes then found him, and her smile grew even bigger. That simple act of assurance settled every one if his nerves, including the ones that had been festering over the seven weeks that he had been away. She was happy to see him, and she was excited to be here. Peter returned her smile and went to step towards her.

But as soon as he did that, his right boot caught his left, and he promptly tripped over and fell down onto the dusty road. His clumsy act caught the attention of his entire family, and Peter wanted to bang his head against the ground. Why was he born without a charming bone in his body?

"Peter, are you alright?" The question was asked by every one of his family members, but he focussed on the soft, accented voice belonging to Belle.

She had raced over to him, kneeling down on the road without a thought for her gown. "Peter, are you hurt?" she asked, her voice filled with concern.

"Only my pride," he replied with a laugh, but he felt her hand on his cheek, and his laughing stopped. Peter looked up into her eyes and he swallowed. Lord, he hoped he would be able to kiss her tonight.

Chapter 21

"May I escort a lady inside?" Peter asked, still rubbing his pride as he climbed to his feet, Belle's posture straightening simultaneously.

Her eyes flicked to both Cecily and Grace, both of whom had joined their gathering. Peter could sense a little bashfulness from Belle all of a sudden, and it frustrated him that she had grown so shy so quickly when she had appeared so excited only a moment ago. He wished she would not allow her nerves to get the better of her.

"I am not a lady," Belle whispered, as though it were a confession.

Peter's face fell as he realised that Belle had grown self-conscious over his use of the word "lady". She observed the ladies around her, and she believed that she did not belong. While his initial thoughts were of his own frustration, Peter had to remind himself that Belle was conditioned to believe this. She had lived most of her life being treated as though she had the worth of a sewer rat.

Before Peter could assure her, Cecily interjected.

"Hogwash!" declared the dowager duchess.

Peter grinned as Cecily's exclamation elicited a jump of surprise from Belle. Her golden eyes flicked back to him. "What is hogwash?" she asked him, again in a whisper. "Hog is pig, no?" Belle's eyes flared with shock at the realisation. "Does she call me a pig?"

Were Peter not already stupidly in love with this woman, that would have been the moment that did it. Belle's expression of horror was terribly amusing, and Peter knew that he would be going to hell for laughing, but he could not help it. Nor could anyone else.

Peter never wanted to surprise Belle with touch, but he put his arm around her in a secure, comforting manner, just as she became terribly embarrassed by the laughs of their party.

"What did I say wrong?" stressed Belle. "Do they all think I am a pig?"

"No, no," Peter promised. "Hogwash means nonsense. What you said was nonsense, rubbish, not true," he explained. "Her Grace was defending you. There was absolutely no mention of pigs," he assured her. "Besides, you are every bit a lady to me."

"Oh, dear Belle, how terribly cruel of us to laugh so," Grace cried, her voice filled with regret, though Peter could still tell that his sister was amused at the situation.

"Well said, Peter," Cecily commended. "You are every bit a lady, my dear girl," she added to Belle. "I have found the best women in my acquaintance to be the ones that society witches would look down upon. You will find that I have marvellous taste," she then said, commending herself, before adding, "and an even sharper tongue. Should you feel that anyone in attendance tonight requires a dressing down, do not hesitate to find me. Have a lovely evening." She smiled slyly. "Adam?" Cecily turned to the duke. "Will you escort Grace and I inside now? I fear blue does nothing for my complexion."

"Blue, however, suits Grace so well, Mother. I thought we might stay out in the cold a little while longer," Adam replied teasingly, before securing both his wife and mother on either arm and leading them towards the assembly hall.

Peter and Belle followed last, following Jem and Mrs Denham inside. The music was merry, and the first dance was already in full swing. The Beresfords were fashionably late to make their entrance.

Belle's grip on Peter's arm was tight, but her expression had returned to that of her original excitement. She was standing up on her toes, attempting to peer over the top of the crowds, though that was quite impossible with her short stature.

"You look beautiful tonight," Peter complimented, bending down to whisper in her ear.

Belle looked up at him and smiled, her golden eyes warming. "You look handsome tonight," she said, returning the compliment.

After they were announced into the ball, the ladies were offered dance card. Belle beamed in anticipation as she held out her gloved arm to the attendant, who slipped the ribbon over her wrist. Her attention was focussed on the card, so she did not see the expression of confusion and judgement on the attendant. Peter glared at him, and his face became neutral by the time that Belle was aware that it was time to move on.

Peter would not allow anything or anyone to spoil her night, or their night.

"The duchess, your sister, she has been very kind to me," Belle said as she held onto her dance card. "She has been teaching me the English dances, so I do not make a fool of myself like I did last time."

Peter realised that she must have been referring to Susanna's wedding. He chuckled. "I enjoyed improvising a dance with you."

Belle pursed her lips, though she smiled. "I enjoyed dancing with you then, as well. But I do so want to be ... ordinary."

Peter did understand her desire. Though considering she was quite plainly the prettiest woman in the ballroom, wearing a garment that flattered her so beautifully it ought to have been a crime, Belle would never be ordinary. But Peter would oblige her, whatever she desired. "May I have the honour of the next with you, Miss Desjardins?" he asked formally.

Belle grinned rather gleefully, and she nodded, holding out her dance card to him so that Peter could sign his name.

Just as Peter had finished writing, Jem seized hold of his arm, hitting him once in the chest, and saying, "Be calm, we are about to be introduced!"

Peter rubbed his chest and resisted elbowing Jem back. "You be calm, you duffer."

The ballroom was clearly abuzz now that the Beresfords had arrived, as the social schmoozing could begin. Peter had watched this sort of behaviour for years from the outside. It was amusing, really, how some people thought that gaining the favour of women like Cecily Beresford, could boost their own social standing ...

Peter then realised that thought was hyper-hypocritical of him. He supposed that he was the evidence of what gaining favour could do. Had his sister, had not two of his sisters married into the family, then he would have never had the opportunity to go to work in London.

"Schmooze away," he muttered under his breath. "Good luck to you all." Peter followed Jem's line of sight, which was, of course, focussed on Cressie Martin.

Cressie was being dragged along by her mother, the dance card on her wrist dangling by her side. Cressie did appear awfully put out, and Peter's previous assumption that there had been a quarrel between the two prior to the ball appeared more apparent.

Peter found himself feeling sorry for the girl. She reminded him then of Susanna the summer before last, when she had been suffering through her last season in London, at the mercy of her mother, and hordes of insufferable suitors.

Mrs Martin appeared very keen indeed to have her daughter introduced to the Beresfords. The vicar was beside Adam, Grace, and Cecily making the introductions of any new residents of the parish, and Mrs Martin and Cressie were certainly new.

No matter how his brother teased him, Peter would always be on Jem's side. "Wait on moment," he uttered to Belle, before left hers and Jem's sides. He manoeuvred around the crowd to come and stand behind his sister, just as Mrs Martin and Cressie were being introduced.

"Your Graces, may I introduce Mrs Martin, and her daughter, Miss Cressida Martin," said the vicar formally. "Mrs Martin, Miss Martin, may I present their Graces, the Duke and Duchess of Ashwood, and the Dowager Duchess of Ashwood."

Mrs Martin and Cressie both curtseyed deeply, and the quarrelsome expression from Cressie's face had disappeared, and was replaced with a respectful, albeit intimidated, smile.

"It is a true honour to make your acquaintance, Your Graces," declared Mrs Martin, seemingly very pleased indeed. She then looked to her daughter, almost nudging her forward.

"Yes, I agree with my mother. I am d-delighted," stammered Cressie nervously.

As Mrs Martin went on to praise the festivities, Peter leaned forward to Grace's ear.

"Do your youngest brother a favour and introduce him to Miss Martin," he murmured.

Grace's expression did not change, save for a very small smile appearing on her lips.

Peter returned to Belle's side, and he spied Jem nervously fretting, a glisten of swear evident on his forehead. He fished a handkerchief out of his pocket and handed it to Jem. "She is not going to want to go near you if it looks as though you've just been swimming."

Jem huffed and quickly wiped his brow, just as they noticed Grace delicately claim Cressie, as though she was taking her under her wing. Behind her, Mrs Martin followed on, utterly delighted at the unfolding events.

Grace arrived with Cressie before Peter and Belle, meeting Peter's eye with an excited glance.

"Miss Martin, I would like you to meet my brother, Mr Denham," she gestured to Peter, "and this is Miss Belle Desjardins. She is a dear friend of my family, and rather a talented modiste as you may have read in the papers, in and amongst the drivel. Peter, Belle, meet Miss Cressida Martin."

Cressie was still very nervously standing in and amongst the party, and she rather reminded Peter of Belle quite a bit. She looked as though she felt a little out of place. Certainly, she did on the arm of a duchess. That part was Peter's fault.

"Delighted to meet you, Miss Martin," Peter said kindly.

"And you, Mr Denham, Miss Desjardins," replied Cressie.

"I would also like you to meet my youngest brother," continued Grace casually. "Miss Martin, meet Mr Jem Denham. Jem, meet Miss Cressida Martin."

Jem looked as though he had swallowed a lemon. Peter wanted to kick him. For how long had he been planning this moment, and now here he was ... looking like that. Cressie peered at him curiously, frowning. It was now that Peter noticed that Cressie had quite dark brown eyes, and they were looking upon Jem for the first time.

"I am sure Miss Martin is truly pleased to make the acquaintances of the brothers of the duchess!" encouraged Mrs Martin from behind her daughter, which prompted Grace to add in her quick introduction.

"I want a sandwich!" Jem rather loudly announced, before he promptly turned on his heel and all but marched in the direction of the refreshment room.

"Good Lord, Jem," muttered Peter under his breath. He would hate himself for that later. He probably hated himself for it right now. He had spoiled their meeting, and Cressie probably thought that he was a lunatic with an insatiable need for sandwiches in the middle of parties.

Peter and Grace shared a look, before Belle murmured, "You should go to him. Go and calm him."

Peter smiled down at her gratefully. "Will you save me the next dance, then?"

Belle smiled, her cheeks warming. "Yes."

Belle watched as Peter walked away, weaving through the crowd in the direction that Jem had escaped. She felt terribly for Jem, as it was very obvious how nervous he was in the presence of such a pretty girl as Miss Martin. Belle understood feeling nervous very well.

She was left standing with Grace and Miss Martin, whose mother flanked her closely behind. Belle met the brown eyed gaze of Miss Martin. She was terribly young, and Belle could sense sadness within her.

Belle would have offered her some word of comfort, but she felt a little intimidated by Mrs Martin, who appeared quite domineering. Belle was unsure if she would have wanted someone like her to be speaking to her daughter. Belle acted with precaution and merely offered Miss Martin a kind smile.

Miss Martin returned the gesture.

"Is not that the way of gentleman nowadays, Your Grace? Always hurrying about one way or another!" Mrs Martin laughed to herself. "When do you suppose your brothers will return?"

"I am certain they will not be long," replied Grace. At that moment, Adam joined her, gently claiming Grace's arm for his own.

"Do pardon me, ladies, but the duchess had promised me this dance." As Adam spoke, Belle heard the music change, and the couples began to gather for the next dance. Adam led Grace away, which prompted Mrs Martin to reclaim her daughter's arm.

Mrs Martin began to pull Miss Martin away, and as she did, she turned over her shoulder and said, "Your dress is beautiful by the way, Miss Desjardins."

Belle was so flattered by the compliment that she couldn't find the English words quickly enough to reply before Miss Martin had disappeared into the crowd.

Belle was alone, as Mrs Denham had gone to sit down on one of the chairs at the edge of the ballroom, and she was joined by Cecily, who had apparently left the vicar.

It was suddenly very daunting standing alone. Though the ballroom was filled with hundreds of people, she felt quite isolated, though by the hairs standing up on the back of her neck, she knew she was not invisible. She felt eyes on her. She could see some of them. There were looks of brief admiration, as well as suspicion and uncertainty ... and, of course, there were distasteful and judgemental expressions, but Belle took no heed of those.

Belle turned her attention to the dancers, ignoring the feeling of being watched. She looked on as the couples jumped and twirled jovially to the upbeat melody of the song. Adam and Grace danced happily in and amongst them, looking just like every other cheerful couple, and not the highest-ranking pair for miles.

Belle had become so distracted by the dancers that she had not realised that she was no longer alone. She felt a large hand on the small of her back and she jumped half a mile in the air.

"I'm sorry!" exclaimed Peter apologetically. "I did not realise that you had not seen me approach."

Belle placed a hand on her chest as she caught her breath. "It is alright. I was ... dreaming in the day ... I think is the English word."

Peter grinned. "I think I prefer it your way," he mused. "I set Jem straight. Poor boy was in a state. If you look over there," Peter pointed into the crowd, "he should be asking her to dance right about now."

Belle stood up on her toes. She did not have a terrific view, but she could just make out the top of Jem's head. She would have to take Peter's word for it.

"But enough delaying. Shall we dance?"

Belle had never had such a terrific time in her life. For the first time ever she forgot about everything, anything that could take her mind from being happy in the present. She didn't think about her past. She didn't think about what anyone else was whispering. She paid no heed to anyone but

Peter, who was looking upon her with such affection that Belle feared she might melt every time she met his gaze.

Though she had been learning, she had not mastered every dance, which gave her and Peter the opportunity to still invent some steps together. This time it did not embarrass her. Belle laughed.

Save for a few rest breaks, Belle danced every dance with Peter, and was quite thoroughly exhausted near the end of the program. She had certainly worn through her shoes, and she was positive that some of her hair had come loose from the pins, as she could feel her curls bouncing.

"I can't breathe!" Belle panted as they finished the quadrille.

"Come with me," Peter urged, as he took Belle's hand and pulled her through the crowd. Belle followed him into the refreshment room, before he expertly, and subtly, led them outside into the chilly night air.

Belle inhaled deeply, filling her lungs. She wore no coat, and in that moment, she did not need one as she had been dancing vigorously. The cold air felt pleasant against her skin. She and Peter were around the side of the assembly hall. In the distance, and illuminated in the moonlight, Belle could see the carriages and the horses belonging to the attendees inside.

They stood in a small garden that consisted of a stretch of lawn, shrubbery, trees and a stone bench that appeared black in the night.

"Will you sit with me?"

"Yes," answered Belle, and they sat down together on the bench.

Peter took hold of her hand and squeezed it tightly. "You really are the beauty of the garden."

It took Belle a moment to realise what he was saying before she understood his reference to her name. She smiled bashfully. "It is dark. You cannot see me properly."

"Hogwash," he said teasingly. "I can see you just fine."

Belle's smile became a grin. "I do not like that pig word, you know," she jested.

"I call hogwash on that, as well." Peter laughed.

When he quietened, Belle sensed a change in him. She sensed it in her chest, and in her stomach as her nerves began to rise.

"Did you enjoy yourself tonight?" Peter's voice was thick, and no louder than a whisper.

"I have been looking forward to this night for weeks," replied Belle, nodding. "I have loved every moment."

Peter lifted the hand that was he was holding, and with the other, he began to run his index finger over her knuckles gently. Belle was suddenly glad for her gloves, as Peter could not feel the goosepimples which now covered her skin.

"I am so proud of you, you know," Peter uttered, still tracing. "I loved every one of your letters. Thank you so much for writing to me."

Belle's heart swelled as she heard his sincerity. She had tried so hard to write him good letters. She had pored over them for hours to write and spell as well as she could. She had wanted to say so much more, but she didn't know how. Hearing that Peter appreciated her letters meant a great deal to her.

"There is something that I have been wanting to do ... if you will let me ... if you want to ..."

Peter's hand lifted to her chin, and he gently lifted her face towards his. Belle's heart quickened when she realised what he wanted from her, but there was no forcefulness. He did not lead her any further. He waited. He was waiting for her permission, for her to decide that it was safe.

Safe. Safe. Safe.

For how long had those words chanted through her brain when she thought of Peter? He was safe, and she was safe with him. She was safe now, no matter what. Belle did not want to wait a moment longer.

As she began to lean forward to close the distance between them, Peter fell off of the bench, taking Belle down with him as he landed on top of her. It took Belle a moment to realise that she'd heard an almighty thud.

It took her eyes a moment to focus from the shock to realise that they were no longer alone in the garden. Peter was unconscious, and someone had struck him. As Belle sucked in a breath, filling her lungs so that she could scream, a rag was placed over her mouth, and she fell into the darkness completely.

Chapter 22

Peter's eyes fluttered, and he felt the odd sensation of something cool, yet rough against the side of his face. There was a loud, thumping noise, sounding from the back of his head. It was as though church bells were ringing from inside his skull.

He groaned, finally able to open his eyes. It took a long moment to realise that he was laying down. He was lying face down on the ground against the short blades of grass. What on earth ...?

Peter slowly moved his hands to place them flat against the earth so that he could push himself up. He was able to move his torso and legs quite easily, but the weight of his head was almost unbearable. It was throbbing uncontrollably. Not only did it hurt, but he felt groggy and slow, as though he had been indulging all evening when he knew that he had not touched a drop. He sat up very clumsily and reached behind his head to press his hand against the site of the pain. The moment Peter's hand touched his head, he gasped, wincing at the pain of an open, weeping wound. His finger felt the wetness which could only be blood.

What had happened to him? Who had done this?

He blinked his eyes over and over, trying to focus on his surroundings, and the moment he realised where he was, he remembered what he had been out here doing, and who he had been out here with. Peter's head snapped around, the pain protesting the sudden movement. Though it was dark, he could still see that he was clearly alone in the garden.

Someone had struck him. Someone had knocked him unconscious. And someone had taken ...

"Belle," gasped Peter.

Panic set in as Peter frantically looked around, searching for any sign of her. As he scrambled to his feet, pushing the pain aside, Peter's hand brushed over something soft on the grass. He seized it, immediately bringing it close to his face so that he could see what it was.

It was a lilac ribbon, the same one that Belle had been wearing in her hair.

"BELLE!" Peter's panicked voice practically screamed her name. Whatever demon had knocked him unconscious had thus been alone with Belle, and she had now vanished.

Peter ran, stumbling with the fogginess of his head, as he desperately searched for any trace. As he ran alongside of the assembly hall, back towards the door that they had come out of, Peter nearly tripped over something on the ground. He seized it, taking hold of a dainty, heeled woman's slipper. He had not seen what sort of footwear Belle had been wearing, but women did not leave their shoes about in public gardens.

"BELLE!" Peter screamed once more. For how long had he been unconscious? She couldn't have got far. Someone had to have seen her!

Peter stumbled around the front of the assembly hall, still clutching Belle's ribbon and shoe, and was confronted by the sight of the parishioners leaving the ball. The business was hectic. People were everywhere, chatting animatedly, footmen and servants were attending to carriages, and Belle was nowhere to be seen.

Peter grabbed hold of the first man he saw and asked him, practically hysterically, "Please, Belle Desjardins, have you seen her? She is missing!"

The man was considerably confronted by Peter's frantic behaviour, and shook him off, before hurrying away. Peter raced as quickly as his unsteady legs would carry him to the nearest carriage.

"Help me, please!" he cried to the driver. "Belle Desjardins, she is missing! Have you seen her? She was taken by a ... well, I don't know by whom ... but she was taken a short while ago. Please, did you see anyone take a woman?"

"No, lad," replied the driver. "It's the end of the ball, isn't it? We're a bit preoccupied. I'm sure your missus is around here somewhere."

Peter swore. Loudly. A nearby woman looked at him with a most affronted expression. He persisted, begging anyone who would listen to tell him if they had seen Belle, all the while keeping an eye out for her. The pain in his head seemed to vanish as he anxiously searched. Peter's heart thundered so loudly it might have alerted onlookers.

No one had seen Belle. No one had noticed her go. No one had noticed the man who had taken her. How could that happen? How could one simply vanish? How could so many people be so oblivious? How was it possible?

Peter was a hysterical wreck by the time he nearly crashed into his own family, who appeared to have been searching for him as well. Jem gripped hold of Peter's upper arms, and his brother appeared quite startled at Peter's appearance.

"Peter, what's the matter with you? You look dreadful! What's happened?"

"Peter? Peter!" cried Mrs Denham from some twenty feet away. Spotting her sons together, she hobbled over as quickly as she could.

Peter searched his family party, spotting Cecily, Adam, and Grace all following Mrs Denham towards Peter. Belle was not with them.

"Belle, have you seen her?" Peter asked desperately, calling out to all of them. "Please, tell me you know where she is!"

"Peter, what's happened?" stressed Mrs Denham.

"We were just looking for the both of you," replied Adam, frowning deeply. "What's happened to you?"

"Peter, what's wrong?" worried Grace.

Peter felt like he was going to be sick. His breathing was entirely erratic as his head grew heavy and his eyes clouded with tears. "Belle and I ... we were in the garden. Someone hit me and knocked me out ... and when I came to, Belle was gone!" Peter held out the ribbon and the shoe in his hands. "Someone has taken her!"

Mrs Denham spied the back of Peter's head and gasped. "Oh, good God! He needs a surgeon!"

Mrs Denham's reaction prompted Jem to look as well, and he shared similar concerns, turning to Grace and saying, "We need to send for a doctor. He's bleeding down his back."

"We shall all go back to Ashwood House, and shall send for the doctor myself," Cecily declared.

"I don't need a bloody doctor!" Peter exclaimed hysterically. "I need a horse! I need to find her! Someone had taken Belle, and God knows what they could be doing." Peter did not need to try hard to imagine. Belle had trusted him with some of the horrors of her past. Peter knew all too well the evils of men. Peter didn't know why she was taken, or by whom, or anything, but he did know that no woman deserved to be at the mercy of a man.

"You are not going anywhere on horseback like that!" Mrs Denham stated firmly.

Peter had never had an ill thought towards his mother, but at that moment, he wanted to throttle her. Did she think that he cared about what had happened to him when Belle was missing?

"I will look for her," Adam interjected. "I will search the village, the surrounding roads. She can't have got far, wherever she is. You need to take care of yourself, Peter. You are no use to Belle, bleeding and as unsteady as you are."

"You will have to tie me down if you think I won't go out looking for her," Peter all but growled. "I promised her that no one would ever hurt her." The words came out of Peter's mouth before he realised what he was saying. A new sort of despair filled his senses as he swore again. He had promised

Belle that no one would ever hurt her again, and he needed to find her before that promise was broken.

Belle felt her body rhythmically moving to the jostle of a carriage. She was sitting on a padded seat and leaning against the soft wall of the side of the carriage, her head gently tapping against the window each time the wheel rolled through a divot in the road.

She frowned before her eyes opened, her mind slowly returning her senses to her. Belle inhaled through her nose, taking in the scents of the carriage. The air was stale, but something lingered, something familiar.

"You are quite the elusive one to find."

Belle's eyes snapped open as her blood ran ice cold. Her heart stopped in her chest and her breathing ceased. The few seconds it took for her vision to focus both frustrated and frightened her. Belle could see a blurry figure opposite her, and the familiarity of his scent became clear.

His voice was cool and formal, speaking French as though he belonged with the nobles and grand blancs. He was a grand blanc.

Slowly, excruciatingly slowly, her vision settled, and the blurriness cleared as the figure across from her revealed himself.

His large frame eclipsed much of the opposing bench, and he sat casually, cockily, with his legs spread and his elbow hitched up and resting on the back of the padded seat. His belly appeared rounder and was highlighted by the deep purple waistcoat he wore, its buttons protesting their master. One of his meaty hands rested on his knee. His thick fingers, which resembled sausages, were still and idle, and yet were capable of inflicting severe pain.

Belle's eyes unwittingly travelled north against her own accord, almost needing to in order to truly confirm it was him. If she didn't look into Satan's eyes, she couldn't know it was him. At first, she saw his jaw, cleanshaven, full and round. Next was his mouth, his thin lips upturned into an amused, ominous smile. His teeth were crooked and were stained yellow by his indulgences. His cheeks matched the roundness of his face, and his nose was long and straight. She could see the lengths of his sandy coloured hair tickling his ears at the side of his head.

And then she found his eyes. Cold, grey, the colour of a dead corpse. He looked upon her with amusement. Those eyes had followed her since she was five years old, and they had haunted her every day since.

Belle looked up the face of the devil, but she would not flinch, no matter how terrified she was.

Jean laughed lightly, musically, as he ran his hand over his jaw. "You certainly appear surprised to see me. Did you really think I wouldn't find you? Did you really think that you could run away and that I would stand idly by?" Jean placed his hand back down on his knee and the leaned forward, the timber of the wooden seat underneath the cushion squeaking under his frame. "I could have you killed for running away, you know." His voice dropped, and his eyes narrowed upon her as he meant to frighten her.

And he succeeded. As much as Belle didn't want to be afraid, she recoiled in her seat, pressing herself as far back into the wall as she could. She had been determined that she would not flinch, and she had failed in mere moments.

"I could have you strung up, a rope around that pretty neck of yours, and the last thing you would hear is the snap," Jean clicked his fingers, "as your neck breaks."

Belle's breathing was shaky and uneven. Her heart beat erratically in her chest. She knew that Jean was not serious. She knew that he would not kill her like that. It was too quick. He would not enjoy that. He would not have tracked her down thousands of miles away simply to kill her.

Jean had other plans.

Belle's memories vividly returned, of every moment that she had begged, pleaded, and wished for death at the hands of Jean, and of men like him. She had wanted to die so that she would not suffer anymore. She had wanted to die so that she would not ever have to be at the mercy of a man again.

Belle could not look away from Jean's cold, cruel eyes. She could see exactly what he was planning just by the way he focussed on her. She could see what he wanted. She had known that look many, many times before.

Every time, every time, she had wished for death. As soon as he would look upon her the way he was now, she would wish for death so that she would not have to experience it another time.

But no such prayer came to Belle then.

Belle didn't want to die.

Belle wanted to live.

She swallowed, inhaling the steadiest breath that she could, and she straightened her posture, coming away from the back wall of the carriage. Belle might have wished for death countless times throughout her life, but she had survived everything that she had been through. She was a survivor, and this man would not take one ounce more of her will from her. Belle would survive this man, and she would get back to Peter.

Jean's eyebrow arched at Belle's shift, and his sinister smile grew more apparent. He almost appeared impressed. "Little mouse thinks she can fight the bear?" he mocked.

"She will try."

Jean grinned, before raising his arm and slamming his fist down against Belle's temple, silencing her, and sentencing her back to the world of darkness.

Chapter 23

Peter never knew it was possible for someone to simply vanish off the face of the earth, but Belle had managed to do just that. She was gone. There was no trace of her save for the ribbon and shoe that she had left behind in the garden.

He and Adam had searched all night, taking the main roads and trails all around Ashwood and the neighbouring villages. They didn't see a carriage. They didn't see horses. They didn't see a girl being dragged down the road against her will. They didn't see anything.

They returned to the assembly hall when the sun rose. This was the place where Belle had last been seen, and they hoped that there might be other clues left behind that they had not been able to see the night before.

"Good God, Peter!" cried Adam, as they approached the bench where he and Belle had been sitting last. Adam bent down to collect something off of the ground. He rose with a small rock, about the size of his fist. Half of it was caked in dark, dried blood.

Whatever had been numbing Peter's pain had dulled. It was as though he had taken an imaginary dose of laudanum to help him on his initial search, but it was waning. Peter's headache was terrible, and his balance and coordination were making riding a horse difficult.

That rock was clearly the weapon that had been used by the culprit to incapacitate him.

"Did you hear anyone behind you? Did you see anyone? Do you remember anything now that you are back in the garden?" Adam asked, frowning deeply as he placed the rock down on the bench.

"I don't remember hearing anyone," Peter replied. "I was preoccupied." He had been determined to kiss Belle, to propose to her if she would let him. He had been so determined to do this that he had brought her outside alone. "I didn't consider the risk," Peter hissed, cursing himself. "I didn't think of her safety at all. I was thinking of myself. I wanted to be alone with her and ... and ..." Peter looked around helplessly.

"You weren't to know," Adam said firmly. "How could you have known?"

"I know what is appropriate," Peter spat back. "I know that bringing a woman outside alone is not, and if I was thinking like a gentleman, and not like a stupid lovestruck boy, I would never have put her in this position." He sucked in a staggered breath. "And now she's gone!"

Adam ignored Peter's remarks and continued searching, keeping his eyes low. "Look here," he called, pointing to an area on the ground. "You can see the indents in the grass and the dirt. Someone was being dragged. Belle was being dragged."

Peter could see the tracks in the grass made by Belle's feet as she was dragged towards the direction of the front of the assembly hall. She had to have been taken in and amongst the chaos of the carriages, horses and drivers. But nobody had paid attention to her. She had been smuggled into a carriage or something, and nobody had noticed. How could this happen?

Peter thought that his head might explode with worry.

"What's this?" Adam wondered aloud. He walked over to one of the garden beds, and picked up a bit of paper that had somehow gotten itself wedged in and amongst the foliage. It appeared to be damp with the dew of the morning. "Oh." Adam scoffed.

"What?" asked Peter. "What is it?"

"It's nothing," replied Adam. "I thought it might have been important, but it is just a bit of old newspaper." Looking down at it, he laughed in an irritated tone. "It's that bloody story that was written after Susanna's wedding. Why does this garbage insist on following us around?"

Peter remembered that story. Belle had kept a copy of it, hoping to read it as it referenced her name and her efforts in designing Susanna's dress. Peter remembered her asking him to read it for her, and he could recall the anger and frustration he had felt in reading the utter ignorance that passed for journalism. As Adam crumped the page in his hand, Peter thought for a moment. That story had been printed in a London newspaper. It was not a paper that was delivered to the Ashwood village. The only reason that Ashwood House had a copy of that paper was because it was specially sent for. Peter could remember, quite mockingly, thinking what precious specimens the Beresfords were for needing their newspapers ironed for them. Grace had told him about it when she had worked there as a housemaid.

So, if Belle had held onto that copy of the newspaper, then what on earth was a scrap of it doing in this garden?

"Wait." Peter held out his hand, reaching for the newspaper.

Adam peered at him curiously as he released it from his grasp. Peter held it in his hands, and he could feel the dampness from the night. He smoothed it as best he could, but much of the ink had run, rendering much of the story illegible. However, there was something that had been added. An annotation.

Peter could see that underneath the first mention of Belle's name in the story, someone had underlined it with a line of thick, black ink. In the margin someone had scribbled something. It was smudged … but it read something like: est-elle votre femme?

Peter did not know what it meant, but he knew it was French. His mind raced with panic as he pondered a thousand different scenarios. But only one made sense. What motivation would an ordinary man have for taking Belle? He thought back to when Belle had told him of her – for want of a better word – husband. She had been so afraid, so terrified, and so completely believing that he still had such a hold over her, such control over her.

Peter had convinced Belle that she was free, that she did not need to be afraid anymore. Who, other than someone connected to her former husband, and her former life, would have the motivation to take Belle?

Peter trembled. He didn't know what he was feeling. It was a combination of fear, panic, guilt, despair and desperation, somehow combined to make a wholly terrified human being. He didn't want to believe it, but it was the only possibility that made any sense.

"Tell me," stressed Peter shakily. "Tell me, do you read French?"

Adam peered at the annotation but shook his head. "No. But Mother does. Peter, you've gone extraordinarily pale. Do you know what's happened? Does this mean something to you?"

"I can't be certain until I know what this says," Peter managed to reply. "But I fear that Belle has been abducted by her former master. The man who forced her to marry him."

Peter told Adam as much as he could on the way back to Ashwood House, and Adam reacted as furiously as anyone would having heard the tale. Belle's coercion into marriage at only fourteen years of age was criminal. For too long she had been at the mercy of a madman, and she could well be yet again.

The Beresfords and Denhams were all gathered at Ashwood House, where they had waited all night for news of Belle, and for Peter's return to have his head looked at. The doctor had been summoned, and he, too, had been waiting all night. The family were all still dressed in their ball attire, and nobody looked as though they had slept.

There was a flurry of questions, and Peter could not focus on a single one as his gaze focussed on Cecily. He still had the newspaper page in his hand, and he walked directly up to her, faintly hearing his mother's fussing behind him for the doctor to make him sit down.

"Please, Your Grace. Adam tells me you know how to read French. Please tell me what this says." Peter showed Cecily the page, pointing to the annotation in the margin.

"Be damned that tasteless article," rebuffed Cecily, before she peered closer. She frowned. "Oh, yes, that is French. Est-elle votre femme?" she read. "It says, 'is she your wife?'"

Peter's heart fell like a stone boulder from his chest to his stomach. The weight of which brought him to his knees. As he dropped, he heard Mrs Denham cry out in fright. He could feel someone touching his head, but he paid them no notice. He did not care about it at all.

He could only imagine, or dread, what had happened to result in that newspaper article winding up in that garden? Had someone spotted Belle's name in the paper and sent it to her husband? Had whomever spotted the name come to take Belle to him? Or had her husband received that article and come after Belle himself?

"For God's sake, Peter, you will lie down this moment!" Mrs Denham demanded. "You are no use to Belle half dead!" she accused fearfully. "Doctor, please, help him! His head had been like this all night!"

"He was struck by a rock, Doctor," Adam informed him. "About the size of my hand." Adam made a fist. "He has been unsteady on his feet the last hour or so, but before that he has been well." Adam paused. "Or as well as can be expected in circumstances such as these."

"We don't know why, but often in times of great shock, the body can mask our pain. That does not mean that the ailment has gone, or that a physician should not be summoned. It is just a phenomenon of the body that we are yet to understand," the doctor explained.

Peter could barely concentrate as he was moved to the settee in the drawing room. He did not feel any pain as his head was cleaned and stitched. He blinked and squinted as the doctor held the flame of a candle before his eyes, but otherwise he was numb to his surroundings.

In the distance, Peter was very faintly aware of Adam speaking. He heard Belle's name, and perhaps that was because he wanted to be attuned to it. Perhaps Adam was telling everyone what Peter had told him. Perhaps Adam was telling them all that Belle had been forcibly married, and that one way or another, Belle was now in that man's clutches.

How could this happen? After everything that precious, beautiful girl had been through, how had she fallen victim to this man again? Why was she not allowed her freedom?

Why had Peter failed to protect her?

Belle deserved more than this. She had barely begun to live before her freedom was quite literally snatched away. Peter prayed for a miracle. He would need one to find her and to bring her home safely.

Belle was awoken by the same familiar jostle of the carriage, only this time, her head throbbed as though she had been kicked by a horse. It did not take long for her memories to fill the gaps in her pounding head. It might as well have been a horse for the size of the fist that had knocked her unconscious.

She was lying horizontally on the seat, and her eyes first focussed on the floor of the carriage where she spotted Jean's court shoes that were adorned with gaudy gold buckles.

"Did the little mouse enjoy her sleep?"

His tone was mocking, goading, but thoroughly amused, as though he thought this whole predicament was a fun, little game.

Belle had spent her entire life training her eyes down. She never dared to look into the eye of a white man or woman. She was well-practised in subserviency.

But Belle would never be this man's prey. Never again.

Belle looked up.

She stared into the corpse grey irises that had so haunted her nightmares, and she felt the fear deep within her bones. But she felt something else, as well. She felt fire in the core of her belly, fuelling her fight.

Jean grinned, before laughing at her expression. He laughed so hard he made himself cough. He beat himself in the chest with his fist to settle his lungs. "You are so different, but the same, too. You have the same witch eyes, the same black skin ... you are fatter, but I don't mind."

Belle's jaw locked. He had a nerve to call her fat when he ate for twelve while the people who laboured for him starved. Belle was eating properly now. She was healthy.

"But you have a spirit now that you never had before. I rather like it." If Belle did not know him better, she would have said that he sounded like he admired her. But Belle did know better. She knew that Jean loved feeling powerful, and nothing would make him feel more powerful that beating the spirit out of a woman.

Belle was determined to hold onto her spirit, her fire, no matter how many punches he threw at her.

"You have changed, too," Belle managed to spit back.

Jean arched an eyebrow. "I have? How so?"

"I did not think it was possible for you to get any uglier."

Jean threw his head back and laughed as Belle's eyes widened at her own gall. She had mocked the devil to his face, and he laughed. And as he did, he moved with quicker agility than a man of his size ought to have as he grabbed a fistful of her hair.

Belle yelped in pain as she was wrenched across the carriage by her scalp, it burning under his force.

"Oh, darling, when I am through with you, you will wish you had never been born."

Chapter 24

Belle was not certain for how long they travelled. The days seemed the blend into each other, and the haze from the two concussions that Jean had bestowed upon her didn't not help with her ability to focus.

She wanted to be able to. She wanted to concentrate on what she could see out the window. She wanted to be able to memorise the roads, any particular landmarks, or special trees, anything to be able to determine her location.

But her mind wouldn't let her.

The carriage only stopped to change horses. Belle was not permitted out of the carriage during these stops, and Jean made sure to wait with her. They didn't stop to rest overnight. And as much as she wanted to remain awake and alert, restless, broken sleep found her.

Jean had not touched her again, most likely because his size made manoeuvring inside a carriage quite awkward and challenging. But that did not stop him from watching her with his corpse eyes, leaving Belle wishing that she had a heavy, thick cloak to wear to cover herself from his hungry gaze.

Belle did not say another word to him. As much as she was glad that she had spoken up against him, she knew that she needed to be smart. She wanted to live. She wanted to go home. She wanted to see Peter again. She needed to keep herself alive.

She would allow Jean to think that she had returned to her submissive demeanour. But Belle would be damned if he ever laid his hands on her again. She would kill him first.

Jean did not refrain from speaking. He filled the silence comfortably, seemingly regaling her with his triumph in locating her after more than a year's absence.

"I am ashamed to say that it did take me a day or two to notice that you have disappeared after the hurricane," Jean confessed. "My mind was elsewhere. The damage needed to be seen to. But when I realised that you had disappeared, I must say that I laughed." Even now, he snickered, his lips peeling back over his teeth in a sinister grin.

Belle said nothing.

"It must have been a little of this spirit that you now have," he surmised, tilting his head a little, his eyes raking over her from top to bottom.

Belle looked away.

"I do like it, you know," Jean reminded her coolly. "It is more fun when they fight."

An icy shiver ran down Belle's spine as bile rose up in her throat. But she didn't say anything, no matter how she wanted to curse him. She wanted to tell this vile excuse for a pig person that he was condemned. She wanted to tell him that he would rot in hell for how he had treated her, and those like her.

And she would. Belle promised herself that she would tell him exactly what she thought when she was in a position of power. She would not remain powerless. She would take the power from him somehow.

"I hate to admit it, but it did take me a little while to track where you had gone. But I wasn't going to let you go. Not you." His voice thickened, and Belle could hear his sickening desire.

He leaned forward, though struggling a little in the small confines of the carriage, and he placed one of his meaty hands on her thigh over her skirt.

Belle reflexively swatted his hand away, like she would if an insect had landed on her sleeve. A deep chuckle gurgled within Jean's chest as he placed his hand back firmly on her leg, gripping the sides of her thigh in a tight vice. His hand was large enough to nearly envelope half of her leg, and she winced as his grip tightened to hurt her.

Jean watched her, smiling, sickeningly entertained, as his grip grew firmer and firmer, to the point where her leg was screaming in protest.

Belle squirmed, writhing, but she kept her mouth firmly shut. He wanted her pain. He wanted a cry. That was what he desired. He wanted evidence of her submission, of his power over her. That made him more excited than anything.

Tears pooled in Belle's eyes, but she clamped them shut, refusing permission for them to fall down her cheeks.

Belle tried with all her might to keep her mouth shut, but as Jean's hand squeezed to the point of crushing her bones, a cry of pain escaped her lips, and Jean let her go. A moment later his hand was rubbing her leg gently, though he was laughing softly, satisfied.

"You went to Portugal," Jean continued, his tone taunting, as though he was mocking her with his clever detective skills. "Did you know that was where you were going? Did you mean to go there? You did not stay there long."

Belle didn't answer him.

"But you were captured again. One of my men, Claude, you remember him?" Belle did known Claude. She would have called him a henchman. She had not seen the driver, but she would had assumed it was Jean's dog who bit others when ordered to. "Claude discovered your name on an illegal ship's manifest, the copy that was not provided to harbourmasters. A copy that was kept by smugglers. You fell into the hands of smugglers, didn't you?" When Belle said nothing, he continued. She could hear the smile in his tone, though she was not looking at him. "You must have thought you were so clever, running away from your master, your husband. But your evil caught up with you."

Evil. Jean was the epitome of the word.

"It took me longer that I would have liked to find out your next move. Smugglers are notoriously sneaky with their catches." He spoke of her as though she were a fish in a net. "You were brought to the British Virgin Islands. And you were sold, weren't you? Sold to a man named Harold Wilkes."

Had Belle ever known his name? She wasn't sure. But she certainly remembered being sold. She remembered being forced to stand there in the middle of a square, naked before all of those jeering people who hurled words at her that she could not understand. The humiliation and the fear haunted her, and it was just another day in her life that she had tucked away in a quiet place in her brain while she prayed that it wouldn't hurt her again.

But Jean had pulled it right back out of her safe spot. She remembered that man, Harold Wilkes, speaking to her in a tongue she didn't know, only know that she could understand, the memories became all the more terrifying.

But Alex had been there, and Alex had been able to stop him. Belle pulled her eyes back to Jean's cold stare. There was no one here to save her, but there was someone here to stop him.

"It wasn't you who killed him, though, was it?" guessed Jean, cocking an eyebrow. "You're too meek for that, spirit or not." Jean did not wait for Belle's answer, even though there was not to be one. "You vanished after that, and it took me a long time to discover what had happened to you next. I eventually found myself in Louisiana. I thought perhaps you had been captured again. There are plenty of slaves on the mainland of America. But it was there that I heard of a wedding. A wedding that was taking place between a negro man and a white lady. I recognised the name of the man. His had been on the manifest beside yours. The same as he had been sold to Harold Wilkes alongside you. It turned out the captain speaking about this marriage was that slave's father!" Jean exclaimed.

Belle felt the blood rush from her face as she imagined Captain Whitfield proudly chatting about his son's upcoming nuptials, very innocently in a tavern or somewhere like it, completely unaware that a man like Jean Leclerc was listening.

"And England became the next port of call. I sent Claude on ahead with instructions to track you down. And that was exactly what he did. When I arrived, he had located you, and so began the reconnaissance, the search for the perfect moment to reclaim what will always be rightfully mine."

Jean spoke almost triumphantly, as though he expected her praise for managing to find her after so many bumps in the road. It was like he had won a prize and wanted congratulations.

"When Claude informed me of your adultery, he offered to kill you for me."

Jean's voice had suddenly become as cold as ice, ominous in warning as he endeavoured to put fear into her, to exert his control.

"He suggested breaking your neck, or stoning you like a Moor."

The mention of a stone stirred a blurry memory in Belle's mind from the night she had been taken from the Winter Assembly. She could remember Peter being struck by something, by someone. And she did not remember anything after that. She couldn't recall him getting up. She couldn't recall him breathing.

Panic began to quicken her heartbeat. Was Peter alright? Had it been Claude who had struck him? The merciless attack dog.

God, let him be safe, Belle prayed.

"What do you have to say to that?" Jean provoked.

But before Belle could answer, or not answer, the carriage came to a stop. Belle's breath hitched in her throat. It had not been long enough to warrant a changing of horses. And it was not a mealtime. Why had they stopped?

"We're here," realised Jean as he peered out the window of the carriage. "Finally. Five days of travel wreaks havoc on the joints," he muttered.

Five days. That was how long they had been travelling for. Five days was a long time to travel, and certainly a great distance had been covered. How many miles was she from Ashwood? Had anyone known which direction she had gone in to follow her? Belle worried for a moment that as she hadn't been recovered, that no-one had noticed her absence. But she knew in her heart that would not be the truth.

When the carriage door opened, a cold breeze immediately blew into the small, enclosed space. Belle could suddenly taste salt on her tongue and realised that they were now close to the ocean. She knew England to be a great island. Which ocean?

The chill in the air chattered Belle's teeth as Jean shuffled awkwardly get up and out of the carriage. He nearly stumbled down the step, before he turned around and looked at her. "Come along now," he beckoned.

Belle didn't move. She was frozen to her seat. Seeing Jean standing out on the dirt road sent a shock of fear through her. He was no longer sitting across from her like a lump of lard. He stood, hulking frame and all, ready to seize her, to take her.

"Claude." Jean spoke his henchman's name and nothing further, but that was enough.

Claude appeared in the doorway of the carriage, blocking out the light from the misty sky. Belle had not seen him for years, but he had not changed at all from the way she had remembered him. Claude was large as well, but his bulk was strength, and not the French menu that Jean indulged in. He kept his head clean shaven as he had once occasionally worn a wig back on Saint-Martin. There was no hint of a wig today. His lips were turned up in a sneer, and his thick, black brows were downturned in a serious scowl as he glared at her.

Claude reached out with one of his tree trunk arms and seized her forearm, his hand fully encircling her, his fingers meeting his thumb. And he yanked. He yanked her so force-fully that Belle tumbled out of the carriage and down onto the dirt, bumping and grazing her legs on the steps. Her shoulder protested the pull he had on her arm.

Belle managed to gather whatever wits she had left to look around her. This had been the first time that she had been allowed out of the carriage save for a relief break in the middle of nowhere occasionally. In the distance, she could see the ocean. It was a ribbon of blue peeking over a grassy hill. The dirt road continued on over it.

The carriage had stopped next to a small house. Rather a shack, really. It was constructed out of driftwood, the salty sea having greyed and weathered the timber. It was small, with two chimneys at either ends of the far walls. Belle counted two small windows on the front of the house, and someone had thought to add flower boxes, though it was not the season for blooms.

"Where are we?" Belle wondered aloud, completely involuntarily.

"Purgatory," murmured Jean in reply, and amused smile on his face. "Allow me to give you a tour." His eyes darkened, and his grip replaced Claude's on her arm.

Chapter 25

Alex and Susanna returned home from their honeymoon journey three days after the Winter Assembly, completely oblivious as to the hellscape that they would be walking into.

The Denhams had essentially set up camp in the Ashwood drawing room, namely because Peter wouldn't leave. Peter had combed through every single one of Belle's possessions, hoping to find the name of her husband, but he had come up with nothing, and he was cursing himself for never asking, even if it would have pained Belle to confess it.

Meanwhile, Adam had travelled to London to fetch the law. Peter had wanted to go himself, but Mrs Denham had all but threatened to throw herself in front of his carriage if he so much as left the grounds in his state.

He'd had a thumping headache for days, but that was to be expected, and he did not pay much attention to it save for the dose of laudanum prescribed by the doctor to manage his pain.

The moment Alex had walked into the drawing room, Peter had all but pounced on the man. Considering that Peter really did not know the man well, it was extraordinarily odd of him to be hanging off of his lapels.

"Peter, what on earth?" Susanna cried from beside her husband.

"Did you know that Belle was married?" Peter cried. "Please, do you know the man's name? Do you know anything about him? Please, he's taken her. I know he has." He spoke so quickly, so frantically, that hardly anything could be understood.

Alex's dark eyes were immediately narrowed, and his brows furrowed with deep concern. He placed his hands on Peter's shoulders and steadied him. Peter was practically bouncing with how quickly his heart was beating against his ribs.

"What are you talking about? What's happened to Belle?" he demanded to know. His eyes quickly flicked around the room searching for her, but, of course, he did not find her.

Peter's legs gave out underneath him as feelings of complete helplessness consumed him. He didn't know what to do. He didn't know where to look. He felt like a complete failure. He had promised that he would keep her safe, and she had been missing for days. God only knew what had happened to her.

Grace quietly intervened, kneeling down and putting a comforting arm around him as she explained what had happened to the grievously concerned newlyweds.

Alex was shocked, furious, and terribly frightened. Peter, in his own despair, could barely concentrate on the questions that Alex was firing at the room, speaking so quickly and emotionally that his words became French.

In the days that followed, as Peter's head cleared, it became apparent that Alex knew nothing of Belle's former life on Saint-Martin. When they had met aboard the smuggler's ship, all he had learned from her was her name. Alex was not even certain of Belle's age. She was very concerned with shielding herself, and Alex knew better than anyone why she was that way. But it also meant that he had no information to offer or add that would aid in locating her.

Their only lead was Saint-Martin. If her husband was intent on recovering her, then it was possible that she would be travelling back there from a port city. That was, of course, if recovery was her husband's mission.

Peter feared the worst. He feared that she was lying hurt somewhere, bleeding, crying, dying, calling out for him, calling out for help where no-one could hear her.

Peter would have travelled to every port city in the country immediately, but his mother insisted that he wait for the law in order to be as methodical as possible. He greatly resented Mrs Denham's rationality.

A week after the assembly, Adam returned to Ashwood accompanied by two Bow Street Runners. They were certainly out of their usual patrol, but Adam had paid them handsomely for their assistance.

The first of the Runners was a man named Nigel Hayfield, who appeared to be around forty years of age. He possessed a lean build and an intimidating height, and had small, sharp eyes. The second was a younger man named Francis Radcliffe. He looked to be in his twenties and was definitely second in command compared to Detective Hayfield.

They appeared to be well briefed on the situation but came prepared with information to add to the legality of Belle's situation.

"The marriage of a slave is not legally recognised. It was not in the British Empire, and I am certain that the French do not recognise it either," Detective Hayfield informed them all. "Whatever ceremony was performed, whatever words were spoken, it is not legal. Therefore, this man is not legally the husband of Miss Desjardins, thus he has no rights to her."

Peter had needed to be told this information twice. It wasn't legal. Her marriage wasn't legal. While that was wonderful news, it didn't help him find her.

"Furthermore, the slave trade is illegal in Britain. Kidnapping persons with the intention of keeping or trading them as slaves is against the law and will warrant an arrest."

Again, Peter had needed that information repeated. Of course, he was pleased that the law was on their side, but how could it not?

"How often do you catch these people?" Alex asked angrily. "I speak from experience. They manage to get in and out of Britain easily. How often do you check their cargo holds?"

"Our jurisdiction is London, Mister," replied Detective Radcliffe. "The control of the ports lies with the Navy and the Army. We mean to assure you all that the law is on your side."

"If this woman was legally married to the man, and she was not a slave, then the law would support his right to claim her," added Detective Hayfield. "But as she is not, it is a kidnapping, made worse by the fact there is potential smuggling involved."

Peter could not even begin to fathom the ridiculousness of the law. Were Belle a free woman, legally married, however forced, it would be perfectly alright to kidnap her? How could women ever feel safe with laws such as those?

"Where do we look then?" Peter pressed. "Where do we start? The bastard can be hung, drawn and quartered for all I care, I just want to find her."

"We have sent detectives on to the major port cities that would have ships travelling to the Caribbean. Southampton, Exmouth, Torquay, Plymouth. There they are to inform the naval and army forces to be on the lookout for smugglers. The Duke has also paid to have the story printed in every newspaper and has offered a reward for her safe return. These papers travel across the country, and with one thousand pounds there for the taking, every man in England will be on the lookout for her. If Miss Desjardins is still not located, then it would be an option to seek passage yourself to Saint-Martin, however if she makes it Saint-Martin where British slave laws do not apply, you might find it difficult to remove her from this man's custody."

Peter would shove the bastard off a cliff if he needed to.

"What I propose is that we follow the detectives," said Adam. "We travel to Southampton and work our way towards Plymouth. We'll travel all the way to bloody Penzance if we have to. I've made sure that this story will fly across this country. She will not leave England."

Belle was dragged into the small house, her heart racing a mile a minute. As soon as she was inside, Jean slammed the door shut and locked it, leaving Claude outside with the horses and carriage.

The house was one rectangular room with a small stove for cooking at one end, and a low to the floor bed and fireplace at the other. A random assortment of weathered timber furniture had been collected to complete the house. There was nothing much in the way of decoration, save for a grey-white ring that hung on the back wall. It looked to be one that was found on ships for floating. Belle could remember floating in one of those when she and Alex had swum from Captain Whitfield's ship to the shore of Haiti.

There was writing on it, but Belle could not read it. She recognised the letters, but she didn't know how to put them together.

Plymouth Harbour 1754

Belle couldn't concentrate on anything else as she was suddenly pressed up against the wall of the house, Jean's large frame completely covering her. He grinned at her wickedly as his mouth immediately accosted hers, his tongue forcing its way into her mouth.

Belle clamped her eyes shut as she panicked, but she needed to think. She needed to fight. Her heart was erratic, and she couldn't breathe. She forced her arms free and pushed against his chest, but her tiny hands could do nothing but tickle him. So, Belle bit down. Hard.

Belle bit down until she tasted blood.

Jean jerked away from her, screaming profanities at her as he spat blood down onto the floor. "You spiteful bitch!" he seethed.

Belle launched away from the wall and ran to the door, trusting that she could outrun Jean, and Claude if he was not expecting her to escape. Belle wrestled with the lock by her hands were shaking. Before she could wrench the door open, and she was grabbed by her hair and yanked backwards, falling to the floor.

Belle screamed as he head was forced backwards, and her eyes found Jean's furious orbs, blood dripping from his lips. "I'm going to enjoy this," he sneered from above her, blood dropping from his mouth onto her forehead.

Jean dragged Belle by her hair away from the door, her curls feeling like they were being ripped by their roots. Belle gripped his hands to fight for any relief from the pain. When she was away from the door and flat on the floor, Jean released her, but only for a moment, before he captured both of her wrists and gripped them in one of his large hands. He loomed over her like a thunder cloud blocking out all the good in the world, and Belle panted as she willed herself to fight.

Belle had been in this position countless times, and each time she had been terrified, just as she was now. But before she had wished to die. She had wished for death to take the pain away. But not anymore. Belle was not going to die, not because of this man. She would not let him hurt her.

With his free hand, Jean gripped the hem of her dress and threw it out of his way, and Belle hated the cool air that she could suddenly feel on her legs. But she pulled them up, pulling her knees to her chest before she kicked with every bit of strength, she had within her. She kicked for Peter, and for Alex, and for Susanna and the Beresfords. She kicked for every person she had left behind in Saint-Martin. But most importantly, she kicked for herself. And when the thought of herself filled her mind, she felt her heel connect with her target, and Jean buckled over, howling in pain.

Belle took the opportunity to scramble out from underneath Jean as he nursed his groin, and this time she ran to the fireplace. Beside the hearth was a stand of tools, and there she found her weapon. Belle seized the fire iron in her hands and inhaled deeply, filling her lungs with determination.

When she rounded on Jean, he had begun to recover, groaning as he climbed to his feet clumsily. She had never seen him so furious, but she had also never felt so strong. Belle would fight him until he had nothing left.

Her grip tightened on the fire iron. "I am not yours," she seethed. "I am not yours to take. I am not yours to own. I am not yours to destroy. You have no power over me."

"What do you think you're going to do with that?" Jean grunted in anger. "You stupid girl."

"You cannot hurt me," Belle continued, staring him right in the eye. "I won't let you. I choose. I decide."

Jean laughed then, almost maniacally, shaking his head. "You choose, do you?" he mocked, before he spat blood on the floor again. "You're lucky I don't choose to string you up. I still might," he spat. "Get. On. The. Bed."

Belle's jaw clenched. "No," she said emphatically, before she lifted the fire iron. "Never."

Jean's eyes flicked to the fire iron before he shook his head. "I'll kill you with that once I've had my fill of you," he sneered, before he lunged at Belle, thundering across the floor towards her, reaching for her throat.

Belle was faster. She ducked out of his reach and stabbed, throwing the fire iron forwards and plunging it into whatever flesh it could find. She hadn't meant to close her eyes, but she had, and she felt the force of the fire iron finding its target reverberate up her arm.

She heard an unholy sound escape Jean's mouth as he shrieked in agony. She had never heard such sounds of pain before, save perhaps from her own lips. When Belle opened her eyes, Jean had fallen backwards on the floor, and he was bleeding profusely. He was bleeding from his groin. Belle still gripped the fire iron in her hand, and she gasped at the sight of what she had done.

But the shock didn't last long. This was her chance. Once again, she flew to the door, and this time she managed to unlock it. Belle nearly pulled it off its hinges as the door swing open. As she did, she saw Claude climbing down from the carriage, abandoning his newspaper as he rushed towards the house.

"What was that noise?" he barked at her.

"Help!" Belle suddenly screamed. "Help him! He's hurt! You must help him!" Belle hid the fire iron behind her back as she pointed in Jean's direction.

Claude crossed the threshold immediately and dropped to his knees in shock at the sight of his master. Belle did not waste any time in striking Claude in the back of the head with the hilt of the fire iron. The force knocked him out cold and he collapsed onto the floor.

"That was for Peter," she said through clenched teeth. Belle still kept hold of the fire iron as she ran out of the house and into the unknown.

Chapter 26

Belle ran.

She didn't feel the pain in her foot even though she ran with only one shoe. She didn't feel the fatigue in her body as though she had been travelling for days in a confined space. She didn't feel anything but determination to put as much distance between her and that house as she could.

Belle ran towards the ocean. The ocean meant fishermen, people, help. She needed help. She prayed for help.

As soon as Belle had crossed over the grassy hill, her eyes took in the great expanse of the sea before her. It was endless. But it wasn't a fishing village. The boats were not fishing boats. It was a port.

Belle had experience with ports. The boats were tall ships, docked in the great harbour. Some flew the British flag, and they looked to be military vessels. Others looked like ... they looked like trade ships. She froze as panic began to cripple her. It began to flow through her veins and paralyse her right there in the middle of the dirt road.

Which way?

Whichever way she ran she could be taken. She couldn't run down into that port and ask for help. She couldn't risk being led somewhere, abducted, forced onto a vessel and shipped somewhere terrible. Not again.

Belle's breaths were shallow as she struggled to suck in enough air to fill her lungs. Without warning, her legs gave way and her knees fell into the stone covered road, digging into her skin and, no doubt, breaking it. Belle tangled her fingers in her hair as she gripped her head, trying to focus, trying to breathe, and trying to calm down so that she could think.

I don't want to be taken. I don't want to be taken.

I don't choose it. I don't want it.

I want to choose. I want to be the one to choose.

"Stop it," she hissed at herself. "Stop it now." Crippling herself in the middle of the road was far more dangerous. She was practically asking for someone to come along and take her. She had already fought, and she had already won. She could do it again.

Belle climbed to her feet and filled her lungs with air, properly this time. She knew what was behind her. She didn't know what was in front of her. As if there was ever a choice.

Belle continued to run, putting one foot in front of the other, bringing her closer and closer to the port town. The smell of salt and fish in the air was intoxicating and Belle prayed that she would find sanctuary.

As she began to pass the first few houses, she realised that she was still gripping the fire iron in her hand, from the point of which dripped Jean's dark red blood. Belle knew that she needed to abandon it, even if it made her feel safer to hold it. She said a prayer to ask for protection as she threw the iron into the long grass on the side of the road. And the moment she did, she wanted to run back after it. She felt naked without it, and the fear began to turn her veins to ice.

But Belle kept moving, determined to steer clear of the dock. She would not go anywhere near a ship, and she would keep her wits about her. She needed to find a way to contact Peter.

The village itself was busy. The wind whipped off of the ocean in a freezing chill, and Belle hugged at her sides for warmth. There were stalls hawking their fresh catches and men selling fishing supplies. Belle recognised the scent of the tavern before it actually came into view.

She hadn't meant to pass by such an establishment, but she had, and she immediately heard the drunken jeers of men who stumbled outside. Belle hurried past them but became highly aware that two continued after her.

Belle's heart, which was already thundering against her ribs, about beat out of her chest. This had happened before. This had happened before. This had happened before. No, no, no. She screwed up her face as her tears began to cloud her vision before she ran again.

"Wait!" shouted one of the men behind her. "Who are you?"

"We just want to talk!" called the other.

Belle ran blindly. She didn't stop. She did not even turn around. Could people not see? Could they not see that she was being chased by these men? She ducked and weaved, forcing her way through the groups of villagers, her teary eyes meaning that she bumped into more people than she meant to.

Belle turned a corner, hoping to evade them, but her heart dropped out of her chest and onto the ground when she realised that she had turned down an alleyway. A dead end. This was how it happened in Portugal. She had been cornered and she had been attacked and she had been taken aboard a ship. A loud sob escaped Belle's mouth as she turned back, but her path was quickly blocked by the two men from the tavern.

Belle's hand flexed around the phantom fire iron, and she took a step backwards. "Stay away from me!" she shouted at them.

But they didn't listen. They loomed like devils, edging towards her with their grins of yellowed teeth.

Belle anxiously looked around her for a weapon, something to wield against them. The alleyway was empty save for some abandoned crates of old fishing nets. Her eyes flicked back to their approaching figures.

"Get away!" she shouted again.

"We've never seen you around here before," called back one.

"We just wanted to meet you."

Belle swallowed before sucking in a lungful of air as she prepared to scream. But before she could, a third figure joined them in the alleyway. At a glimpse, Belle could see that he wore a fine blue coat.

"What do you two think you are doing to this poor woman?" His voice was fine, his accent reminding her of the way the duke spoke.

It took a moment in her heightened state of panic to understand what he had said. But she did, and his commanding tone forced the two would-be devils to stop in their tracks.

"Just showing her the way is all, Lieutenant," the man on the right muttered.

"Be on your way then," commanded the lieutenant.

The two men were quick to scurry out of the alleyway, leaving Belle alone with the lieutenant. He stood with proud, perfect posture, his hand on the hilt of the sabre he wore on his belt. The moment Belle caught sight of his weapon, she felt a searing pain across her belly.

Her hand instinctively went to the scar that marred her skin there, the one that had been placed there by a weapon just like that one, when she had been hiding from the lynch mob aboard Captain Whitfield's vessel with Alex.

"Are you alright, miss?"

The man's tone sounded sincere and concerned, but Belle could not feel safe when she was cornered like she was. She moved forward tentatively, walking towards the mouth of the alleyway, but quite nearly hugging the wall on the opposite side from the lieutenant.

He stood completely still.

When she came out into the light, she could see the face of the soldier clearly. He was young, perhaps only a few years older than she was, with a fair complexion and ashy coloured hair underneath his hat. He was watching her with his pale blue eyes.

"My name is Lieutenant William Harrow. You look as though you have had quite an ordeal, miss. May I be of some assistance to you?"

Every instinct of Belle's was to never trust a man. They were not safe. This man had sent the others away, but that did not mean that he was safe. She could not afford to make such a mistake.

"Do you have some family nearby? Someone I can send for?" he pressed further. When Belle said nothing, he asked, "Can you understand me, miss? Do you speak English?"

"Yes, I can understand you," she replied tentatively. "Where is it? This place, where is it?"

Lieutenant Harrow frowned a little. "This is Plymouth, miss. How have you come to be here?"

Plymouth. She remembered that the word on the ring in Jean's house began with 'p'. Had that word said Plymouth? But she couldn't remember how to spell it. If she managed to get her hands on some paper and ink then she would have to ask someone to spell the word for her.

"Have you been brought here against your will, miss?" Lieutenant Harrow continued to press. A flash of something crossed his face. "Were you brought here aboard a ship? I can hear an accent. Where have you come from?"

There were too many questions for Belle's racing mind to translate. "Slow!" she begged.

The lieutenant took a breath. "Have you been brough here against your will, miss?" he asked again, this time much more slowly.

Belle nodded.

She heard him swallow. "Were you brought here aboard a ship, miss?"

Belle shook her head.

"Where have you come from?"

Belle knew that he most likely meant to ask from whence she had come from originally. She very clearly did not appear to be of English blood. But she had come from her new home, and she wanted to return there. "I live in Hertfordshire," she replied softly.

Lieutenant's brows furrowed a little. "Hertfordshire?" he repeated, but he nodded. "And who brought you all the way to Plymouth from Hertfordshire?"

"A monster."

Belle looked into the lieutenant's eyes. She could see confusion and apprehension, but she could see no malice. Her instinct was never to trust. But in this instance, she had to. She needed help.

"I was kidnapped by an evil man." Belle would not call him her husband. Husband was a title reserved for an honourable man. "He took me from my home, and he meant to force me back to Saint-Martin, to be a slave." She prayed this lieutenant would be able to help her. And if he couldn't, or if she was wrong about him, she was no longer cornered in an alleyway. She was fast on her feet.

"This man meant to smuggle you?" Lieutenant Harrow asked sharply, his eyes narrowing.

"Yes," confirmed Belle.

The lieutenant's already perfect posture straightened. "You are safe now, miss."

Safe. This was her favourite word, and her most fervent wish. "I want to go home to Hertfordshire. Is there a carriage? Or somewhere I might write a letter?"

The lieutenant escorted Belle towards a small building with a sign that read: Royal Mail. Belle struggled to read the sign but recognised the interior as a postal service. Inside was a large wooden counter with a small stack of parcels and a collection of newspapers. Behind the counter were a series of shelves, on which letters and parcels were organised in neat piles.

The lieutenant kindly gave the postal worker a coin and he provided Belle with a piece of paper, a quill, and a pot of ink.

"Is this the latest?" he asked, gesturing to the pile of news-papers.

"Arrived this morning," confirmed the postman.

Belle took a breath and concentrated.

Peter, she wrote.

I am in P –

"Excuse me, would you please spell this town for me?" Belle murmured to the postman.

"Plymouth? It's like it sounds," he replied gruffly. "P-L-Y-M-O-U-T-H."

It certainly was not like it sounded. There was a 'y' in the word. But nonetheless, Belle copied down the letters he spoke.

– lymouth. I am saf.

Plez get to Plymouth.

Belle

Belle shook the piece of paper in the air to dry the ink before folding the letter. The postman provided her with wax and a seal before she flipped the letter over to address it. That was when she froze. She only knew of Peter's address in London. How would she write to him in Ashwood?

"Are you in the custody of the Duke of Ashwood, Miss Desjardins?"

Belle gasped as she looked up at the lieutenant. He had lowered his newspaper to the look at her. She had not told him her name. How had he known that? And how had he known about the duke?

"Your ordeal has been reported in the paper," the lieutenant clarified. "I am terribly sorry for what has happened to you."

"What?" The postman frowned as he snatched another of the newspapers off of the counter.

Belle, too, peered over the counter to look at the paper.

DUKE OF ASHWOOD OFFERS £1000 FOR SAFE RETURN OF BELLE DESJARDINS

Much of the headline was a muddle for Belle. She couldn't read it save for her name. But the duke had put it there. They were looking for her.

"A thousand pounds?" gasped the postman. "For her?" He motioned to Belle. "You're the woman in the article?"

Belle said nothing. She didn't like this man's tone. It made her uneasy.

"Are you claiming the reward?" he asked the lieutenant.

"That would be immoral," retorted Lieutenant Harrow. "Kindly send Miss Desjardins' letter."

Belle could see gold in this man's eyes, and not the gold that was in hers.

"It's not addressed," snapped the postman.

Belle quickly wrote Peter's name before she looked to the lieutenant. "I do not know the address."

He clearly thought that was odd.

"I cannot write it," she explained further. "Please. I need this to be sent to Peter Denham. Ashwood House, Ashwood Parish, Hertfordshire."

The lieutenant gallantly took the quill and addressed the letter for Belle, and the postman took it from her. He looked very sad to see them ago, as though his biggest payday was slipping away from him.

The moment that Belle and Lieutenant Harrow stepped out onto the street, however, there seemed to be quite a bit of commotion about. She could hear shouting, and a large gathering of people had formed some fifty feet away.

Lieutenant Harrow placed his hand on his sabre as he uttered, "Wait here, Miss Desjardins." He walked over to the gathering with authoritative purpose as he commanded people to move out of his way. The villagers cleared quickly, and that was when Belle caught sight of him. She caught sight of Claude.

Claude was huffing and puffing, ranting and raving, and his clothes were stained red with blood. With the villagers cleared, however, Claude was able to set his eyes on Belle. The minute he saw her, he pointed at her. "There she is!" he shouted in his heavily accented English. "Arrest her! She is a murderer!"

Chapter 27

Peter stared blankly out of the window of the carriage; his mind long lost to the roads of south-west England. He had no idea for how long they had been travelling. It could have been weeks. It could have been months. The days blended into one another and it was easy to lose track when one's focus was elsewhere.

Adam's article had done its job. Word was everywhere. Of course, their care was not for Belle's safety, but for the Duke of Ashwood's one thousand pounds. But Peter did not care a wit, for if that money led to Belle's safe return then it would have been worth it.

Every man in Southampton and Exmouth seemed to know Belle's name, but they had not seen her. She was not there. Though they were travelling with the Bow Street Runners, Adam, Peter, and Alex were the ones to run about each harbour questioning and bribing captains and harbourmasters for information.

And they learned nothing.

Peter was a wreck.

Alex was dangerously silent.

Adam had to be the optimist. He had to assure both men that the fact that nobody had seen Belle at these ports meant that she had not left the country from them. She had to still be in England.

Peter prayed that she was, and that she was unscathed. But he knew as the days passed, that the likelihood that she was unharmed slowly but surely diminished. That man, whatever his name was, would be damned to hell for whatever he did to her, and it would be done to him tenfold.

"Have you slept, Peter? You look terrible," Adam murmured sympathetically.

"I can't sleep," he muttered in reply. Peter did not remember the last time he had slept.

"We'll find her," Adam promised him.

Peter's eyes unwittingly flicked to Alex, as they seemed to whenever Adam made such promises. This was where Alex's silence frightened Peter. Alex said nothing, but he did not need to when his eyes spoke for him. He had been in Belle's position before. He and Belle had met in these exact circumstances. He knew what it was to be taken, to be smuggled on a ship, and to endure the horrors that man subjected his fellow man to. Alex knew it all.

Their luck changed when they reached Torquay. Of course, Belle's story had reached the port. But the whispers were different. Belle had been sighted in Plymouth only a week earlier. As soon as Peter had received that information, he had not needed to hear another word. The men piled into the carriage and the driver was ordered to take them directly to Plymouth without delay.

Belle had been in Plymouth. Belle was still in Plymouth, as Adam would positively say. She had been sighted a week ago. Peter needed to think coherently.

"It is December," Adam said, seemingly reading both Peter's and Alex's minds. "There are few, if any, ships crossing the Atlantic at this time of year. It is highly likely the man will be hiding her until they can seek passage across."

"For the right price, a smuggler would risk an Atlantic crossing at any time of year," Alex said intensely. "We are a valuable cargo."

A chill ran down Peter's spine and Adam paled as he looked upon Alex sympathetically.

Sometime along the journey, when Adam nodded off, Alex whispered something to Peter. "You must tell Susanna that I love her, and that I am sorry."

Peter's eyes narrowed.

"I will be hung for what I will do to that man if I get my hands on him." For a man who had black eyes, Peter had never seen them so dark.

"You will have to beat me to it," he replied vehemently. It was clear that Alex had ten years and perhaps four stone in weight on Peter. But he was no less serious.

Alex's dark eyes flicked over Peter's person, before he simply nodded, and returned to his startling silence.

Peter felt like to hope was to tempt fate when the carriage finally rolled into the port village of Plymouth. The harbour was nearly at capacity with tall ships stationed for the winter, and the town was busy with villagers and navy men alike.

Their first port of call was the harbourmaster, as it had been in each port they had visited. A donation of five shillings had secured them the information that no ships had departed the harbour bound for the Caribbean in the last month. As Belle had been sighted a week ago, that had to mean that she was still in Plymouth, or at least, still in England.

"It is Belle Desjardins you seek?" the harbourmaster inquired. The man was dressed in clothing much finer than his station, or his rate of pay. It was clear that his brass buttons were paid for by his many bribes of captains intending to smuggle goods in and out.

Peter shuddered to think of people as cargo.

"Yes," he confirmed. "She was sighted in Plymouth a little more than a week ago. Do you know her whereabouts?" Peter could not help but sound utterly desperate. He probably looked like a madman with the bruise-like shadows under his eyes.

"I don't know," replied the harbourmaster. "Do I?"

"This is a young lady's life we are discussing," Adam hissed as he went to slap another five shillings into the harbourmaster's hand, but Alex stopped him by grabbing his arm.

Alex stepped in front of Adam, standing directly in front of the harbourmaster, engulfing him with his intimidating height and brawn. "Your money will not buy this man a conscience," Alex said, eerily calm. "Tell me where the lady is."

The harbourmaster recoiled as he felt the weight of Alex's presence. "I am but a humble businessman," he stammered.

"You are a weed," spat Alex, "and if you do not tell me where the lady is, I will drown you."

"You ... you wouldn't do that! You'd be hanged! The Navy are but a shout away!"

"I would strangle you with that pretty cravat before you could shout for your mother."

"Gentlemen!"

Their attention was captured by the voice of Detective Hayfield, who was flanked by Detective Radcliffe as they marched down the pier. Alex took a subtle step backward from the harbourmaster.

"We've found her," Detective Hayfield told them seriously.

His tone was not one of elation, but of caution. It immediately put Peter on edge.

"Where is she?" he demanded to know.

"With the magistrate," Detective Radcliffe replied. "It seemed the wisest course of action for an investigation into Miss Desjardins' whereabouts in this port, and it turned out to be the correct one. Miss Desjardins was arrested and has been remanded until a judge can be brought from London for trial."

"Arrested?" gasped Peter.

"For what?" cried Adam.

"Attempt to kill and causing grievous bodily harm."

Peter stormed into the magistrate's office and found it to be a small stone building with very simple furnishings. A small man sat behind a desk laden with papers, and the sudden intrusion of three men and two Bow Street Runners made him drop his teacup which shattered into pieces on the wooden floor.

"You would knock!" cried the magistrate.

"Mr Ennis," Detective Hayfield said, stepping forward. "Allow me to introduce the Duke of Ashwood. Miss Desjardins was in his custody."

"The Duke?" repeated Mr Ennis, his eyes widening. "So, you are the one offering the reward?"

Out of the corner of his eyes, Peter saw Alex ball both of his hands into fists. His own jaw clenched.

"I would very much appreciate if Miss Desjardins could be promptly returned to my custody," Adam spoke formally, pleasantly, and was much more amenable than either Peter or Alex would have managed to be.

"I am afraid that is quite impossible," Mr Ennis said regretfully. "She has been placed under arrest. A judge has been sent for and we expect him in the coming days. She is to stand trial for her charges. Fear not. I doubt she will be convicted of the attempted murder. She will not be hanged. I expect transportation for what she did to that man." The magistrate shuddered.

"Transportation?" exclaimed Peter, losing his composure. After everything, she could not be shipped off to the bloody colonies! Whatever Belle had done was absolutely deserved. Peter was certain.

"What does that mean?" hissed Alex.

"It means she will likely be transported as a convict to Australia to serve hard labour," clarified Detective Radcliffe.

"Mr Ennis," interjected Detective Hayfield, "there has been a misunderstanding, and there could be a grievous miscarriage of justice. Miss Desjardins was kidnapped from her home in Hertfordshire by a man intending to smuggle her as a slave. As I am certain you are aware, this is an illegal practice."

Mr Ennis sighed. "Yes, yes. I have had this from the lieutenant who was with her when she was arrested. I sympathise with the young woman's plight. She is lucky, to be certain. She was accused of murdering the man! That would have meant her execution! She is fortunate that her husband survived the attack."

Flashes of violence flooded Peter's mind as he imagined what could have transpired leading up to Belle defending herself. And that is what it would have been. She would have been defending herself from that man. "He is not her husband!" he snapped.

"Theirs was not a legal union," clarified Detective Hayfield upon the magistrate's confusion. "Miss Desjardins is a victim of a great crime. If her captor survived, then it is he who will be brought up on charges of kidnapping and smuggling."

"And he will be when the doctor releases him," confirmed the magistrate. "Though I do not know when that will be. The girl rendered the man impotent." He shuddered at the thought.

All five men gasped at the revelation and gravity of what this meant. Peter was quick to decide that impotence was only the beginning of what that man deserved.

"It was cleared done in an act of self-defence," Adam insisted.

"Belle was held by this man for God knows how long!" Peter cried. "He'd attacked her, abused her, for years, before she escaped him. And here she is, taken by him again, and she manages to fight him off! That is the only explanation. You ought to be congratulating her, not arresting her!"

"It is her word against his," Mr Ennis replied. "Unfortunately, with no physical evidence of abuse, or a witness to testify to it, the charge stands."

Peter wanted to throw something. Alex actually kicked the wall which earned him a scolding from the magistrate. How could this be possible? How could this be justice? How could a judge be summoned to sentence a poor, brutally illtreated woman to transportation as a criminal when she had endured as much as she had?

It wasn't fair. It couldn't happen. Belle deserved more than this! She had to know that there was more to life than suffering! She deserved a good life, and Peter wanted to be the one to give it to her! He wanted to show her that life could be beautiful and full of opportunity for those with ambition. He wanted to help her achieve every one of her dreams.

Instead, she was sitting in a cell suffering yet again. God, he willed, if you help her, I will never let her know another day of suffering.

"I will employ a solicitor immediately," Adam informed the magistrate.

"I want to see her," Peter demanded.

Mr Ennis seemed to look upon Peter with pity. "Alright," he allowed. "Five minutes." He collected a set of iron keys from his drawer and stepped out from behind his desk. He then led Peter, Alex and Adam through a door and down a poorly lit hallway that housed three doors, all made of iron bars.

Through the bars, Peter could see a small gaol cell, entirely stone and terribly filthy, most likely owing to the drunkards that frequented them. The first of the cells was empty. The second was occupied by a man who was sleeping on the small cot in the corner of the cell. He was mostly covered by a blanket that appeared rife with smallpox.

When they came to the third cell, Mr Ennis fiddled with the keys as he searched for the right one. Peter anxiously looked through the bars and spotted a tiny figure on the cot, like the man in the second cell. All he could see of her was her head, but he would know those black curls anywhere.

It was her.

"Belle!" Peter cried out.

"Belle!" Alex was next to anxiously call her name.

Peter expected her to stir from her sleep, to turn over and look upon them with her haunting golden eyes. But she didn't. She stayed facing the wall.

"Belle?" Peter called again, firmer this time. "Belle, it's me. It's Peter."

At that moment, Mr Ennis found the key he was after and he put it into the lock, turning it over before he pulled it open. Peter was so desperate to get inside that he nearly bowled the magistrate over. He fell to his knees beside Belle's cot and placed his hand gently on her side, before immediately regretting it. She would not want to be touched, especially not without warning.

But she didn't flinch. At least, not violently. It took a moment for Peter to realise that Belle was moving. She was shivering.

"Belle?" whispered Peter fearfully as he reached for her face. He meant to turn her face towards him, but the moment he touched her skin, it nearly burned him. "She has a fever!"

Chapter 28

Belle was ill. She was desperately ill. Peter cupped her face in his hands and felt the beads of sweat beneath his palms. Belle's eyes were closed as she shivered. He could hear the chattering of her teeth.

"You didn't know she was ill?" accused Adam. "How could she be left in such a state?"

"She needs a doctor!" Peter cried. "Immediately!"

"She was fine this morning when breakfast was delivered," replied Mr Ennis, anguish in his voice at the clear panic and anger of the men in the cell.

Out of the corner of his eye, Peter spied a rather filthy looking tray with a bowl of grey broth and a piece of bread left virtually untouched. He rather doubted that Belle had been properly checked on that morning.

Peter could not believe that after all their searching, he finally had Belle back within his grasp, only for fate to be so cruel to her once more.

"The only doctor for twenty miles won't see her!" Mr Ennis stressed. "He doesn't treat people like her." His eyes almost fearfully flicked to Alex. "Like them."

Peter looked back down at Belle, shivering and small as she was, and his heart tore in two. She was innocent but broken, cruelly mistreated and undeservedly so. Her only crime, in the eyes of the sinful, being that her skin was a beautiful, cool brown. How could people not see it as beautiful? How could a doctor refuse to treat an innocent woman because of her skin?

"I am certain I could persuade him," Alex seethed through clenched teeth.

Adam placed a hand on Alex's forearm to calm him. "I will double his fee," he told Mr Ennis. "I will triple it. I am a member of the bloody House of Lords. I will command him to treat her if I have to."

Mr Ennis finally relented, passing on the address of the doctor to Adam, before he and Alex departed directly. Peter refused to leave Belle's side, and so Mr Ennis locked him in the cell with her. Did he really believe that Belle was in a state to get up and run away? Though Peter couldn't deny that the temptation to carry her out of there would have been great had the cell been left unlocked.

"You have to be alright," Peter whispered to her. He rested the back of his hand against her forehead, still feeling the searing heat of her fever. "You have so much left to do." Peter removed his hand and rested it against her voluminous dark curls. "We have so much left to do together if you'll let me."

Belle whimpered, though her eyes were still closed.

"Hear my voice," he whispered. "Stay close to me."

Belle was perhaps the smallest woman he had ever encountered. Peter wondered if her life before coming to England had contributed to her small stature. His mother had always scolded him as a child if he did not finish all of his vegetables, warning him that leaving them on the plate would stunt his growth. He had always thought her joking, but was there some truth to it? Belle had no doubt known the pain of hunger, in and amongst the pain of her enslaved existence. And yet despite this, despite her tiny stature, she had found it in her to fight off the evil, black-hearted swine once and for all.

Lord, he was so proud of her. Peter bowed his head, gently resting his forehead on her belly. He was so, so proud of her. Such strength, such spirit and fight deserved reward. She deserved the life that she wanted. She did not deserve to die in a gaol cell.

Two agonising hours later, Adam and Alex returned with an elderly doctor whose nose was scrunched up in such a way that it appeared he was permanently smelling a terrible odour.

The doctor placed his medical bag down on the floor of the cell and looked over Belle briefly. He did not even bend down to feel her temperature.

"She's full of disease," he grunted, firming his assessment. "She must be bled."

"What?" snapped Peter. He looked to Adam for affirmation. "How could you know that? You have barely looked at her!"

The doctor ignored Peter's protestations and bent over his medical bag, opening the clasp and removing a leather pouch of surgical tools and a bleeding tray. Peter's stomach turned. No, this wasn't right. He wasn't a doctor but bleeding a woman in Belle's weakened condition could not be the right course of treatment. He and his siblings had all suffered from fevers throughout their childhood and they had never been bled.

"What are you doing?" Alex demanded to know as the doctor opened his pouch and removed a surgical knife.

"Certainly a more thorough assessment is called for, Doctor Meacham," interjected Adam, stepping in between the doctor and Belle.

Doctor Meacham glowered at Adam. "Bleeding is standard treatment for fever," he snapped. "It lets out the disease."

Peter couldn't make sense of it in his head. His ever instinct was begging him to stop the doctor from touching her. But what if the doctor was right and this was the way to save her? Before he knew it, the doctor had seated himself on a stool and had rather roughly grabbed hold of one of Belle's arms, extending it outward. He placed the bleeding tray underneath her elbow and brought the knife to the crook of her arm. He pressed down enough for the blade to slice through her skin, and a red river of blood began to seep from the wound he had created.

"You butcher!" accused Alex.

The moment Peter saw it, he felt sick, and he knew it was wrong. Belle whimpered again as if to affirm his thoughts. "Stop that!" he hissed. "She is too weak for this! Stop the bleeding this instant!"

The doctor held the tray in place, collecting Belle's blood. "Of the two of us, boy, whom do you think belongs to the Royal College of Physicians?"

"I do not care if you belong to the Royal College of the Moon," Peter spat back. "Stop it this instant!"

Doctor Meacham turned around and looked to Adam. "I see my expertise is not wanted, Your Grace. It matters not to me, but the boy will be the one to kill her."

Peter knew that couldn't be right. Her fever would break. It had to. Bleeding would not help to hasten her healing.

The doctor was quite happy to gather his things and leave them standing there in the cell. The moment the path was free, Peter ripped a handkerchief from his pocket and pressed it against the seeping would at her elbow. "Have I done wrong?" he asked Adam and Alex worriedly.

Alex fell to his knees and began uttering things under his breath in French, while Adam put a comforting hand on Peter's shoulder.

"You protected her. That is all you can do. When Perrie was ill with fever, Grace and I simply had to wait. We had to wait and hope."

There was no persuading the three men out of the cell, and Mr Ennis was quite at a loss to know what to do or say. Peter wagered that he only hoped for the judge's swift arrival so he could be rid of all of them. Peter hadn't even begun to think of what he would say to the judge. What he would beg.

"No."

Peter awoke with a start. He had not realised that he had fallen asleep, but he had. He was lying in a very awkward and uncomfortable position alongside Belle's cot. Adam and Alex were similarly lying in varying degrees of misshapen awkwardness within the cell.

For a moment Peter thought that he must have imagined a noise, but this notion was quickly disproven when Belle spoke again.

"No, no."

Her voice sounded laboured and scared and not at all coherent.

"Belle?"

"No, Jean!" Belle mumbled, frightened.

Peter didn't know that name, but it did not require a lot of deduction to wager a guess the identity of the man haunting her nightmares. Peter reached for Belle's forehead again and breathed a sigh of deep relief when he felt that her searing temperature had settled, and her fever had broken.

Though it was dark, Peter was able to hold onto her arm and gently shake her. "Belle," he whispered. "Belle, wake up."

Belle stirred groggily, and the moment her coherency returned, he felt her stiffen. "Qui êtes-vous?" she asked fearfully.

Peter did not know what she said, but all he could do was let her know he was there. "Belle, it's me. I am here. Thank God you are alright!"

"Peter?" Belle gasped.

Behind him in the dark, Peter could hear both Adam and Alex stirring from their own slumber. A moment later, Peter was knocked over backwards by Belle launching herself at him. He fell flat on his back, Belle landing on top of him, as she scrambled to hold onto any part of him that she could in the dark cell. She finally managed to grip hold around his neck, and he felt her press her head tightly against his chest. Not a second later did he wrap his own arms around her, returning her embrace just as fervently.

"Belle, are you awake? Are you alright?" Adam gasped, his voice thick with sleep.

Alex similarly asked something of her in French.

"Yes, oui," she said to the both of them, her head not shifting from Peter's chest. "You are all here," she whispered to herself. That thought seemed to stick with her, and a few moments later, Belle suddenly sat bolt upright, nearly kneeing Peter in the gut in the process as she could not see anything. "Ow! My arm ...?" she began, but she seemed to dismiss the thought. "You're here. You're all here. How? How are you here? How did you find me? No, why are you in here with me?" And then she gasped. "Peter!" she cried. "Peter! Are you alright? Are you hurt?" Belle practically threw herself back down on top of Peter, hissing at the pain in her arm, but seemingly needing to feel that he was real to convince herself that he was there and that he was fine.

"I'm fine," Peter promised. "Perfectly fine." A concussion and stitches were nothing to worry her about. "It doesn't matter how we found you. What matters is you. Are you alright? Are you hurt? Did ..." but Peter couldn't finish the question.

Belle seemed to read his mind, and he felt a shudder from her before she uttered, "I stopped him. I won. He can't hurt me. He can't hurt anyone."

Peter reached for her in the dark, finding her face and cupping it with his hands. He felt the wetness of her tears as they spilled down her cheeks. He wanted to tell her how sorry he was for failing to keep his promise, for failing to keep her safe. But her words echoed in his ears. "You won," he repeated. Belle had fought and she had won.

A fresh tear fell against his hand as she whispered, "I'm not sorry." It sounded like a confession one would make to a priest. Her voice trembled, and Peter believed that she had forgotten that they were not alone. "I'm not sorry I did it and they're going to kill me for it."

Chapter 29

Belle could not believe her eyes. She had to convince herself that she was not dreaming, and that Peter was really there with her. But it had to be real. Belle's dreams were rarely of the good.

She felt dreadful. She felt tired and weak, her stomach felt empty and heavy, and there was a strange pain in her arm. But she paid no attention to any of that, not while Peter was there. She had been so frightened that she would never see him again, that her letter would find him too late.

Belle knew that they were going to kill her. That was what white men did when a slave attacked them. It was allowed. It was lawful. Had she not been with the lieutenant at the time of her arrest, she was certain that they would find the nearest tree and strung her up just like every other poor soul before her who had tried to fight back.

"You shall never need to be sorry for what you did," Peter promised her quietly.

But Belle felt it in her bones that if she found some ounce of remorse that she might be able to plead her case as a moment of insanity or something. But she couldn't. She was physically incapable of feeling any sense of guilt. And she worried if that made her wicked. Not as a victim, but as a human who harmed another.

Adam and Alex huddled over her then, and she finally could comprehend that there were three men in her tiny, filthy cell. They had all come for her, and they were all frightened for her. More tears fell from her eyes then, and they were not tears of sadness.

"I don't want to die," Belle managed to say, her voice cracking as her eyes returned to Peter.

Peter's large hands cupped her face then, and his thumbs brushed away her tears. "You are not going to die," he promised her.

"It is not a death sentence you face," added Adam. "The magistrate believes your punishment would likely be transportation to Australia."

Australia. Where on earth was that? Was it far? Was it in England? For how long would she have to go?

"But you are not going anywhere," Peter said firmly. "When the judge arrives, everything will be put right. I'm certain of it."

Belle got a sense that Peter was trying to convince himself as much as he was trying to convince her. Whatever the charge, it was inevitable that she would be punished. Punished for fighting. Punished for winning.

"Tais-toi et laisse-moi dormir!" shouted a voice that echoed along the corridor outside the cells.

Belle gasped.

"What is it? Who is that?" pressed Peter.

"Claude," replied Belle with a whisper. "He is ... he is Jean's right hand." Belle had pleaded her case with the magistrate when she had been arrested, but she hadn't known that he'd listened and had actually arrested Claude as well. Did that mean that Jean was also somewhere in this building? The very thought made her blood run cold.

Alex leapt up and gripped the bars of the cell in his hands and rattled them with such force that the entire wall shook. With such strength, he would have been able to break through the door with enough effort.

"Je vais te teur!" Alex bellowed out into the darkness.

So vicious was his tone that Belle believed him. Had Alex been able to get his hands on Claude in that moment, he would have killed him.

"J'aimerais te voir essayer!" came back Claude's taunt.

Alex smashed his hand against the bars of the cell in anger, and Belle jumped unintentionally.

"Alex, that is hardly helpful," Adam urged in warning.

Alex swore filthily in French.

Mr Ennis returned the next morning and, seeing as Belle was no longer deliriously ill with fever, he forced Peter, Adam and Alex from her cell. Peter cradled Belle for a long moment, before he reluctantly obeyed the magistrate.

As she door of bars closed behind him, Belle wrapped her fingers around them. Peter was quick to cover her hands with his own. "Do not lose hope," he willed. "You are a survivor, a fighter. He won't win."

Belle nodded, praying that he was right.

When he was gone, Belle couldn't help but sink to her knees, her weight becoming too much for her legs to bear. She pressed her forehead against the bars of her cell and concentrated on breathing evenly. It was the one little thing that she could control. The rest was out of her hands. And that fact was terrifying.

The following two days could only be described as utter madness. Culminating in a sentence that Belle would have never, not in her wildest dreams or nightmares, have ever thought she'd hear.

"We are going to have Claude Laurent testify on your behalf." The words were spoken by a Mr George Webb, a solicitor employed by Adam to defend her at her looming trial.

Peter had been back and forth to the gaol, as had Alex and Adam. Mr Webb had been to hear her story the day before and had returned to share what could only be described as an idea of complete lunacy.

"He would never!" exclaimed Belle through the bars. "He is responsible for bringing me to ... to ..." Belle couldn't say his name. "And he struck Peter in the head!"

Mr Webb nodded with pursed lips. "I have spoken to the magistrate who has agreed to lessen Mr Laurent's charges in exchange for his testimony. What he has to say might well benefit your case and put the nail in the coffin of the impotent one."

Claude knew it all. He had been Jean's lapdog for years, and he had never lifted a finger to stop any of it. Such was his level of respect for the people like her. Belle didn't know what Claude would say, but nothing in her experience with him could lead her to believe he would offer her case any benefit.

It was hard for Belle to have faith in such a thing as justice when it never served the truly oppressed.

"Tell me honestly. Do I have any chance?" she asked fearfully.

Belle saw a mixture of thoughts, both positive and negative, cross the eyes of the solicitor. But he did not answer her question. Instead, he said, "The judge is expected imminently. You ought to rest, Miss Desjardins."

And with that he left. Belle's stomach twisted in anxious anticipation of what was to come. She knew she ought to prepare herself for the worst, but she did not know what it was.

Peter felt ill as he watched Belle be brought into the public hall before the Honourable Justice Percival Steele. The judge had arrived that morning and had promptly called the arraignment trial, as well as instructing the magistrate to assemble a jury of twelve eligible men.

Belle looked so unbelievably small as she walked behind Mr Ennis, her tiny wrists in irons that were so ill-fitting, she might have slipped out of them if she had wanted to. Her golden eyes were wide and frightened as she searched the room, before she quickly found his. Peter saw every ounce of her terror in her gaze, and he would have done anything to take it all away.

What they had done over the past few days was everything that they could do to secure a favourable outcome, complete with Alex swallowing his urge to crush Claude Laurent's windpipe with his bare hands, in order to convince the man to testify on Belle's behalf.

Without a witness, it would have been her word against her captor's. Peter would not call that man her husband.

Belle was brought to stand next to the solicitor Adam had retained, Mr Webb. She did not sit down before the judge. A smartly dressed clerk, who had travelled to Plymouth with the judge, stood and began reading off of an official looking document.

"The accused, Miss Belle Desjardins," read the clerk phonetically, butchering her French name, "has been arrested and charged with the alleged assault and subsequent grievous bodily harm of Mr Jean Leclerc. How do you plea?"

Just hearing the man's name made bile rise in Peter's throat. He stared at the back of Belle's head, knowing that it would have the same effect on her.

Belle was to plead not guilty. And then they would all pray fervently that their self-defence argument worked.

"Not guilty," replied Belle, her voice soft and fragile, tears very evident in her throat.

The arraignment trial was brief, and after Belle's plea was entered, the judge was informed of what evidence would be provided to prove Belle's guilt. Namely the doctor who had treated Jean would be there to describe the injuries inflicted. And then the meeting was adjourned.

The following day the trial began. Peter, Adam and Alex returned to the hall and were seated on one of the benches that looked to belong to a church. There was little more they could do now but wait and pray that what they had done would work, and that justice would be served to the right person.

The first person to enter the hall under the escort of Mr Ennis was not Belle, but a man whose waist circumference rivalled that of his height. He was dressed in luxurious finery, though he walked with a considerable limp as he hobbled down towards the chairs before where the judge would preside. This man was not Claude, so he could only be Jean Leclerc.

Peter's blood ran cold as he looked upon the face of Belle's torturer. In knowing what he was capable of, Peter could not find one redeeming feature on him. He was an ugly man whose devil horns could not been seen by the naked eye. The picture of evil.

Peter noted that Jean's hands were also in chains as he gripped the underside of the bench to stop himself from launching at the man. Lord, it made him angrier than he had ever felt to know what that man had done to Belle, to know the pain he had inflicted upon her, both to her body, and to her soul.

Alex, however, did not possess Peter's self-control. He stood up and hurled vicious French at Jean. Though Peter did not speak the language, he understood Alex perfectly well. Jean's head looked back, and one of his eyebrows rose and he looked upon Alex was an amused expression.

Adam yanked Alex back down and hissed, "I imagine you threatened to kill him in a rather colourful way, but such threats are illegal and could wind up with your own life in the hands of a judge. Hush."

Mr Ennis then escorted Belle into the hall, and her face was startlingly grey. She was wearing the dress and spencer coat that Peter had purchased for her, no longer having to wear her once lovely ballgown that had been ruined by her ordeal. It was certainly too big on her slender frame, but at least it was warm.

Jean turned around and watched Belle walk inside. Despite what had happened to him, and deservedly so, he still found it somewhere in his sick and twisted mind, to offer her a sinister smile. Peter could see that Belle's eyes were averted from him. It made her sick to be even in the same room as him.

Belle was once more brought beside Mr Webb, and that was when Peter noticed that the jury of twelve had assembled to the side of the judge's bench. The men were dressed in their Sunday best, and sat stoically as they prepared for their role in the proceedings.

Peter wished that women were allowed to serve on juries. Surely women would be more sympathetic to Belle's suffering at the hands of that blackguard.

Peter, Adam and Alex were not the only members of the public in the hall to view the trial. Every available seat had been taken by Navy men and villagers alike. This trial had certainly been everywhere along the south-west coast owing to the fact that Belle's name and kidnapping had been in newspapers everywhere. It was the story of the century, and there were most definitely journalists in the hall who were seated in eager anticipation with their pens ready to note down all the sordid details.

The clerk announced the judge's arrival and everyone in the hall stood. The judge was clad in his formal robes and looked upon Belle and Jean with plain indifference. They were then allowed to take their seats once more.

The clerk once more read out the charges before the victim prosecution was to begin. The very notion that Jean Leclerc was first invited to speak as a victim made Peter's skin crawl. The depths of Hell awaited that man as he struggled to his feet to address the jury.

Chapter 30

Belle imagined herself to be quite in a hellish trance as Jean related his story to the jury, painting her as an insane runaway determined to maim her innocent husband.

She could hardly focus on anything. She could barely construct a coherent sentence in her head to muster up a defence to any one of his outlandish and utterly untrue statements. Luckily that was not her job.

"I rescued this woman," Jean declared to the jury in his very heavily accented English. Belle had never known that Jean spoke the language. "She was owned by my father and I rescued her, I made her my wife. I took a negro like her and put her on a pedestal. I gave her the life of a white woman, and this is how she behaves? She is obviously unhinged and could have very well taken my life. She practically has already."

Belle's hands were shaking so violently that she hid them in her lap. She could not look anywhere but at the table, where she counted the grains in the wood to keep her mind from doing exactly what Jean was accusing it of. She did not want to lose her sanity. She did not want to cry in this makeshift courtroom. No matter how broken she was, she wouldn't cry in front of Jean.

She felt Peter's eyes on her, but she did not turn to look at him. Belle had seen him out of the corner of her eye when she had entered the hall and seeing Peter and Jean in the same room together filled her with such a level of disgust and shame that she had never felt before.

To have the epitome of good look upon the epitome of evil and know what he'd done to her made Belle feel entirely filthy.

Twenty-seven, twenty-eight, twenty-nine ...

Belle continued to count the grains to occupy her racing mind.

She was unsure of for how long Jean spoke. It might have been hours. But one small glance at the jury as Mr Webb stood for her defence told Belle all she needed to know. She looked upon the faces of twelve men who were convinced of her guilt.

Mr Webb cleared his throat as he stepped out in front of the jury. "What a fairy tale you have just heard, gentlemen," he quipped. "And I do say fairy tale, as it is utterly fictitious in every sense of the word as Mr Leclerc would have you believe that he is a victim of Miss Desjardins. I will have you all know that it is quite the opposite. Miss Desjardins has suffered grievously at the hands of this man," he pointed a firm finger at Jean, who had returned to his seat, "culminating in a final act of self-defence to save her own life. Mr Leclerc would have you convinced that he is the husband of Miss Desjardins. Tell me, which of you would allow your daughters to marry at the age of fourteen? For that is the age in which my client was forced to marry this man. But his abuse started long before this sham of a marriage took place. I was disturbed and seriously grieved to hear that Jean Leclerc, a grown man in a position of power, first violated Miss Desjardins when we she was but five years old."

Belle's eyes closed as all blood drained from her body and she became as cold as ice. Of course, she knew that this would be spoken of. She knew that Mr Webb would use this in her defence. But to hear it, to see it in her head, to have everyone there know, made her feel so ashamed.

"For such an accusation, there must be unmitigated proof," Justice Steele said firmly.

"My client will testify, Your Honour," replied Mr Webb, "and I have a witness to prove her claims."

Belle's eyes were still closed, but she could hear the shocked whispers inside the hall. Her mind could not help her distinguish what anyone was saying, but it made her feel sick to her stomach to know that they were no doubt speaking of the very worst thing that had ever happened to her.

"Jean Leclerc's years of abusing Miss Desjardins when she was but a child culminated in an illegal marriage. The marriage of a slave is not recognised, and so Jean Leclerc has no legal marital claim over my client."

Mr Webb had a confident and commanding voice in that hall, and he told Belle's story to the jury, as well as assuring the judge of its relevance, with an impassioned theatre. Belle soon found herself seated beside the judge, in full view of the jury, preparing to be questioned.

Belle had tearfully confessed when she had been discussing her case with Mr Webb at the magistrate's office that she wasn't certain of her ability to speak without breaking. Mr Webb has promised to lead her. But she could also clearly recall their last conversation. Despite his talent as a solicitor, he was not confident in their success.

"Miss Desjardins, can you please enlighten the jury as to how you first escaped from your enslavement in Saint-Martin."

Belle took a breath. She willed herself not to cry. "There was a hurricane." Her voice was barely audible.

"Louder please," ordered the judge.

"There was a hurricane," Belle said again, her voice a little stronger. "I used it as my opportunity to escape. I stowed away on a ship to take me ... anywhere. Anywhere that wasn't Saint-Martin. Somewhere far away from ... from him."

"Up until that brave escape, for how long had Mr Leclerc kept you as his illegal wife?"

"Four years." Belle's voice shook. She looked directly at Mr Webb, and nowhere else.

"And during that time, can you confirm for the jury that the abuse continued? Can you confirm that Mr Leclerc committed heinous acts of rape against you?"

Belle would not cry. She forbade herself from crying. Her hands began to shake uncontrollably as she clapped them together, setting them in her lap in an attempt to stop them. She felt weak, and so, so afraid. She had felt this way so many times before, for years at a time.

Her mind suddenly took her back to Alex and Susanna's wedding, to the first time that she had spoken about any of the terrible things that had happened to her, and how she had told them to Peter. She had felt weak and afraid then, too. She had so wished to be brave.

"You are brave," he had told her. "You are a survivor, a fighter. I can see it in you."

Belle was alive. Despite everything, she was alive, and she was here. She had survived everything that had happened to her, everything that Jean could ever do to her, and she was here.

"The shame is not mine," she realised aloud. "It is his." Belle took in a deep breath as she looked up and found Jean's cold glare upon her. "Yes," she said in answer to Mr Webb's question. Her eyes then moved away from the empty wasteland that were Jean's eyes, and instead moved to the ocean blue irises of Peter. He was seated rigidly, his hands gripping the pew in front as he watched her with anxious concern. When their eyes met, he gave her all he could in that moment, a look of reassurance, and a word.

He mouthed what could only be combat. Fight, he willed her, and he had said it in French.

Belle answered every one of Mr Webb's questions about Jean's abuse, and she fought through the pain of every one of the answers, until finally came the questions surrounding her kidnapping and journey to Plymouth.

"I will once again remind the jury that Mr Leclerc is not the legal husband of Miss Desjardins, and so the abduction of forced removal from her home in Ashwood, Hertfordshire, was entirely illegal. Miss Desjardins, did Mr Leclerc bring you to Plymouth with the intention to return you to Saint-Martin as a slave?"

"Yes," Belle confirmed.

"Not only has Mr Leclerc committed heinous crimes against my client, but Britain's laws on the illegality of the slave trade. Kidnapping persons with the intention of keeping them or trading as slaves is illegal," Mr Webb declared to the jury. "My client was brought to this port against her will by a villain who had wielded his power over her since the tender age of five. In a final act to save herself from further unthinkable abuse, my client used whatever weapon was nearest to defend herself and to save her own life."

Belle was finally excused from testifying, and Mr Webb called on their witness, a man whose hands Belle would have never thought to place her life. When Claude was brought before the judge, he was accompanied by a man Belle did not recognise, but who was quickly introduced as the translator of Claude's testimony.

When Claude emerged, Belle caught sight of the blood draining from Jean's face. Until then, they'd had no way to prove their claims against Jean. It was her word against his without a witness.

But with the promise of one year of penal servitude instead of seven year's transportation, Claude was prepared to testify on Belle's behalf.

She prayed this would save her. She prayed that Claude would put right one of his countless sins and save her.

Once Claude was sworn in, Mr Webb began listing every one of the heinous accusations that had been brought against Jean, and he confirmed everything.

"He liked the little ones," Claude had said in response to the accusation of Belle's abuse as a child. "They don't fight."

When the translator told the jury what Claude had said in response to this charge, they were visibly shocked and disgusted. As was everyone in the hall.

"He treated her the worst of any of them. What he did to her ... she was no better than a beaten dog. But his dogs ate better. His dogs slept better. He enjoyed her pain. He loved her pain. You should see her back. It's a mess."

Belle had already confirmed the fact that she had been lashed on several occasions, and hearing Claude state, in such a blasé fashion, that Jean had loved her pain sickened her.

But to hear someone describe her as a mess wounded her. The accuracy wounded her. It also hurt to know that Peter heard that.

Mr Webb continued to ask Claude to confirm every point that he had made during Belle's testimony, and he did, right down to Jean's intention to smuggle Belle out of the country. He did this, of course, without further incriminating himself.

The moment Mr Webb's questioning concluded, Jean was given the right to cross-examine Claude. He struggled to his feet in an almost dramatic fashion.

But gone was Jean's nasty, confident demeanour. He was pale and almost appeared in shock. He had not cried out an objection throughout the testimony and had sat in stunned silence at what had unfolded before him. He had witnessed his own downfall.

"You're lying," Jean accused in French, before the judge reminded him sternly to speak in English. Jean was reaching for anything that would help him in that moment. Jean repeated his accusation again in English, his voice shaking.

Belle had never heard Jean sound like this. She had never before seen him weakened, not even in the state that she had left him in when she had run from the small cottage, leaving him wounded.

"Mr Leclerc, do you have any evidence to offer that disproves Mr Laurent's testimony?" asked Justice Steele.

Jean looked between Claude and the judge with such a helpless expression. Belle's breath caught in her throat. She didn't know what to make of it all. She didn't know how to feel. But she wanted to hope.

She was brave. She was a survivor. She was a fighter. And she wanted to hope.

"He's lying!" Jean cried to the judge. "She's lying!" he accused, rounding on Belle. "You all know what she did to me!"

"And now we all know what you did to Miss Desjardins, Mr Leclerc!" retorted Mr Webb.

Jean glowered at Belle, his hands balled into fists at his sides, his chest puffing as he sucked in angry breaths. In two strides, his enormous frame was suddenly towering over her, and he wrenched the table out of his way, flicking the wooden piece of furniture across the room as though it weighed nothing.

Jean's quick actions sent the hall into chaos. Belle jumped so violently that she fell backwards in her chair, and as her head fell back, she saw Peter leap out from his seat and run towards her, crying out. Peter's voice was drowned out by the cries from the jury, and the banging of the gavel as Justice Steele tried to regain order.

Jean managed to clench one of his large hands around Belle's neck moments before Mr Ennis at the judge's constables pulled him away. Belle had been deprived of air for only a few seconds, but she sucked in lungful after lungful in shock as she heard the sounds of handcuffs being secured.

Peter fell to the floor beside Belle, crouching over her protectively as he pulled her into his arms. Belle melted into his embrace and covered her neck with her own hand as she shielded her face in Peter's chest.

Jean was secured to his chair and his ankles were subsequently bound in chains.

Peter helped Belle to her feet as the judge began to summarise the evidence according to his notes. Belle was in a haze as she listened to Justice Steele repeat the evidence in his view and opinion to the jury. She heard words like "abuse", "heinous assault" and "grievous mistreatment". Were she able to concentrate, it would have almost sounded like the judge was instructing the jury to agree with the defence.

She vaguely remembered Mr Webb explaining this part of a trial to her before it began. The judge would take notes throughout the presentation of evidence and would summarise a case for the jury at the conclusion, often giving their opinion as to the verdict. The jury would then depart to decide on the defendant's innocence or guilt.

And no sooner had the thought entered her mind, the judge dismissed the jury to deliberate, and the twelve men rose and exited the hall.

Chapter 31

"Are you satisfied that you have reached a unanimous verdict?" the judge asked the jury once they were returned.

Belle stared at the twelve men intently, her heart having long stopped beating. They had been gone a mere twenty minutes. She was not sure of the normal amount of time that it took for jury deliberation, but Mr Webb seemed to think that it was awfully quick.

It terrified her that, even after all this time, her life was still in the hands of white men.

The first juror rose to address the judge. "We are, Your Honour."

"How do you find the defendant?"

"We, the jury, find the defendant not guilty, Your Honour."

Belle's bones vanished from her legs as they buckled beneath her. She completely missed her chair and she crumpled down onto the floor. She pressed her hands against the rough timber of the floor and watched as her tears fell freely, dampening the wood.

Not guilty.

Of all the English words she had learned, to her, there would forever be a beauty about those two words when place together.

"Oh, dieu merci," she whispered under her breath.

Belle felt tender hands on her back and shoulders, and she knew it was Peter. She could hear the noise of the hall all around her. People were crying out, cheering, protesting ... she could hear Jean protesting. But Belle turned into Peter's chest and her whole body shivered. His arms enveloped her as one of his hands cradled her face.

Safe.

That familiar, beautiful feeling of Peter returned, and Belle wasn't afraid anymore.

"Please stand, Miss Desjardins," the judge commanded.

Belle's body shook as her eyes lifted to meet Peter's. "I need help," she whispered. "My legs ..."

Peter beamed, his smile bigger than any she had seen before. She could see his youth once more on his tired face. His ocean eyes were endless and were only for her. Belle could see his constancy as clear as anything. Such overwhelming feeling did not help with her legs.

Peter helped Belle to stand, and he supported her weight as she faced the judge. In turning away from Peter, she could properly see what was happening around her. The judge's constables were holding Jean to his chair as he cursed at them in French. The judge banged on his gavel to silence the noisy hall.

"I will have order!" he cried, and the noise immediately ceased. He then looked upon Belle with an almost sympathetic gaze. "Belle Desjardins, you are acquitted of all charges. You are a free woman."

Peter's grasp around her tightened as Belle whimpered with joy.

"Jean Leclerc," Judge Steele continued, his voice hardened to one laced with disgust. "I hereby order your arrest, where you will be charged with kidnapping, smuggling and rape, including the unforgiveable and damnable offense of the rape of a child. If and when your guilt is determined, I will have you hanged by the neck until you are dead, and I will see to it personally that your sorry soul is hand delivered to Satan himself."

Peter went to pull Belle away, but she found her feet then, and stood firmly as Mr Ennis came to take Jean away into his custody. He was already in chains, but Mr Ennis helped the constables to pull Jean to his feet so that he could be removed to the gaol.

Jean met her eyes as he was pulled away and cursed her.

"Sorcière!" he cried.

"Et tu peux aller au diable," she cursed right back.

When Belle stepped out onto the street, she inhaled deeply, having never loved the scent of salt and fish more. She was flanked closely by Peter, Alex and Adam, all of whom surrounded her like a live barrier, protecting her from anything and everything. Belle turned towards them, before she stepped forward and hugged Alex for the first time. Belle had never purposefully touched Alex before, nothing less than was necessary.

But it was alright now. She felt that in her bones.

Alex held onto Belle tightly, before she felt him press a soft kiss to her forehead. She could feel that he knew the significance of this touch as she did.

When they parted, Belle looked to Adam. He smiled at her, and he nodded reassuringly as he captured both of her hands in his.

"I don't know how to thank you. All of you," she said to them, her voice shaking.

"You don't owe us any thanks, Belle," promised Adam.

"I don't think you realise just how far this boy was willing to go for you," Alex added, nudging Peter with his elbow. "I'd wager he would have leapt off the ends of the earth if that was where you were."

Belle smiled as Peter chuckled bashfully. "I'm so grateful you came to find me."

"I'm so proud of how you fought," he countered immediately. He pursed his lips as his hand cupped her cheek. "You are brave. A fighter. A survivor."

"I didn't want to ..." Belle's voice trailed off, and she couldn't utter the word "die".

Peter seemed to be able to read her mind. Belle had confided in him before of her wish to die when something terrible had happened. "I'm proud," he said again, ever so sincerely.

"Good day to you all."

Their embrace and celebration were disturbed by another joining their party. Belle turned to recognise the lieutenant who had helped her when she had first fled the shack Jean had brought her to.

"Lieutenant Harrow," recalled Belle.

"Miss Desjardins," Lieutenant Harrow greeted as he removed his tricorn.

She could feel Peter, Alex and Adam's eyes upon them both questioningly.

"Please let me introduce you to the Duke of Ashwood, Mr Peter Denham, and Mr Alex Whitfield. This is Lieutenant Harrow," Belle introduced.

"Your Grace, Mr Denham, Mr Whitfield," Lieutenant Harrow greeted them all.

"The lieutenant helped me, he saved me, when I first escaped from ... I never properly thanked you, sir."

"No thanks necessary, Miss Desjardins. I am just glad to see justice served."

Peter extended his hand to the lieutenant. "You have my eternal gratitude, Lieutenant. I thank you."

Lieutenant Harrow shook Peter's hand and nodded. "It was my honour to be of service to the lady."

Though Belle was free, she was forced to recount her story once again for Jean's trial, which began two days later just as soon as legal counsel could be sourced. Mr Webb refused the case.

Claude was once again persuaded to testify with a yet again reduced sentence. His one year became six months, and his confirmation of Belle's accusations made her case a very simple one. She couldn't be torn down. She wouldn't be made to feel like Jean's actions were somehow her fault. Jean was condemned, and it was only a matter of time.

The jury had taken twenty minutes to deliberate on her verdict. They had needed only ten minutes to deliver Jean's guilty one.

Belle left the hall for good just as the judge laid down Jean's death sentence. Instead of listening to his fate, he screamed, "Sorcière!" over his shoulder, over and over.

They left Plymouth that very day, with one last stop at the harbour so that Adam could leave a one-thousand-pound cheque with Lieutenant Harrow. Of course, he had tried to refuse the reward money, but Adam had insisted upon it. The money would be there once he had finished his career to fund a comfortable retirement for his chivalrous and hon-ourable service.

Their first stop on their journey back to Ashwood was in Torquay. After paying an innkeeper for rooms for the night and eating what was perhaps her first decent meal in weeks, Belle asked Peter if they might go out for a walk.

And at her request, she watched the blood drain from Peter's face as he turned ashen white. Peter looked out the window of the inn dining room at the setting sun and shook his head.

"No," he said firmly. "It is going to be dark very soon. I won't have you out at night."

Belle could see the fear on Peter's face, and she knew where it had come from. Perhaps it would have been wise for her to be afraid also, but she wasn't. It was exhilarating to not feel afraid for perhaps the first time in her life.

But she could see by the look on Peter's face that he was afraid. She could see the sleepless nights underneath his eyes. He looked exhausted and wrecked, and it was Belle's disappearance that had done this to him.

"I hope you do not blame yourself," she murmured fearfully.

As soon as the words escaped her lips, the flash of an expression across Peter's eyes confirmed it for her. Belle's face fell.

"Peter," she appealed.

Peter averted his eyes from Belle's. "I know that what he did ... I know it was not my fault, the same as it is the furthest thing from being your fault. But it was me who put you in the position to be taken in the first place. I took you out of the assembly. I placed you in danger, and I am not prepared to do that again. I made a promise to keep you safe."

Belle wondered if Peter had slept at all since the night she had been abducted from the assembly. Had he spent all this time punishing himself? Belle reached out and pulled on his arm, her hands sliding down to entangle her fingers with his.

"He told me ... oh, I don't know the English word ... se vanter." Belle thought hard with frustration. She so desperately wanted to make her point and she could not find the word. "When you ... when you laugh and speak," she muttered, "and tell a story but laughing and speaking because ..." Belle stopped talking and turned her head, searching the room quickly and finding Alex sitting beside Adam at the bar, both quietly enjoying a drink. "Alex!" she called.

Alex turned immediately, with an almost alarmed expression on his face, as though he was ready to throw his fist. How terribly she had frightened everyone, it seemed. "What is it?"

"Se vanter," she called to him. "What does this mean?"

Alex's brow furrowed, but he sat back down on the stool and let out a breath. "To brag, do you mean?"

To brag! "Yes!" she cried, before she turned back to Peter and exclaimed, "brag!" She gripped his hand tightly. "He brag to me," she insisted. "He brag that he knew where I was, that he knew every place I had been. If it was not at the assembly, it would have been somewhere else."

Peter shook his head as he used his free hand to tuck one of her curls behind her ear affectionately. "Why, oh why, am I allowing you to make me feel better after everything that you have been through?" he asked rhetorically.

"You cannot always be the one looking after me. That would hardly be fair."

Peter chuckled and Belle beamed. She had made him laugh.

"I'm free," she uttered, "and I am not afraid. I have nothing to be afraid of anymore. I fought and I won. You said so yourself."

"You are free to do whatever you please," Peter said quite serenely, "and I am honoured that you would exercise your freedom to walk with me." His voice then grew firm, but Belle could still see the warmth in his eyes. "There is perhaps a half hour of good light left. Can we return then?"

Belle grinned as she nodded.

The tide was rolling in along Babbacombe Beach, and there was very little of the pebbled shore left exposed. Belle loved it, nonetheless. She had sailed the Caribbean and had experienced some of the most beauteous places that the Earth had to offer, and yet as the sun set in the horizon and bled glorious pinks and oranges into the sky and across the ocean, she was quite certain that God had touched Devon. At this time of day, it was quiet, save for the sound of the wind whipping around the cliffs and the soft waves breaking over the rocks. Belle had removed her shoes and was walking over the smoothed rocks enjoying the feeling of the freezing water as it brushed up against her ankles.

Perhaps it was a little insanity to be dipping her toes in the ocean in December. The water was icy, the air even more so. But she didn't care. It made her feel alive.

"Before travelling to Plymouth, I'd never seen the ocean before," Peter confessed as he walked beside her. He, too, had removed his boots and had rolled up his breeches. "I don't think the Thames counts. It's filthy. The sea, though. It is remarkable."

Belle looked out on the ocean and marvelled at its expanse. It occurred to her then that perhaps she saw more beauty in it now then she ever had before because she was truly free. Why, on Saint-Martin, the ocean had been like prison bars surrounding the island.

"I think, in a way, I am seeing it for the first time, too," Belle replied.

They walked in comfortable silence along the beach, and when the feeling began to disappear from their toes, they made their way back to the stone retaining wall that separated the shore from the street.

Belle spied Peter watching her out of the corner of her eye as she stepped back into her stockings and tried to awkwardly maintain her modesty in a public area as she pulled them up her legs. Despite her slight embarrassment, she was reminded of the reason why she had wanted to be alone with Peter, why she couldn't wait until they were returned to Ashwood. If she'd left this weighing on her for the rest of their journey, then she would have certainly gone mad.

"I wanted to ask you something."

"What is it?"

"Why haven't you asked me anything?" That actually hadn't been her question, but it had escaped her lips without her realising. And as soon as she'd asked the question, she was glad. She certainly had been wondering that, too.

Peter frowned helplessly. "Asked you anything? Do you mean about your experience? What happened to you while you were ..."

"Yes," she interjected.

"Belle, I have a thousand questions that I want to ask you. I have a thousand questions that I am afraid to hear the answers to." He flicked his eyes away, and Belle could have sworn for a moment that she saw them become glassy. "But you shouldn't have to answer them to pacify my curiosity, my anxieties."

"I fought and I won, remember? I didn't let him hurt me." It seemed clear to her that Peter's worries, and indeed his guilt, centred around the possibility of her assault.

A sound escaped Peter's mouth that almost sounded like a hiccough. He groaned, before snatching her and pulling her into his arms. Belle didn't shy away. She never would again. She snuggled into his embrace.

"Yet again," he mumbled against her hair, "I cannot believe that it is you who is comforting me." Peter kissed the top of her head, and Belle felt a shiver flutter down her spine. "I'm so proud. So proud," he whispered.

Belle smiled against his chest. She felt his hand rub over her back, and her eyes opened, and she was reminded of her original question. "Peter," she whispered.

"Mm."

"I have another question."

"Yes?"

"Did you hear ...?" Belle swallowed nervously. She didn't quite understand why this of all things made her nervous and apprehensive. Of all the things that Peter had learned about her, from her own lips and from the trial, this was hardly the worst. And yet, it was troubling her. "Did you notice what Claude said ... what he said about my back?"

Belle had been the one to first state that she had been lashed while enslaved. But Claude had been the one to insinuate, or state very plainly for all to hear, that her back was a mess. Sadly, he was not lying.

Belle felt Peter stiffen against her and his hand froze on her back. However, she felt his fingers spread against her ribs.

"Yes," he confirmed quietly. "I cannot tell you how sorry I am that such a terrible thing happened to you. I wish it hadn't. You cannot know how I wish it hadn't, how I wish that none of it had happened."

"I don't remember much of it happening," she confessed. Belle had passed out from the pain after only a few minutes. What she remembered most was the pain afterwards. How one of the wounds becoming putrid had nearly killed her with fever had one of the other women not treated her with an old remedy. How she had been unable to sleep on her back for months.

And while it didn't pain her any longer, she could still feel it. She could still feel the hardened tissue against her clothing or when she laid down at night. Belle didn't like to look at it in the mirror, but when she did, it sickened her.

Belle suddenly felt very vain to be fretting like this. But she couldn't help it. She was the farthest thing from a debutante lady, from someone like Susanna. "I ... I don't want you to be shocked ... or repulsed ..." A deep blush filled her cheeks as she realised the presumptuousness of this conversation. They were not engaged. Their courtship, if it even had been one, had not been made official.

"Stop," Peter practically commanded.

"They are not even the worse ones," Belle continued in a ramble, ignoring Peter's instruction. "There is a terrible, awful scar here." She ran her hand over her abdomen. "It was where a sabre sliced me when Alex and I were hiding on his father's ship. Perhaps the cut would not have been so bad had they not burned the wound closed. The burn is the worst part –"

"Belle, for God's sake, stop." Peter silenced Belle by capturing her jaw in his hand and lifting her face to his. He was looking down upon her intently. "Hear me," he insisted, "you are beautiful. You are the most beautiful woman that I will ever lay eyes upon, and no scar, inside or out, will ever change my mind." He squeezed his hand so that her lips puckered, and she let out an unwilling raspberry. "Do you understand?"

Belle nodded.

"Good."

"I want you to understand something else," Peter continued. "I even learned it in French so that nothing could be lost in translation."

Belle's lips were still embarrassingly puckered in Peter's grip, and she could see his amusement. But there was a seriousness, a fierceness in his eyes as something took over him.

He released her just as he uttered, "Je t'aime."

Belle's mouth opened in shock, and when she couldn't speak, Peter paled.

"Oh, God. Did I say it right? You do understand, don't you? Don't tell me that I accidentally insulted you by muddling up a word. Of course, I managed to do that. Managing anything remotely suave or romantic is simply not my forte."

"Stop!" Belle cried as she found her voice. Her eyes indeed welled up with tears. "You said it right! I understood. Your accent is terrible, but I understood." She laughed as the tears rolled over her eyelids and fell freely down her cheeks. "Do you mean it? Really?"

"If you are going to laugh at my French accent then I might just take it back," Peter teased.

"No!" Belle exclaimed. "No, you can't! I won't allow it."

Peter chuckled. "Yes," he confirmed, brushing over her cheekbone with the back of his knuckles. "I mean it. Terrible

French accent and all. Je t'aime. I love you. Every beautiful, incredible part of you."

Belle closed her eyes as she allowed Peter's words to rush over her. It felt very much like the waves capturing her ankles, only this time the feeling was warm and intoxicating. "Je t'aime," she murmured, her smile so wide her cheeks were hurting.

"Are you correcting my accent, or telling me that you love me?"

Belle's eyes snapped open as a laugh escaped her throat. "I love you," she said again, in English this time.

"You do?"

"I don't want anything to get lost in translation," she replied, grinning as she used Peter's words. Peter quickly returned her smile, his eyes lighting up, beautifully reflecting the brilliant oranges across the sunset sky.

Peter's eyes dropped to her lips for the briefest of moments, before he looked back into her eyes, silently asking for permission. Belle was so used to being afraid when it came to any sort of physical touch, even if it had only been the kind hand of a friend. There was once a time, not even that long ago, when she was quite certain that this would never be a possibility for her.

Belle could not change the past. There was nothing that she could do to go back and stop what she had endured. But now she was free. She was free to choose to her own path, her own life, and the deep privilege of that fact would never be lost on her, not knowing that there were so many like her without that luxury.

Peter was her choice, and she could feel it in her bones that he would be a choice that she would never regret making. Belle closed the distance between them before he could, and she kissed Peter with everything that she had.

Chapter 32

"Peter," cooed a soft voice. "Peter, wake up. We are returned."

Peter stirred from his groggy slumber. Certainly, it was the first decent sleep that he had managed to get in what felt like a year. His eyes fluttered open. His head had been resting against the window of the carriage, and he could see the familiar grounds of the Ashwood estate passing them by as the carriage travelled swiftly towards the house.

There was frost on the grass, or a light dusting of snow. The clouds were low, and rain seemed inevitable, but Peter had never been more glad to see the miserable winter weather of Hertfordshire.

Peter's head turned back to Belle, as she was sitting beside him. He could see the warmth, the excitement, and indeed, the relief in her golden eyes. He needed to stop starring at her. Peter had made a terrible habit of it over the last five days on their journey home, but he had not been able to help it. His eyes, with a mind of their own, searched for her. And when they found her, he felt a remarkable sense of wonder. And love. Indisputably.

Peter did not think that he would ever be able to fully comprehend just how brave Belle was, the same as he was certain she would never be able to fully comprehend just how remarkable he thought she was. Though he knew more than most, he knew that there were some atrocities that Belle kept buried deep within her for her own sake and protection. For her to smile as she was, despite the suffering she had endured, kept him in awe of her. Peter was quite certain that he would spend his life trying to deserve Belle Desjardins.

"Perhaps it will be a white Christmas this year," Adam observed looking out the window.

It was hard to believe that it was only a mere two days before Christmas, and that they had all been away for over a month.

The carriage came to a stop before the grand steps of Ashwood House, and the driver and footman jumped down to open the door and let down the step. Adam climbed out first, and he assisted Belle down. Alex and Peter followed, stepping out into the chilly morning air.

Peter watched as Belle's chin lifted as she took in the sight of the great house, as though she was looking upon it for the first time. He stepped beside her, offering her his arm. "Are you glad to be home?"

"I am glad that you are with me," she replied peacefully as she threaded her arm through his.

The Duke's unannounced return quickly sent the servants into a frenzy, for usually there would be a reception planned to greet him or a member of his family. As it was not yet ten in the morning, the house was not yet fully awake.

This was a fact that did not at all bother Adam. He was quick to ascend the stairs to head towards the bedroom he shared with Grace, as was Alex when he learned that Susanna had been staying in her old room during his absence.

Peter and Belle were very quickly standing alone in the grand foyer of Ashwood House.

"It's going to be alright now, isn't it?" There was a beautiful innocence in the tone of Belle's voice as she asked the question. It was the voice of a woman who hoped, something that she would have scarce been able to do before.

"Yes," Peter promised her, as visions of the plans that he had begun making trickled back into his mind. "Everything is going to be alright now."

"Belle!"

Both Peter and Belle's heads turned towards the first-floor landing, where a woman in a white nightdress had suddenly appeared. Susanna had flown onto the landing, her golden hair still fixed in rags. Alex soon appeared behind her, wearing a bemused expression.

Peter chuckled quietly. This was obviously not the reunion that Alex had been envisioning as Susanna sprinted down the stairs, taking them two at a time, before she threw herself into Belle's arms, capturing her in a vice grip hug.

"Oh, thank God you are alright! We have all been so worried!" Susanna cried as she held onto Belle.

Belle returned Susanna's act of affection, and Peter did not even see her flinch. "It is so good to see you, my friend."

When Grace suddenly appeared on the landing, not quite in the state of undress that Susanna was, but closely followed by Adam and his frustrated expression, Peter openly laughed.

"Dear Belle!" Grace declared as she reached Belle and Susanna once down the stairs. "I cannot tell you how glad I am to see you home safe. Are you well?"

As Belle began to recount a very diluted version of events for Grace and Susanna, both Alex and Adam came to stand with Peter.

"What are you smirking at?" Alex grumbled.

"Nothing. Nothing at all," replied Peter innocently.

"Just you wait. Soon you shall be married and then your wife won't care a wit about your comings and goings," teased Adam.

Grace heard the comment, and she turned around with her hands on her hips. "Oh, dear me. I've wounded you, Adam!" she realised with a facetious smile.

"Yes, you have. Terribly so," confirmed Adam as he nodded and folded his arms across his chest.

Grace rolled her eyes as she crossed the small distance between herself and Adam, before she stood up on her toes, grabbed a hold of his lapel, and brought his face down closer to her. She then kissed his cheek, eliciting a laugh from Adam as he captured her jaw in his hand and pressed his lips down to hers softly. Grace grinned as she turned her back on Adam, only to lean back into his chest as he wrapped his arms around her in such a familiar way.

Alex then cleared his throat, but Susanna pretended not to hear him.

Peter watched as an expression of pure amusement spread across Belle's face. He was not at all certain about what he had expected from Belle upon returning home, but this silly antics by the husbands who had missed their wives were just the ticket. It wasn't serious. It wasn't demanding. It didn't frighten her. It was just that: silly.

When Susanna did not go to Alex, his long legs marched towards her in three strides before he collected her in his strong arms. Susanna squealed as Alex spun her around and Belle laughed at the sight.

Adam had jokingly made the comment, but Peter knew he was right. Soon he would be married. Just as soon as the time was right to ask Belle.

Belle's return had set the gossip mongers within the Ashwood parish positively ablaze. The popularity of the story, and Belle's sudden celebrity, had made the gossips quite forget that they had once discarded Belle's value because of her race.

Though she still could not read the newspapers properly, her name seemed to be all over the papers that Adam had delivered from London, even a week after returning home. She was still learning, but seeing her name splashed about as it was made her feel a little relieved that she could not be tempted to read what they were saying about her.

As Belle sat down to breakfast beside Adam, his newspaper was open and raised in front of his face. Once again, she saw the bold headline which contained her name.

JEAN LECLERC HANGED. BELLE DESJARDINS VINDICATED.

She was not sure of the other words but did not doubt that they were speaking of her kidnapping, the trial, or about what had happened to her. The journalists that had been inside the hall had been fuelling the gossip that was being spread about her. She supposed there was some grace in the fact that their stories were sympathetic and blameless towards her, but it still made it terribly difficult to even want to step foot into the Ashwood village.

When Adam heard Belle's chair being pulled out by a footman, he lowered his newspaper and greeted her with a smile. He folded the paper in half and stowed it on the table as he speared a piece of ham with his fork.

"Good morning, Belle," he greeted.

Before Belle could even return his sentiment, there was a knock on the dining room door as Mr Cole entered.

"Pardon me, Your Grace. Mr Denham has arrived. Shall I direct him to your study?"

"Oh, yes. Thank you, Cole." Adam quickly drained the rest of his tea and popped an entire boiled egg in his mouth as he rose from his chair.

The Mr Denham in question was Jem, and not Peter. She had learned that after Christmas dinner, Jem had asked Adam for some advice in how to rise up in the world. He had finished his education but had not the means to attend university. Jem was a proud and determined young man, and would not accept what he had not earned, which was why he had refused Adam's proposal to fund his higher education. Instead, Adam had taken on Jem as his steward.

Peter had later explained this role to Belle and had told her that it was a job well suited to second sons of the lower to middle classes. To be taken on as the right hand of a gentleman was a great honour indeed, and one could rise up to manage great estates. Peter had observed to Belle that he had seen a want of maturity in Jem for the first time. He had always been youthful and energetic, but he seemed determined to make something of himself. Peter was his kindred spirit in that respect.

"I do apologise, Belle. Do excuse me," Adam said apologetically.

"Not at all." Belle shook her head, smiling.

And with that, the duke departed, and Belle was alone in the dining room. She helped herself to an egg, some ham, cheese, and bread, all the while watching the folded newspaper out of the corner of her eye. When she had buttered her bread, her curiosity could no longer be suppressed.

Belle unfolded the newspaper and was quite confronted by the image below the headline that bore her name. It was of a man, a large man, standing on the gallows with a noose around his neck. The artist had captured his evil eyes well as Belle traced two other words in the headline with her index finger. J. Jean.

The third? "H ... ha ..." she whispered under her breath, before the picture made it clear. "Hanged."

Jean had been hanged. The execution had taken place. He was dead. What followed this realisation was an immediate feeling of relief, which Belle prayed was not some terrible sin. To be relieved at the news of a man's death seemed horrid, but certainly God could understand. An unwitting tear rolled down Belle's cheek as she folded the newspaper over and tossed it onto the floor. She would feel bad for creating something for the footmen to pick up, but that was where she felt Jean's likeness belonged.

As she made the conscious decision that this would be the last time she would ever voluntarily think of Jean Leclerc, she wondered how possible such a commitment would be in a little village like Ashwood. She had only been into the village once since returning, and that was to attend church for the Christmas service.

She could not blame the parishioners for their curiosity, but some of their questions were tactless and overly familiar. Belle did not think that it would ever be possible to once again sit at her little table in Mr Andrews' shop and sew buttons for the villagers.

But that was all she wanted to do. After everything she had been through, all she wanted to do was to do something that she enjoyed.

There was another knock on the dining room door then to interrupt her thoughts, and Mr Cole entered once more. This time, his eyes were for her.

"Pardon me, Miss Desjardins, but Mr Denham has arrived." Mr Cole suddenly paused. "That is, er, your Mr Denham," he corrected himself.

A smile spread across Belle's face. Her Mr Denham indeed.

Chapter 33

Belle abandoned her breakfast and darted out into the foyer to meet with Peter. The moment he saw her, he smiled.

Belle felt such warmth and security when she was in Peter's presence, especially now that she had returned to Ashwood. Though she knew that she was safe here, and that no harm would ever befall her, it was another thing entirely to be beside Peter.

She supposed that this was what it felt like to be in love.

Peter's arms opened, and it felt like the most natural response in the world to jump into them, her arms fixing themselves around his neck as he gripped around her waist and spun her.

Belle still feared touch. She hoped one day that this fear wouldn't trouble her. It was a reminder of her past and seemed to be the one that would not go away. But Peter's patience had been exactly what she had needed as she learned to trust him, and her fears did not trouble her when she was with him.

Belle and Peter had only parted the day before, but their reunion seemed as though they had been separated for months. It did not bother them, though. They had known what it was to be separated, and unjustly against their will.

When Peter returned Belle to her feet, still holding onto her waist, he looked over her shoulder and said, "Could I please trouble a servant to fetch Miss Desjardins' cloak, Mr Cole?" he asked politely.

The butler bowed his head once and replied, "Of course, Mr Denham."

Peter's eyes returned to Belle's, and he said, "There's a little break in the drizzle today. Would you like to take some air with me?"

Belle nodded.

Mr Cole returned promptly with Belle's cloak, and Peter helped her to put it on. Belle fastened the buttons before she took Peter's arm as he led her outside.

It was indeed very cold outside, but the air was fresh, as it always was after rain. The drizzle had washed away the dusting of snow that had fallen overnight, and the great lawns before Ashwood House were green and glistening. The clouds hung low, and the air was indeed very grey, but Belle saw great beauty in it. There was always beauty in the land of which one could walk upon it as a free woman.

"How are you this morning?" Peter asked her as the descended the stairs towards Ashwood's gravel driveway.

"I am well," she replied. "I am with you." Belle's cheeks flushed with colour. She hadn't managed to stop herself from uttering something so forward.

But Peter didn't mind. He never seemed to mind. He seemed to enjoy when it was not him blushing. Peter grinned down at her. "I do so love when your cheeks are rosy."

"It is becoming a habit."

Peter chuckled. "One I quite adore."

They stepped off of the driveway and onto the lawn. The dew of the morning immediately soaked through the hem of Belle's dress, but she didn't mind very much at all. She just naturally leaned into Peter's side as they walked, as though they had been walking together all their lives.

"I ran into Mr Andrews this morning," Peter told her, and his change in tone told Belle that this was something that he had been mulling over telling her about.

She focussed her eyes forward. "Oh? What did he say?" Belle had seen Mr Andrews at church on Christmas, but she had not spoken to him. She had actively tried to avoid everyone in the village save for the Denhams.

"He wondered at your return to his shop," replied Peter as his lips pursed into a firm line. "He asked me if I would pass along the message that you have been asked after by everyone."

"I'm sure I have been," murmured Belle. She paused, and Peter immediately stopped walking to round on her. He placed his hands on her upper arms, before he lifted her chin gently with one of his fingers.

"I can see that you do not wish to return," he said softly. "And it is quite alright, and more than understandable."

"It is not because I dislike the work." Belle sighed. "Honestly, nothing would be more fulfilling than to occupy my hands with work that I am good at. I would sew buttons for the rest of my days if I knew that someone would not walk up to my table and ask what it was like ... what any of it was like."

Belle felt a sudden pang of guilt for her sensitivities. She had once observed the innocence and the unworldliness of the people in the Ashwood village, and she had been glad for them because of it. These people could not comprehend the experiences of a woman like Belle, and they were curious and could not help themselves.

Belle just did not want to be a circus attraction.

Peter brushed Belle's cheekbone with the backs of his knuckles and exhaled. "I can see the guilt in your eyes, and I wish it was not so. I know this community does not deserve you. I can only hope to."

Belle bit down on her lower lip as her cheeks filled with colour once more.

"Will you sit down with me?" Peter then asked. "I want to talk to you about something." He gestured to the stone bench that was situated underneath and evergreen tree.

She nodded.

Peter took Belle's arm once again and led her through the wet grass towards the bench. When they reached it, the rain had left the stone glistening, and moss had grown up the sides. Peter dropped her arm for a moment as he unbuttoned his coat, before he threw his coat overtop of it so that she could sit down.

"Don't be silly!" Belle exclaimed. "It is too cold out to be without your coat. I can sit down on a damp bench."

Peter merely placed his hands on his hips and stared at her with a challenging brow before she conceded and sat down on the warm, woollen coat with a sheepish smile. Peter then sat down beside her.

"I've had an idea," Peter then said, taking her hands between his and warming then. There was an excited energy about Peter as he began to speak. "I believe that you are far too talented to settle for sewing buttons, no matter how you say it would please you. You once told me that it was a dream of yours to have your own shop, to be a modiste. That was before you quickly dismissed it as a fantasy that could never be possible."

Belle remembered their conversation vividly. She would be lying if she said that she did not think often of owning her own shop where ladies could come to buy a couture gown made by her.

"I want to make this dream of yours a reality," Peter continued eagerly. "I know that Ashwood, perhaps, is now a little too small for you to live the life that you want comfortably. What about London?" he suggested hopefully. "Would you consider it? Would you consider establishing your own shop right in the heart of Mayfair? It would be right where the ladies would come every summer season. There is a location that I have in mind, and it has a very comfortable flat above it."

Belle was not at all certain of what Peter was proposing. Was this his very idea of that? Was this a marriage proposal? She was not sure that it was, and that made it very difficult to imagine that she could simply open up a shop in Mayfair, wherever that was, as she had no financial means to do so.

As it was, the financial limitations were not her only hindrance anymore. "No one would come," Belle said dejectedly. "They might have done after the reception to Susanna's wedding gown, but my name is all over the papers, and is had been for over a month, and not because of my talent as a dressmaker. I feel like my name is tainted."

While Belle's name was taken from her unfortunate beginnings, it was hers. She felt a great deal of her own identity within her name. Belle Desjardins. Beauty of the Gardens. It was perhaps the very first thing that had ever belonged to her.

"Then you shall have to make a gown to surpass Susanna's," Peter encouraged. "You, my darling, possess the power to change the narrative. You have power, and I cannot wait to watch you wield it."

A smile tugged at Belle's lips as her face fell forward into Peter's chest. He chuckled as he wrapped his arms around her securely.

"Will you try?" he pleaded. "I know you will be great. I have such faith in you."

Belle could feel that faith in her bones. It couldn't quell her fears that perhaps her reputation was irreparable, but it did not stem the hope. Of course, she hoped.

"Of course, I want to try," she mumbled against his chest. "I suppose I need a client then, don't I?" And the financial means to go to London. Peter hadn't proposed. She was quite sure of that.

"I had thought that you could be your own first client," Peter replied. "I am certain the wedding gown you would make for yourself would be absolutely exquisite."

But then she heard that comment, and her back immediately straightened as she sat bolt upright. She stared at him, her eyes wide with shock. "My wedding gown," she gasped. "Why ... why would I have a need for one of those?"

Peter frowned, his brow very deep with confusion. He then suddenly, very aggressively, slapped the breast pocket of his jacket, before he jumped up from the bench. "Only I could forget to propose!" he admonished himself, before he took a breath and looked at Belle.

She could not help herself. A wicked smile had spread across her face as she heard his curses. She had not been wrong after all. Her stomach fluttered, and yet she felt more amusement and excitement.

"Hush!" Peter demanded of her, his own cheeks reddening, as he leant down to take her hands so that he could pull her to her feet.

"I never said a word!" exclaimed Belle as Peter began searching his coat for the pocket he desired.

Peter flipped his coat and finally found the breast pocket that he was after. He then reached inside and pulled out of it a small velvet pouch that was fixed closed with a golden drawstring. Peter quickly returned his coat to the bench and positioned Belle back where she was, before he again sat back down beside her, velvet pouch in hand.

He slapped his hand to his forehead and frustratedly said, "I was so excited to tell you about the shop idea that I forgot to ask you to marry me first. Forget I said anything about the shop, and I'll start again. I've made such a mess of this. Of course, I have. It's my talent. You can sew, and I can make a right fool of myself."

"You hush!" Belle commanded, shuffling closer to him, causing the coat to bunch between them. "I love that you were so excited to share this with me." Belle only wished her thoughts had not been so initially self-deprecating. "I love that you want to make plans with me, and to help me establish something of my own. I won't forget any of this. That I can promise you." It was her turn to hold his hand, though only one of his would fit between hers. She leant down and kissed it, before offering him a heartfelt gaze.

Peter's smile returned, before he shook his head. "You must have thought me a little mad to be talking about a shop without explaining that I planned on us establishing it together."

"Wonderful," she promised. "Never mad."

Peter removed his hand from hers, only to pull open the little velvet bag. "I really had no idea of your taste in jewellery, so I did not want to present you with something that you might dislike. But then I had a better idea. At least, I thought you would appreciate this more. My father was a tailor, and he passed away while I was still a boy. I really do not have much that belonged to him, but I have always had this. He gave it to me the birthday before he died, as he had always planned to teach me his trade. I never learned. I'd always thought my future lay elsewhere. But when I thought of giving this to you as an engagement gift, it almost makes me feel as though my father might have known that my future bride would have need of it." He chuckled. "Is that silly? This is small and not at all expensive, but ..."

Peter tipped the little object out of the bag into the palm of his hand. There Belle saw a little silver thimble, ornately decorated with branches of oak leaves. It had been polished, and it shone against the pale skin over his hand.

Belle leaned over and peered at it, and it wasn't until a droplet of water hit Peter's hand that she realised that she was crying. Peter immediately used his other hand to brush away her tears.

"It's not silly at all," Belle all but blubbered. "I love it!" How had she been smiling wickedly only a few moments ago? Lord, she loved him. She loved him with every bit of her heart, and she could not imagine being presented with another more perfect.

Peter smiled. "I love you," he countered. "And I will always. Will you marry me?"

Belle helplessly nodded. "Oui, oui," she stammered as she got up on her knees to hug him, before she kissed him softly. Belle felt Peter's hand on the back of her head as he deepened the kiss, enduring the wetness of her falling tears.

When they parted, Peter captured her left hand and delicately touched the silver thimble to each of her fingers before placing it onto her ring finger. They both laughed together as Peter leaned forward to kiss her forehead. "Perfect fit."

Belle and Peter decided to keep their engagement a secret for the remainder of the week, choosing to announce it at the family dinner the following Sunday evening. It was a combined celebratory meal for the new year, as well as for Adam and Grace's wedding anniversary, but they thought it was the perfect time to tell everyone altogether.

Owing to the occasion, a special meal had been prepared, and Belle was filled an anxious excitement as the hours ticked away. She and Peter had spent nearly every day that week together, quietly planning and talking for hours.

Belle had learned that Peter had scouted the location for her shop when he had returned to London after the wedding, and that his elder sister had helped him. It was a settling feeling to know that Peter had been thinking of these plans, and their future, for so long.

Mrs Denham, Peter, Jem and Amélie arrived first, and they were closely followed by Jim, Kate, and their young son, James. Jack and Claire and their two daughters were already in residence at Ashwood House as they had been staying for the festive season and were due to return to London in the coming days. Alex and Susanna were the final party to arrive.

When the children were all put to bed upstairs in the nursery, dinner was announced, and the large family party took their places in the dining room. Adam was seated at one head of the table, and Cecily at the other, as she always was. Peter and Belle were seated beside each other, and they exchanged an excited glance. As soon as the wine was poured, Peter planned to stand up and announce. Belle gripped the underside of her chair in anticipation.

The conversation at the table was animated and lively as everyone caught up with one another over the goings on of the last week. Cecily and Mrs Denham were deep in conversation about something, and at the other end of the table, both Adam and Grace appeared to be discussing something seriously.

Jack caught Peter's attention with a comment about the book that they would be publishing in the coming weeks, just as the footmen appeared with the wine. Belle watched as each of the glasses around the table were filled quickly with the deep burgundy liquid.

Peter lifted his glass as he finished his conversation with Jack and collected his spoon to draw attention. But before he could call the table's focus, another had the exact same thought.

It was Grace, and she had stood up from her seat, wine glass in hand. But Grace was not the only one to stand up. Susanna did also, as she left her seat to flit to Grace's side. The two women looped arms around each other.

"If I could please have everyone's attention for a moment," Grace called. "Susanna and I both have some rather exciting news."

Belle's breath hitched in her throat.

"It's been our little secret while both Alex and Adam were away," added Susanna. "But now that they know, and the doctor has assured both of us that we are healthy, we can share our happy news with everyone."

"There are to be two new little ones born this year," Grace announced with a serene happiness about her. "I expect in June, and Susanna in July."

The table erupted in applause and cheers of congratulations. Jack practically climbed on the table to shake Alex's hand as everyone left their chairs to congratulate, hug and kiss the expectant mothers and fathers. Amélie was in tears after Alex called to her the news in French, but no one was more excited than Cecily.

The authoritative grandmamma could be heard above all declaring a half a dozen new remedies that she had heard of to ensure a baby was a boy and was quick to snatch the arms of both Grace and Susanna to sing the virtues of stewed gizzards.

Belle and Peter could only look at one another and laugh.

Epilogue

3 Months Later

March 1812

Mayfair, London

"Oof!" exclaimed Peter, as he all but dropped a large wooden case on the counter of the shop floor.

Belle heard the noise from across the room where she had been organising bolts of fabric. "Careful!" she exclaimed, abandoning her project and flitting to Peter's side to ensure its contents were safe.

"What is even in that thing?"

"Buttons."

"Are they made of lead?" Peter complained as he rubbed his hands together.

Belle giggled, and Peter's blue eyes found her immediately, daring her with a challenging smirk as he arched an eyebrow.

"Are you laughing at me, wife?"

"No, I wouldn't dare," Belle replied innocently.

"I don't believe you," Peter retorted in good humour as he suddenly charged at her. Belle squealed as she ran around the counter, but Peter's long legs were quick to catch her.

He wrapped his arms around her waist, crushing her back to his chest as he lifted her off of her feet.

When Peter finally released her, he spun Belle around just so that he could capture her lips with his. He held her cheeks with his large hands, and she could feel him smiling against her.

"Let that be a warning to never again laugh at your husband," Peter murmured as they parted.

"Oh, never." Belle smiled coyly. "Be gentle with my buttons."

"Whatever you say, Mrs Denham." Peter winked.

Belle was still unused to her married name, and to hear it spoken aloud filled her with butterflies. She had made the decision to retain her maiden name professionally. It would be the name of her business, after all. But privately, she, Peter, and their family one day, would share a name together.

They had been married a week, and this was their version of a honeymoon journey. Peter had gone on to London not long after their engagement was announced at the family dinner a week after the announcements of Grace and Susanna's pregnancies.

While in London, Peter was able to secure the shop and the flat above for them, while simultaneously returning to his work at Beresford Press in preparation for the publication of "Confessions of a Lady". The book performed terrifically well amongst women, and Peter's advertisement plan had ensured that the first run of copies were highly sought after. It seemed that only two months later there were already plans for a second edition.

Their communication reverted back to their correspondence, as it had the first time that Peter had returned to London, and Belle became determined to improve herself day in and day out. If she was to operate a business in London, then she needed to be literate. She read every day, and she spent an hour a day practising her letters to improve her penmanship.

While she would not consider herself fluent, reading became less of a struggle, and she found that she could read words incidentally now, without having to think about them.

When Belle wasn't reading, she was designing and sewing. Being her own client was alarming difficult, and Belle had never been more self-critical in her life then when she was trying to create her own wedding gown. The stress of which was exacerbated by the tight time frame. They had planned on a short engagement so that Belle could be in business before the start of the next summer season in April.

Cecily had gifted Belle a bolt of French silk which she had ordered from London as her engagement gift, and Susanna had allowed Belle to use the leftover pieces of lace from her wedding dress. After stitching, unpicking, pulling apart, and stitching again, Belle had finally completed her ocean blue masterpiece.

It was a beautiful creation that she had designed to resemble a waterfall. The softness of the silk cascaded down her front in purposeful pleats, with a long train at the rear embroidered with dozens of forget-me-nots. Susanna's lace was sewn into the collar and sleeves and when it was completed, Belle was certain that it was perfect.

And it had been. Despite no members of the aristocracy being present for her wedding, Cecily had still wielded her influence and there were stories praising Belle's dressmaking prowess once more, with connections made back to the press that followed Susanna's wedding. Of course, Belle's story was still of interest to the public, and there were definitely people in London who would know who she was when they learned her name, but when Belle walked down the street in London, she did not feel as though everyone knew what had happened to her.

To be certain, people stared at the black woman on the arm of a white man, but their ignorance could never take away her freedom or her happiness. There was far too much good in her life to dwell on little people. But she would always be glad for them in knowing that they had never endured what she had, just as she had been glad for the villagers back in Ashwood.

When Peter and Belle had arrived in London the day after their wedding, he had brought her directly to what was to be her shop and their home. Belle had been busy marvelling at all the buildings and people, carriages, roads ... so many buildings! She had never seen anything quite like London in her life! She had been so busy staring around her that she had not noticed the sign on the front of the empty shop.

DESJARDINS

Modiste & Couturier

Belle read the sign over and over, completely in awe of the intricate way her name had been painted. Her name. There she was with her title and everything. She was a modiste and a couturier. And thanks to Cecily's prowess with the papers, she had already been contacted by several debutantes wanting to commission gowns for their upcoming seasons.

Which was why their honeymoon would be spent establishing her shop, and not off in some other part of the country. Perhaps there would be time for a trip somewhere else after the summer season had concluded.

The shop floor was a mess of supplies, trunks and crates. Peter's brother-in-law, Jim, had been kind enough to make them some furniture as a wedding gift, and the large counter, which Belle planned on using as her sewing table, had travelled with them from Ashwood.

Peter had sourced the rest of the furniture while in London, and the tables, chairs, cupboard and armoires were dotted around the floor without any real organisation. The shop itself consisted of two rooms. The larger front room Belle planned on using as her sewing room, but also a place to display her designs, fabrics and catalogues. The smaller back room she planned on converting into a private room for fittings.

The upstairs flat was, indeed, very comfortable, and like the shop, was still a mess of their belongings. But Belle and Peter would make it their home.

They spent the rest of their day organising the front room, working together to move furniture, unpack supplies, and to make the room looking like a workable space.

At five in the afternoon, Peter left to walk the short distance to Jack and Claire's home to collect dinner for the both of them. They were yet to tidy the kitchen upstairs, or to brave the old stove.

While he was gone, Belle was sweeping the floor for about the fourteenth time that day. Dust seemed to emerge and remerge when pushing about heavy furniture.

As she finished sweeping, there was a knock on the door. She smiled. Why was Peter knocking? Belle leant the broomstick up against one of the walls and removed her apron, just as her stomach grumbled. She pulled open the door but was surprised to see that it wasn't Peter there with a basket of supper, but two women.

One older, one younger, a mother and daughter pair. They were immediately familiar to Belle, and she furrowed her brow to try and place them.

"Do forgive the imposition, Miss Desjardins," the mother stated. She was an elegant woman in appearance and in dress. She was fair, with light hair and pale skin, and her eyes were a grey green. Belle could see that her gown had been amended to reflect the high waisted fashions, but that this dress appeared to be reflective of the '90s waistlines. The gown appeared to have once been made from expensive patterned silk.

Her daughter was dressed more simply in a lilac coloured linen. She was lovely, and she had inherited her fair complexion and golden hair colour from her mother, though her eyes were a dark brown in contrast.

It was the nerves and apprehension on the face of the daughter that triggered Belle's memory. They had been introduced at the Winter Assembly last November. This young girl was Cressie Martin.

"Mrs Martin," Belle recalled, "Miss Martin. What a surprise to see you both in London." And she was genuinely surprised.

"We are here for the season," replied Mrs Martin. "But of course," she added. "Cressida is to debut." She placed a hand on the small of her daughter's back.

"I congratulate you," Belle told her with a smile. "What an exciting time."

Cressie did not appear at all excited, and Belle could not help but feel terribly sorry for her. At the assembly, she had appeared to have been dragged around by her mother, and today seemed no different. The reason that Belle had been so surprised to see them in London was because they had very abruptly left Ashwood several months ago to stay with relatives. This was while Belle had been away herself, and so she had not learned of it until later. Jem had been quite forlorn at his time with Cressie being cut so short with little chance for redemption after what sounded like an awkward first encounter at the ball.

Jem had since been determined to better himself and to establish himself as an adult with a living. He had been working under Adam for several months now as his steward and by all reports was doing very well.

"But of course," Mrs Martin agreed. "Terribly exciting. Cressida is very eager to make an impression come April."

Cressie's dark eyes lowered.

"Miss Martin is very lovely. I am certain she will make an impression wherever she goes," Belle murmured as she watched Cressie sympathetically.

When Belle spoke, Cressie looked up, and her rosy lips upturned in a slight smile.

"Thank you, Miss Desjardins," she said softly. "You are too kind."

"Am I to assume that you require a debutante gown?" Belle asked, her attention returning to Mrs Martin.

Mrs Martin nodded. "Yes. Yes, we do. When we heard that you had become a modiste, it seemed only right to renew the acquaintance. It could only be you who could design a gown for Cressie, you both once being Ashwood residents. Everyone knows of Lady Susanna's wedding gown. I can only hope we could come to an arrangement to create something divine for my daughter."

Belle could read between the lines. She had already seen it in the economy of Mrs Martin's once expensive gown that was now twenty years out of fashion. Mrs Martin had not the funds to purchase a debutante gown from anyone else. Perhaps her flattery was exaggerated, but Belle wouldn't do it for Mrs Martin. She felt inclined to help Cressie. Her heart hurt for women who were not free, and she recognised that look in Cressie Martin's eyes.

"Would you both come back tomorrow?" Belle asked. "I am not yet set up for customers, and I expect my husband imminently."

Mrs Martin appeared relieved, and she nodded with a pleasing smile. "Certainly. We wish you a good evening, Miss Desjardins ... or should I say Mrs ...?"

"Denham," replied Belle.

Cressie's eyes widened as Belle spoke the name, recognition flooding her face, before she quickly masked it.

"Well, good evening, Mrs Denham." Mrs Martin nodded her head at Belle before she led Cressie away down the street.

Peter returned not five minute later with a basket laden with food. It smelled delicious, and as soon as he crossed the threshold, he stowed the basket on the counter so that he could kiss her softly.

"I hope you are hungry," he murmured against her lips. "We've an entire pork loin."

Belle pulled away, still quite shocked at what had just transpired. Peter frowned at her expression and he cocked his head.

"What is it? What's the matter?"

Belle gripped onto Peter's arms as she cried, "You are not going to believe who just came by to commission a dress!"